Kidnapping Steve

C. JULIANO

Kidnapping Steve
© 2022 C. Juliano

Paperback: 979-8-9860837-0-4
Ebook: 979-8-9860837-1-1

Cover art by C. Juliano

Dedicated to bad ideas, and to Billy.

Contents

This is a work of fiction.

Prologue

The night's dark disguise is pierced by flickering lights, red and blue. As 1:59 turns to 2:00, the police officer's a.m. sorties target burned-out head lamps, busted taillights, speeders, punks, and drunks.

Late-night revelers empty into the street, every labored movement a celebration, every good-bye a promise. A weathered door creaks open and the windows clap shut. An air conditioner is switched to high and the music plays low. Conversations, laughter, complaints, and accusations grow louder until—"Shh—careful not to wake the Weavers." They rise early to peruse North Atlantic Avenue in search of lost change, a hobby that's paid for more than a couple of tanks of gas.

Dawn arrives like an angry reminder of wasted time. Salt blankets the town like a heavy quilt. The clutter of old surfboards colors thin, dusty streets, while scenic neighborhoods reach across the river like fingers cut from muck.

The beach: where the retired, the inspired, and the uninspired reside; where the lucky and the unlucky live. A place for the cursed and the privileged, the poor and the prosperous, those in hiding and the ones who want to be seen.

Children play until dusk in a battered seaside field. Waves pound the shore like ancient warriors beating out an ominous rhythm. Night descends on a small town as the small sounds give way to silence. Even the ocean seems to rest.

Beneath the shifting coastal skies, something happened. On the back roads in a beachside apartment, something went wrong. He should have known better. She should have seen the signs, and the others should have just stayed away.

It began with a phone call, a bad idea, and then a book. "This is a work of fiction," the disclaimer simply stated. Deliberately vague, it was meant to render the work closed but maybe open. Ending or perhaps just beginning. As a harmless declaration of innocence, the intent was to tell the story as it truly happened.

Like a short flight in an old plane or a swim just a little too far out, the danger seemed slight. For something that was never supposed to occur, the risk appeared minimal. But as an ill wind blew, what should have died off grew; what could have flamed out caught. A glowing ember turned into an inferno and burned everything in its path.

In the darkness even a dim light seems bright. There's magic in the smile of a stranger, majesty in the conquered, tenacity in the ones who can't change, and pride in the ones who don't want to. Hidden in the eternal hum, a pulse exists, an awareness creates, a flow decides, a universal truth affirms that without a bottom, there would be no top.

PART I:
BILLY'S BRIGADE

In the Beginning

*I*n the beginning there was a feeling. One they shared. It was like nothing else, ever, for anyone. Their love was the greatest—for all they knew, anyway—better than the rich people up the road, more compelling than the middle class stuck in suburbia, and a heck of a lot more civilized than the shriveled-up drunks at the bar. At least that's what they thought, in the beginning.

Since they were riding bikes to the beach and walking hand in hand, how could it fail? They were young. She was beautiful and he curiously handsome. There were no responsibilities—none but to eat and drink to the fullest, to laugh the loudest and never have any regrets. That's how it was in the beginning. But over time he grew sensitive to her nagging and she to his lack of depth. She expected too much, and he didn't have enough. She worried, and he needed a plan.

It was a long shot for an exotic catalog model turned college student to end up with a lanky self-proclaimed prodigy. An unlikely couple at best, Rita Polli and Billy Winslow were sure to create their fair share of chaos.

A sleek sophisticate from Chicago, Rita had tasted the finer things in life. She knew there was a Van Gogh housed in the Art Institute and that a glass of red wine marked with thick liquid streaks was good.

In true eclectic fashion, Billy rejected the trappings of society. Cut from the cloth of an action comic antihero, he held the weight of the world. Banished, forced to go it alone, he was a beast corralled by a fair maiden; a creature from the deep made whole by the soft touch of a sultry nymph.

Born under the same sign yet still so distinct, their colorful contrast seemed to make sense. Their different styles seemed to connect. What they had was real, and above all else, they made each other laugh. Rita got a dolphin tattoo on her left hip, and Billy painfully inked a yin-yang on the top of his right foot, which he regretted almost instantly.

Billy liked to fish, and Rita liked to sunbathe. The only problem was that he usually stayed on the water a lot longer than she stayed at the beach. And there she was, walking barefoot through a field of daisies, her long, full hair moving in time with a confident stride. Her clothes fit just right, and her complexion was utterly flawless. With piercing blue eyes, she was as perfect as the sky. Only one thing was missing—a smile. She was upset. Billy barely made it ashore before she yelled, "You locked me out of the house!"

Rita stood on a cool patch of grass as Billy recalled locking up her flip-flops. It wasn't his fault she couldn't keep track of her shoes.

"You should have worn your shoes to the beach."

"Is that so?" she snapped. "Guess I should have taken the refrigerator and the shower to the beach too."

"You could have hosed off."

"You hose off. I shower. And where might the spare key have wandered off to again?"

He had a feeling. From a pocket bulging with receipts and spare change, Billy extracted an odd, ridged item and held it weakly aloft.

"Just like I thought, the key to the manor hidden in plain sight."

Now she was mocking him. His residence wasn't the most palatial, but it was comfortable nonetheless.

In the beginning, Billy could just be himself, which by any other standard was quite unremarkable. From the beaches to the quiet side streets and stunning sunsets, everything was new. Angry and emotional, with a critically ill father and a bad attitude, Rita was swept away by the vag-abond charm of a guy named Billy. And with a name like Billy—a half name, an unfinished moniker—nothing good could come of it. But against all warning signs, in she dove, end over end, head over heels. He was handsome and kind, and, above all else, when she needed him, he was there.

So there she was: the sunshine of his life, the apple of his eye, showering him with even more kindness. Through the years, Billy had learned that the best way to combat incompetence was with indigna-tion. While effective at times, it had a rather short shelf life, but, as a true maverick, he'd persisted. Couldn't a guy even go fishing without being harassed?

"After everything I've done for you, Rita, that's how you're going to treat me?"

Head cocked to the side, he let it sit there, a festering question, a sad commentary on all her ingratitude.

Rita didn't flinch. At an earlier time, she might have showed com-passion. In the beginning she may have cut him some slack, but not now. It was way beyond that.

With arms wide and chest forward, she answered, "What have you done? You've been late. You've been unreliable, you've been insensitive and, for the most part, absent."

"But I've loved you," Billy solemnly replied.

No longer the lonely waitress with a headache and an empty pack of cigarettes, Rita wasn't so easily appeased—and to think she could have fallen for a billowy blond, chronically tan lout. At times, though, Billy could be persuasive.

The sun shone brilliantly off the rippled gray water. Rita was also radiant, more a deliberate work than a divine accident.

With curled lips and hands on deliciously wide hips, she said, "Anyone could do that."

That was Rita.

As an aspiring chef courting a grief-stricken waitress, Billy quit his job to walk a sad girl home—to his home, as it turned out. He woke and she was gone, as was the awkward morning after. "Had to get to the hospital," read a hurriedly scrawled note with her phone number in parentheses.

Billy called, Rita answered, and so began their time of beaches, blue skies, late nights, and low wages—coastal living at its finest, except with a twist. She stayed in Florida, and he made the biggest mistake of his life.

Rita sighed as Billy tied off the boat. Tall, lean, and deceptively strong, he showed a certain air of invincibility. With light eyes and a concerned smile, Billy was genuinely sorry to have let her down again.

Rita's thick brown hair made a statement as she fought it back to a single strand. Her shapely legs stood firm as she waited for something. He needed to say what she needed to hear.

"I'm sorry, Rita. It was my mistake."

She acknowledged his admission with a nod as they drew closer.

"A little consideration goes a long way."

"I'll tell ya what else goes a long way," grinned Billy, "a great big bear hug!"

Rita wheezed and pulled away, but it was too late. She was literally off her feet as he carried her home caveman style.

"Put me down!" she chortled along the way.

"Not a chance, gotta save your energy for later."

It sounded good to her.

"Oh, and Rita," said Billy as he labored down the road.

"What?" replied Rita in the midst of being jostled from head to toe.

"I love you."

"I love you too, Billy."

The Call

Sharp crashes and raspy fragments of conversation permeated Billy's chalky-white rental. He knew the sound, but it was a different story for Rita. The steady unnerving clatter was getting under her skin as she finally yelled, "So, what's with the Wonder Twins now? Smashing windows instead of slamming doors!"

"Sounds like Eddie and Horse are breaking beer bottles again. It could go on for a while. They drink a lot of beer."

"Well, can't you just ask them to stop, or at least suggest they recycle?"

"That probably wouldn't go over too well," replied Billy with a slight wince and a moment's reflection on the human condition. "But once again, you've inspired me to innovate."

Now on the move, he feverishly announced, "The Blast, whaddya think of that!"

"Not a whole lot," replied Rita.

"Picture this, a trash can that explodes when hit with anything recyclable!"

"Explodes?"

"With sound."

"With sound?"

"Ahh, an alarm."

"An alarm?"

"Why do you have to repeat everything I say?" he asked.

"I guess because it's so absurd," she conceded.

"Absurd, eh?"

They could have continued and in most cases would have. *Ridiculous, idiotic,* and *utterly insane* were a few other choice adjectives, but rather than elaborate, Rita calmly said, "For being a self-proclaimed inventor, you sure come up with some stupid inventions."

"I never claimed to be an inventor, merely a man of vision."

"Well, an exploding trash can isn't exactly visionary."

"You'll see," he said in a low, trailing voice.

"Blah blah blah," muttered Rita.

Still annoyed, Rita heard something, or rather she heard nothing. It was quiet. Eddie and Horse had flamed out, so Rita could finally turn in early. With a satisfied nod came a yawn, and then the phone rang, over and over again—seven times to be exact—before she snatched it up and answered, "Hello. Yeah, of course, he's here."

"Don't say I'm here before you ask," hissed Billy.

Rita glared. It seemed like he was here. She was staring at him.

"You can't answer the phone in the evening, it's when *they* call," he sputtered, as if the "they" in question was a dangerous cartel or sinister governmental agency.

Rita wasn't buying it. She'd heard the same song and dance before.

"If you don't want to take calls, you shouldn't have a phone, and I'm not going to lie for you."

"You don't have to lie, just don't answer."

"I'm not going to sit there and listen to the phone ring off the hook," replied Rita. "Do your own dirty work, moron!"

Billy shook his head and then said, "Hello."

"Hey, Billy, it's Van."

"Van who?"

"It's Van Dalton, man, what's your problem?"

"At the moment it's you," answered Billy, "so keep it short."

"Well, it's this kid named Steve," snarled Van. "I don't like him, and I saw a television show where some good guys down on their luck changed it all by kidnapping a neighborhood schmuck. Nobody got hurt, you know. They were all in on it. We should snatch the kid, Billy. He's spoiled and his dad's got money."

Immune to the insanity, Billy paused. Considering a few different insults, he finally said, "While I appreciate the offer to participate in a major felony, Van, the first of many problems with such a plan is that you're an idiot, it wouldn't work, and above all, kidnapping isn't really my forte."

Not to be outdone, Van deviously asked, "What exactly is your forte, then, Billy?"

The scathing inquiry forced a sudden moment of introspection. The words stung Billy's ears like the piercing blare from his boxy brown inherited alarm clock, discarded most likely in favor of a newer model with a more hospitable chime. Maybe some soft bells or a pretty song, but not for Billy; he'd suffer rather than slog through an obnoxiously bright store, checking the overhead directories while Rita suggests some mint chocolate chip ice cream. "Yes, yes, we'll get the ice cream," he'd say, "but where are those stupid clocks? I've got to be on time tomorrow."

Then came the daunting task of sifting through the stacks of plastic clocks assembled in a faraway Asian place, conveniently priced, waiting for the kind of person who goes to a drugstore for an alarm clock upgrade and a cheap pint of fluorescent-green ice cream. That loud, old secondhand clock would work for now, but back to what Van had said.

Billy quickly ran through the time of trial and error that had become his life. The search, or better yet, the journey, had galvanized his character, it had strengthened his resolve. It taught him not to pin his hopes on any star-studded, last-chance, long-lasting, money-making TV commercial. The spirit was speaking, and Billy was finally listening.

"You still there?" barked Van.

"You bet," chimed Billy, "and for starters, I've spent the last ten years cooking for busloads of hungry kids, beachside buffet-goers, and late-night stragglers. I've prepared the finest delicacies in the state for scores of upscale clientele. I've fried, broiled, and sautéed things that you've never even heard of. I've crossed the ocean, drank the finest wine with rich men, and broke bread with the common folk. I've been up and I've been down, with and without. I've held on too tight and I've let go. I've been a wise man, a fool, a vagabond, and a beggar, so if you ever again find yourself wondering what my forte is," preached Billy, "my forte is this: realization, organization, and motivation, Brother Van!"

"I appreciate the sermon, there, Brother Billy, but what do you know about kidnapping?"

"I know everything about kidnapping!"

"So, does that mean you're going to help me?"

"You're gonna help me."

"But it's my idea."

"It was your idea. Call back in three days for further instruction," chuckled Billy before cradling the phone with a stern click.

"Three days!" exclaimed Rita.

She wasn't amused. Checking the locks and latches, she announced, "We need to change the phone number."

"It wouldn't help. Van's compulsive, and he's got a bike."

Now contemplating the dangers of a compulsive cyclist, Rita stalled.

Being from Chicago, she would have understood if someone said, "He's compulsive, and he's got a gun!" or even "He's compulsive, and he's got a knife," but a bike? She was at the beach, though, so she'd have to take it in stride. The rules were different. If he wasn't worried, she wouldn't worry, but if something was up, she wanted to know.

"Well, you sounded angry."

"Inspired actually, bought some self-help tapes from the Reverend Gill Wonder Gil, powerful stuff. Had to use your credit card, though, it was kind of an emergency," muttered Billy, gently extending the flimsy plastic article.

"You should try getting a job and using your own credit card," snapped Rita.

"I got a job!"

"Get a real job. Get a career instead of a hobby. I mean, who in their right mind is going to be impressed by a prep cook?"

She sure had a funny way of putting things. But it didn't end there.

"Get into something more permanent. You seem to be out of work every other week and above all," added Rita, batting her eyelids, "to leave a pretty girl stranded every weekend is virtually criminal."

Billy couldn't object. He instead stood firm and wondered how to address this latest barrage. Rita was hard to handle at times, but he could usually even things up.

"I'm not a prep cook. I'm a cook, there's a difference. And after all, you need someone to be better than, so here I am!"

"I could be better than any number of people, but I chose you, so you need to come through."

"Well, what do you think might wow people, professor? How 'bout a kidnapper?"

Rita's face shriveled and Billy was delighted. She moved and he followed. She told him to stop, and he said he was just getting started. As they tumbled through the apartment, he playfully growled, "A rough band of beach mongers raised on surf wax and sand embark on a dangerous journey of their own. Down on their luck and not too smart, they plan to solve their problems with a kidnapping!"

"Did some writing in high school, I see," quipped Rita.

"Yep, had my paper on the corkboard for a week," grinned Billy, imagining himself hunched over a typewriter, banging out the murky details of a crime gone wrong.

Suddenly nostalgic, Rita recalled how she'd first been drawn to Billy: insanity, hers. But if he said he was going to do something, it was almost guaranteed not to happen.

"Down on their luck and not too smart, eh?" repeated Rita. "Sounds good, honey, now how about a kiss?"

Meanwhile, on the other side of town, Van ducked into Keller's trailer.

Keller's Place

Down a gravelly shoulder of road over a stretch of parched pavement, they walked. A glance of something unfamiliar, something different—that's what he was, that's what they were: barren, a mystery to most, well known to only a few, the misplaced or maybe the unjust.

Where were they going? What were they doing? Who were they in love with, or could they even be in love anymore? With thin, strong arms and wrinkled, brown skin, through a distant searing mirage they traveled—to the store on the corner and then back to Keller's place.

It was a familiar slog through an odd part of town. Small, dark yards dotted the eerily overgrown thoroughfare. Faded pink flamingos fell haplessly together, aged and unmoved for years. Littered with soggy newspapers and busted trash cans under mildewed awnings, the park now marked a stark departure from what it once was, when the grass was green and the lawn ornaments reflected the sun instead of soaking it in. When neighbors shared fishing stories, and trailer parks didn't attract so many storms. A time when the residents were either building rockets or transplants attracted to the warm weather and cheap rent. Now with a smattering of cagey tenants and aging owners, the strange neighborhood had been left to fend for itself. And in the deepest, darkest corner of the trailer park, beneath a twisted live oak, stood Keller's place.

As Van approached, his thoughts returned to Billy and how he sometimes liked him and sometimes didn't. Maybe he didn't like him at all. It was a circular argument, one that was never quite resolved.

With his spiraled hair exploding out of a ball cap, Van knocked and waited. He knocked and waited again and was eventually welcomed by a slight, feminine voice.

"Come in," she said, and Van obliged.

The shadowy room smelled heavily of incense and weed as Van stood cautiously in the doorway. Sitting in a lotus position, wearing drawstring pants and an army surplus button-up, Keller looked menacing. On the floor he looked like a big ugly kid, a juvenile delinquent who'd long moved out of adolescence. A flamed NASCAR bandanna wrapped his coarse dreadlocked hair while jagged, self-inflicted tattoos covered most of his muscled body.

Ignoring the intrusion, Keller stared intently into the television. A thin shaft of light cut across a pretty girl's face, giving it the look of something modern. The place was full of stuff but seemed empty, hollow even.

Van took a seat opposite the girl and wondered what to say.

"My name's Van, what's yours?" is what he eventually offered.

"It's Emily," she answered.

Seductively attractive as a trophy on someone's sofa, Emily was pensive. Together they looked like statues, comfortable doing nothing. Keller shifted but still didn't speak. It was spooky, and although Van had just gotten in, he wanted out.

"Well, it was nice talking with you guys, but I gotta run."

As he swiftly made for the door, Keller patiently asked, "So, what brings you out of the woodwork today?"

"Ahh, just thought I'd stop by, was kind of in the neighborhood, you know."

"No, I don't know, Van. Maybe you could explain it to me."

Reluctant to discuss anything more, Van warily said, "Cool bandanna, Keller. Didn't know you were a race fan."

"I'm not a race fan, Van. It was a gift from my lovely girlfriend, Emily. She says that it fits me quite well. I'm glad you concur."

"I'll have to get one, maybe with some different kind of stuff on it, maybe lightning bolts instead of flames," he added, inching steadily toward the door.

Keller then sprang into action, his thin athletic frame coiled at the ready.

"I've never known you to casually make a social call. Most people don't just show up here. They always come over for a reason. They always have an agenda. They always want something or they want to give me something, so which is it, Van?"

Van found himself in a tight spot, staring straight at Keller's chest— any closer and they would have been connected. He decided to hit the reset button, although it hadn't quite been his choice.

"I had a plan."

"Ahh, do tell."

"Gimme some space, bud, you're getting a little too intense," warned Van.

"I'm a criminal, Van. I'm always intense!" exclaimed Keller, edging even closer.

At this point Van knew there'd be trouble. He knew something else too. He knew that Keller hated Billy Winslow with a passion. Rather than suffer the full brunt of Keller's fury, he'd ease Billy into the cross hairs. It was the least he could do.

"Well, it's something that could make us a lot of money, an easy gig. I ran it by Billy earlier, but all he did was laugh."

Van spoke and then watched as the wheels slowly started to turn. Once Billy's name came up, something derogatory was sure to follow.

"So, what's that fake engaged in these days? Helping little old ladies cross the street or maybe at this very moment he's rescuing a cat for a pretty girl with pigtails in her hair and a tear in her eye, that two-faced lowlife," fumed Keller. "You do understand that I must be thorough when faced with unsolicited guests, but since I doubt you're sophisticated enough to do any real harm, I shall listen to this ever-important matter of our fiscal futures."

With Keller finally at ease, Van callously said, "Well, it's this waiter named Steve. He's a waste of space, doesn't even need to work, just comes in to be a pain. I saw a show where some good guys changed their luck by kidnapping a neighborhood schmuck. Nobody got hurt, you know. They were all in on it. I want to kidnap the kid. He's spoiled, and his dad's got money, lots of money."

"I know the type," sneered Keller. "The dear child is working his way through college to learn the value of a buck, an all-too-common theme in the lives of common people doing common things to yield such a common result. He'll complete his studies without much trouble and meet an attractive girl who wants something more. As the wedding bells chime, he'll stroll into his first real job, where the boss is sure to arrive with a helping hand and a quick reference to his ever-so-marvelous family. He'll then sit at the same desk for the next forty years and when the sun sets and the drinks flow and his friends are all adequately impressed, he'll regale the distinguished guests with stories from his days as a waiter."

"Wow, what do you think he'll be making by then?" asked Van.

"My synopsis of Steve's future was hypothetical at best, chronicling a voyage into mediocrity, so to speak."

"Sounded pretty good to me: hot chicks, cold drinks, and a job."

"I didn't say his wife would be hot—I merely said she'd look good enough," strained Keller, "but more importantly, you're wasting my time with a dangerous plan from a stupid show that you most likely watched when you were inebriated. You need to come to me with something developed, something feasible, not more babble for me to decipher. I'm quickly losing interest in this conversation!"

"Well, maybe we could nab Steve and find some way to blame it on Billy," blurted Van.

"Nab Steve and blame Billy," repeated Keller, gazing skyward as if the words were divine rather than dangerous. It was a call to action, a chance to move his crew into a more powerful position, to get them out of petty theft and small-time drug deals. Maybe it wasn't such a bad idea after all, and what if it held the promise of an even better outcome?

"What if we were to carry out a kidnapping and have Billy arrested for it, wouldn't that be fun?"

"That's what I said," replied Van.

"You simply said to blame Billy and, as usual, I took a good plan and made it great. Have Billy arrested for it. Lead the authorities to the false conclusion that Billy Winslow was the mastermind."

"And furthermore," ordered Keller, "you two shall be working together."

What? thought Van. So now he'd have to work with the guy he was selling out? He wanted to just hand it off and get out of the way, but this guy Keller was for real.

"You will continue to associate with Billy and to solicit his assistance as you already have. He'll be only too happy to attempt a so-called 'kidnapping.' His ego won't allow him to say that he wouldn't, or that he couldn't, succeed. But also trust him to stay at arm's length and expect him to slide out at the last minute."

To Van, it sounded like Billy would double-cross him anyway. It made sense.

"You'll need two other operatives, neither of whom knows Billy, nor that he's being set up. It's your choice, so choose wisely. With Billy supposedly in charge, you'll be working both sides. As my closest confidants, Randall and Freddy will handle security. I'll be calling the shots. Is that understood?"

"I guess," answered Van. Between Billy and Keller, there was no good choice.

"If you agree to the terms, contact Billy for phase two and report back to me to begin phase three. If you no longer wish to cooperate, after a thorough debriefing, you'll be free to go."

Van could live with the second and third phases, but the debriefing didn't sound too good.

"Don't just sit there looking stupid," growled Keller. "Are you willing to work within the parameters of this design, or will you be shuffling off into the next failure?"

"OK, OK, I'm in, man," stammered Van, "but you gotta promise me that no one gets hurt."

With his head reared in laughter, Keller replied, "Of course, Van, there's no business in that anyway. He should make a wonderful politician once the trauma wears off."

"Trauma?" echoed Van.

"Spiritual growth is what I meant to say," said Keller with a grin.

Billy's Pad

It was another spectacular spring afternoon. A cool north wind clipped the coast, and the sun baked only a few special places. The neighborhood hummed with the sound of lawn mowers and rickety trucks towing trailers as Rita pulled her Camry up to Billy's pad. She recalled with a smile how the car had become hers; Billy had recommended it.

"Check it out. Toyota makes a good car. You can't beat the price either, it'll pay for itself in a month."

That's what he said before she bought the car and a bit before the timing belt ruptured.

"Even with the fix, you paid way below book value."

He said that right before the radiator exploded.

"I don't know, maybe you just bought a lemon."

Rita recalled him saying that as she sat in the driveway idling. She was steamed that day.

"You're the one who suggested I buy this lemon. You practically sold it to me. With the way you talked it up, you should be a car salesman of crappy cars."

"Easy," he'd said. "You can't blame me for a random act of God."

"That's not a random act of God, that's you telling me to buy an old worn-out car. You're supposed to know about things like that and, in case you didn't know—flash floods and earthquakes, those are acts of God!"

It didn't end there, she remembered. But the car had been running well since the repairs. With Billy around, there were always repairs.

So, Rita hopped out of the car, keys and bracelets jangling, with her thick, curly hair held back by a pair of sunglasses. In cutoffs and flip-flops, she was somewhat disappointed to still be walking up to a rental, but at least it was a nice one. Tucked neatly into a quiet side street, tropical shrubs and a stretch of green grass gave way to a charming ranch-style duplex. It was a comfortable living space, aside from the shipping crates that Billy used for shelves.

Of course, when Rita asked about the decor, Billy shrugged. "Beats buying something new that's going to fall apart in a few years."

What could she say to that?

"Sounds like the voice of a man stuck in a rut."

"If being stuck in a rut means I don't have to buy a bunch of flimsy furniture, in a rut I'll remain, or better yet I'll wallow in it."

"There's some good stuff out there that doesn't cost an arm and a leg," she chuckled.

It made no sense to Billy—he was off to the next garage sale or garbage pile, whatever came first. Rita's one stipulation was that all "treasures" be free of insects before being carted into the house. She hated bugs, especially the ones that waited for the most inopportune time to attack: in the bathroom, before bed, or in the darkness even. The house was full of cracks and crevices, and it was Florida, so Rita's vigilance toward keeping things clean was anything but misplaced.

Now through the door, she trampled a threatening line of ants, begged forgiveness from the ant gods, and walked over to Billy. In checkered slacks and a chef's coat, he lay snoring amid the industrial clatter of the day.

"Hey, honey," offered Rita as Billy moved to turn off the television. "The TV isn't on."

"What's all the racket, then?"

"People working, lawn mowers, landscaping. Why are you here anyway? Aren't you supposed to be at work?"

"They didn't require my assistance."

"What, for the day?"

"Yeah, for the day."

"But you're working tomorrow, right?"

"Not exactly," replied Billy. "But what's with the sudden interest in my work status? People get sent home early all the time. Maybe I called in sick."

"Oh, so you got dressed to call in sick?"

"Maybe I wasn't feeling well when I got dressed. You should be asking if I'm all right."

"You looked fine when you tried to turn off a television that wasn't even on. As a matter of fact, you looked stoned—that's something a stoned person would do."

"That's something a sick person would do."

"Are you sick, Billy?"

"No."

"Why don't you tell me what's going on, then?"

"What's going on is that you look completely gorgeous, and I'm not just saying that because I got fired."

"You got fired? I thought things were going well. The owners liked you. You were doing a great job."

"I didn't really get fired, you know. I got let go, kind of in a nice way."

"Are you ever going to be able to work there again?"

"It's not likely."

"Then, you got fired. What happened?"

"It's a long story, and I don't really feel like talking about it."

"I've got time. You've got nothing else to do, and I need a freakin' laugh. It's been a hectic day."

Between a couple of jobs in the service industry, most every day was hectic. As was the fact that while she regularly had two jobs, her significant other could barely keep one.

"Well," began Billy in a somber tone, "I got fired because of a haircut."

"It doesn't look like you got one," remarked Rita. "Nope, still bleached and matted."

"I appreciate your tenderness at this pivotal moment in my life, but it wasn't my hair that got me fired, it was Ed's."

"Ed. Who is Ed?"

"Ed lives in the park. We give him food and let him stay on the deck every now and then. Anyway, he needed a haircut and couldn't afford one, so I took up a collection."

"That's so sweet," cooed Rita, completely warmed by her man's thoughtfulness.

"So, I collected the money, but then completely forgot about Ed's haircut. In other words, instead of donating the money, I spent it."

"So, you gave everyone their money back?"

"I didn't have their money."

"But you had money to replace it, right?"

"Sure, but that would have left me short, so I gave Ed the haircut myself. I just cut it down, kind of like chopping some overgrown hedges. It's gonna grow back, right?"

"Have you ever given anyone a haircut?"

"No."

"Well, what happened next?" Rita cautiously asked.

"What happened next is that he started yelling about his hair. Then I said, 'Hey pal, it's not like you got a hot date or a new job or something.' And that's when he went to the owners about going to the newspaper. Then came the pat on the back, you know, the fond farewell type stuff. They knew I wasn't there for the long haul anyway. Probably figured I'd split for the next best thing."

"So, you stole the money for Ed's haircut, gave him a bad haircut, and then insulted him?"

Billy rubbed his creased brow with a calloused hand. Everywhere he went Ed would show up, and every time he tried to do something nice, it backfired.

"It didn't start out that way. The whole episode kind of snowballed. I truly forgot about the money. And how hard could it be to give a guy a simple haircut?"

To hear the explanation was a laugh, but it wasn't funny. She knew things could take a toll. But a light still shone in his eyes, a majestic glint. His smile was untarnished, so she knew that he wasn't damaged, but he couldn't have been happy. She wasn't.

Then the phone rang as Billy boldly announced, "That might just be the next best thing right there!"

Van

ello."

"Hey, Billy, it's Van."

"Van who?"

"It's Van Dalton, man. You told me to call you back in three days. We had something to discuss—a financial matter, a business venture," growled Van. "Well, it's been three days and I'm calling you back."

To Billy, Van was a neighborhood crank not to be taken too seriously. To Van, Billy was a friend—a friend who could just as easily be an enemy.

With kinky hair and gritty brown skin beneath a sleeveless T-shirt, Van carried his slight frame with pride. As a member of an exclusive club burned into existence by the hot Florida sun, he spent his days at the beach. His nights were a different story.

Van toiled relentlessly in places where dreams become distant memories replaced by hard, thankless labor. After years of long hours in hot kitchens, he bought a metal detector.

"There's Spanish gold out there," he said.

The problem being that it was completely, in a literal sense, "out there" and not on the beach. Weekend after weekend, he'd show up with a bucketful of trinkets that hadn't even paid for the stupid thing yet.

Then the magical Ernesto made Van's down payment on a shack in Costa Rica disappear.

"A first-class illusion," he'd later say, after enough alcohol had soothed his anger.

Luckily, he had a short memory and a lot of ideas. The only problem was time. With a sink full of greasy pans and more on the way, Van figured to have about three good years left.

It was seven o'clock on a Friday night, and the house was packed. No one else would be seated after nine, and Van would be lucky to be out by eleven. Restaurants were either too busy or not busy enough; there was no in-between. The ones that weren't busy didn't stay in business, so there were no easy shifts at a good restaurant.

Van could perform under pressure. His thoughts were clear. He was calm in the middle of chaos. He was winning, until Steve poked his pointy head into the dish room and yelled, "Where's the damn silverware, Van?"

Of the servers that Van didn't like, Steve topped the list. The kid didn't even need to be there; he had money socked away. *The ultimate insult to the plight of the working man*, thought Van.

A drag from a cigarette and a suggestion from the subconscious is all it took. He went from thinking, *That kid needs to be gone* to *What if he was gone, only temporarily of course, not for good, maybe for money?* Van scoffed at the notion. "Ha," he chimed. But as the night wore on and the dishes piled up, Van began to plot. As the silverware crashed to the floor, he began to scheme. As the glasses rattled noisily through the hot silver dish machine, he began to dream an ugly dream—one where he took something from someone else without a shred of remorse. He laughed again, but this time a sinister cackle. The word *abduct* popped into his head, and then Steve. It seemed to make perfect sense, the sure thing he'd been waiting for. *Worth dealing with Keller, and also the betrayal of Billy*, thought Van as he planned to pipe his new and improved plan through the receiver.

All Billy heard was Van's gravelly bark saying, "It's been three days, and I'm calling you back!"

"Congratulations, dumbass, you did something right for once."

"Yeah, well, after speaking with Keller, I wanted to make sure I got back to you," sneered Van.

Now prompted by a name—a highly toxic one at that—Billy remembered an earlier useless phone call: a kidnapping, an exposé, and an insider's perspective. Capitalize on the idiocy of others—if it's good enough for the nightly news, it's good enough for me. Rita wouldn't be too happy, but she wouldn't complain once the checks started to roll in.

"That's right. You called when I told you to call. An operation like this requires perfect timing and full disclosure," ordered Billy before asking, "So, what business did you have with Keller?"

"We had something to iron out, a minor misunderstanding," answered Van, proving early on to be quite the lethal double agent.

"Well, from now on, due to the sensitivity of this mission, it'll simply be called code name K," said Billy. "And we're gonna need a gang. Any thoughts on that?"

"I got a couple of guys in mind. One's called the young bum, and the other's name is Edwin Slack, an ex-military guy," replied Van, not really convinced of Edwin's military service, but it sounded good.

"Don't believe I've met an Edwin Slack or a young bum. You mentioned Edwin served in the military. What branch?"

"He's some kind of a secret agent, says he can't talk about it, though. He's got some army stuff, that's all I know."

Wonderful, thought Billy, *a delusional general. This keeps getting better.*

"I need a cover, Van, something that's gonna get me close to Steve."

"They're hiring a cook at the Chowder House. Steve's a waiter, and I'm in the back of the house. The manager's around most days at noon."

"Sounds good, Van, I'll check out that job while you gather the troops."

"10-4," answered Van.

Suddenly inspired, Billy cradled the receiver and on the back of an overdue bill wrote:

"An Idiot's Guide to Kidnapping"

Steve

Billy approached the Chowder House with the same expectation of success as usual: not that much. He knew the drill. The manager would act laid-back and flexible, saying, "This is a fun place to work. We're all kind of like family here."

He'd heard that one before.

The sun blazed in its peak position as Billy stepped into a dark dining room. While his eyes adjusted to a stained painting of a shrimp trawler, the methodical movements of a restaurant coming to life were just visible. A blackboard with the lunch specials and a message to seat yourself leaned against a vacant hostess stand. "Best Buffet on the Beach," is what the sign said.

Billy waited. The emptiness of the room gave him a way out. His instincts told him to go. He was about to do so when a swiftly moving gentleman in an apron said, "Hey, Billy, glad you could make it. Van said you'd be in at lunch. Have a seat at the bar, and I'll be right with you."

Now he was stuck. He couldn't say anything, not even that he wasn't Billy. Luckily, he was there on assignment, so there was no pressure to make a stellar first impression, hence the Hawaiian shirt and sunglasses.

"I see you favor the casual look," began manager Phil Easton. "I like that in my staff, laid-back, relaxed. Unfortunately, I have to wear this sale-rack gear, semirespectable, I guess, but I'd be just as happy in a pair of checks working the line."

"Yeah, I was in a hurry—had another job interview this morning, cabana boy at the Hilton or something like that."

"Working at the beach, eh?" continued Phil. "Well, we could use you here if that doesn't work out. I'll just need some kind of a résumé or an application that we could put on file. I mean, you came highly recommended."

"I've got this here," said Billy said as he calmly slid a piece of paper across the bar.

Phil retrieved the wrinkled artifact with a nod. "You've got some good work experience, so I don't think the volume here'll be a problem. Although I see you've listed your occupation as 'A Man of Vision.' This is a restaurant, and we are hiring a cook."

"I could function in that capacity. It's more a title than an occupation, a minor detail compared to opposing forces in constant conflict," added Billy, as if any explanation were needed.

It was obviously a push. Phil was desperate for help, and Billy knew it. No bet would be paid. No one would come out on top. They'd both simply settle to break even.

"Although you seem to be a bit unusual, I believe you'd be a good fit for us."

Unusual in an understatement, thought Billy before muttering, "Well, when would you like me to start?"

"We could use you now if you're not too busy. Just get a little dinner prep done, and we'll put a schedule together."

"OK," surrendered Billy, as the reality of getting used to another hot kitchen set in.

This one would be hotter than most.

As Phil handed Billy a lunch menu, Van tossed him an apron.

"I guess you know him," said Phil, motioning toward Van.

"I'm afraid I do," answered Billy.

Phil took it as a joke between friends, but it wasn't, as the declaration of, "Hey, Phil," rang out from a thin server with spiky blond hair.

"Sorry I'm late, got stuck in Cape traffic."

"That's fine, Steve."

Phil couldn't demand too much of Steve. After all, he was working his way through college.

Never apologize for being late, thought Billy as Phil quickly said, "Billy, this is Steve, best waiter on the staff and soon-to-be proud college grad. Steve, meet Billy, chef extraordinaire and friend of Van."

"Wow, Van has friends? That's news to me. Just what we need: another burnout," replied Steve.

Billy winced. It was a hard first hit.

Phil then paused to say, "You'll have to excuse Steve. He's kind of a wiseass, you know, still in school."

Now, if one were to wonder why Billy held such deep disdain for common employment, here was a perfect example. He was first introduced as Van's friend, which he wasn't. He was then called a burnout, which wasn't completely true, and next reminded that Steve had an excuse because he supposedly had a future.

Desperation suddenly replaced promise as Billy was betrayed by the facts instead of the fiction. The fiction had replaced what had once been true: that he was going to hit it big. He still would. After all, he was writing the story.

"Hey, Steve, you're a funny guy. If that school thing doesn't take off, you should try comedy."

"I'm going to be a doctor."

"What kind?" asked Billy.

"The kind you seem to need most, a psychiatrist."

Feeling the sting of yet another insult, Billy edged forward.

"Easy there, Billy," said Steve. "I was just standing my ground. It's not every day that you get to meet an ass-kicking local in the flesh."

"What, you know me?"

"Yeah, I'm a big fan of your work, *28 Days without Waves*," he said, which was a lie. He'd found the old surf flick by mistake and actually watched it, which quickly proved to be a second mistake. Steve had no qualms about lying to this latest deadbeat, though. After all, he wouldn't be around long. They never were.

Billy was startled by the praise. The movie had been panned, laughed at even, but he felt compelled to share an insider's perspective anyway.

"It was supposed to be *28 Days with Waves*. We only had the equipment for twenty-eight days and it turned out to be flat, so we spiced it up with a bikini contest and a few surfing pictures. Got some other stuff going on now, though. You should be able to check it out here pretty soon. It's gonna be big," added Billy as an inside joke that wasn't too funny.

"Cool," said Steve before lowering the boom. "My dad was a professional wrestler for years—a champion, no less."

Following the stunning admission, Billy stepped back. In a strange way, the tables had turned. The joke now seemed to be on him. He knew of the sport, or the show, or whatever else it could be called; caught it one night while flipping through the channels. It was hilarious. With heroes and villains and plenty of tortured story lines, the colorful trash-talking characters could fight. Anything could be used as a weapon, even the coveted championship belt. He also recalled with an alarming clarity that the wrestlers were all big, strong, fast, and tough.

"Wow!" exclaimed Billy. "I've seen it before."

Then as the first ticket arrived, he dismissed Steve to make a Monte Cristo sandwich, their top seller, he'd been told. With a crackling sear, Billy added the battered mess to a hot pan, then rushed to ask Van a simple question.

"Why didn't you tell me that Steve's dad was a professional wrestler?"

"You didn't ask."

"I didn't ask?"

"Yeah, you didn't ask."

"How am I supposed to know to ask a dumbass question like that?" hissed Billy, as he suddenly remembered who he was talking to. "I mean, don't you know the kind of problems a detail like that can create? The guy's probably a damn local hero, a big and mean local hero."

For the first time in their short conversation, Van leveled his bloodshot eyes on Billy and said, "We're not kidnapping his dad."

Van's logic, twisted as it were, held just the right amount of truth.

"The guy's dad was a damn professional wrestler," muttered Billy, settling in for what was sure to be an interesting night.

Irritated and tired—despite Van, Phil, and Steve—Billy survived his first shift. He entered the house just as Rita exited the shower, and just in time for her to rebuff a halfhearted sexual advance.

"At least clean up before you suggest that," she said, pinching his cheek on her way to a glass of wine.

Lately the smell of fried fish and hush puppies was more a deterrent than an aphrodisiac. It didn't matter before. It had been like making love to the catch of the day.

"No time for that," answered Billy as he wrote, *And the reluctant hero of the story, Billy Winslow.*

He then paused. Something didn't sound right. He needed a name—preferably one that wasn't his.

"What's a good name for a book, Rita?"

"I don't know," she replied. "*The Iliad*?"

"No, I mean for a character in a book."

"Male or female?"

"What do you think?"

"If it's you who's writing the book, it would have to be a male," she guessed, "most likely a stupid one."

"Whatever," groaned Billy. "What's the name, Rita? I need a name."

Borrowing from a *Wheel of Fortune* answer and a grammar school teacher, she yelled, "How about Flash Shackelford?"

"Flash Shackelford," he repeated.

He liked it.

Needing a bold title for a dangerous new character, Billy hurriedly typed:

"A Kidnapping in Paradise"
featuring Flash Shackelford

Steve's Dad

The event that ushered James Elliot Linon into the world was a painful beginning to a life destined only to increase in discomfort. It was 1954, and the birth of James was deemed an event by the doctors and nurses alike, but mostly by his mother, Evelyn. Even at birth, James could be described, in a word, as big.

He had a big head, twice the size of any normal noggin.

His hands were big.

He had big feet.

He had a big mouth, but more importantly, he had a big heart.

James turned into Jim in the ninth grade when his parents finally let him play football, something that he was, of course, destined to do. He led his high school to the state finals twice, won it once, and then accepted a scholarship from the University of Georgia to play for the Bulldogs. At six foot five and two hundred and fifty pounds, he looked to be a shoo-in for the pros. A high-profile signing seemed to be a sure thing. Fame and fortune would surely come. It was all just a matter of time. It was all just a matter of time, that is, until the injury.

Scouts from nearly every pro football team in the nation were in attendance when Jim blew out his knee. And the cheerleaders, thank God for the cheerleaders, at least they were happy. They cheered as the crowd grew silent. They moved but seemed still. The pain was intense. It made everything else dull.

From the sideline, Jim gazed at the scoreboard as a cheerleader named Donna Grey threw her pompoms high into the air. Still on his back, he suddenly noticed the distant, floating objects start to fall. Slower at first and then accelerating, the pair of red-and-white pompoms split the night and hit him square in the head. Despondent, and now rather disgusted, Jim rode all the way to the hospital with the pompoms wedged between his neck and an uncomfortable stretcher. Whisked from the ambulance and wheeled into a waiting room, he'd now go under the knife.

The operating room buzzed with a certain urgency as Jim lay help-lessly awake. Staring into the eyes of an anesthesiologist, he counted backward as the doctors prepped for surgery. Beneath the bright lights, amid the clatter of trays and sharpened steel, they poked and prodded, but he didn't feel a thing. And with the cuts sewn, and the doctors slowly coming back into focus, Jim was carefully rolled away.

Bleary eyed and bandaged in a small, colorless room, he gave a nod as the beautiful Donna Grey sheepishly invited herself in. She'd been at the hospital the whole time, twenty-four hours in all, waiting to apologize. Through a medicated fog, the banged-up all-star quickly eyed another prize, an attractively repentant cheerleader.

"You threw the pompoms at me," guessed Jim, beginning to put two and two together.

"I'm so sorry," replied Donna. "I was excited, they slipped, you were there. I feel so bad to have hit a man on the brink of losing everything."

Jim wondered if she'd talked to the doctors or something. He kind of hoped not to have lost everything. He was thinking therapy and a comeback. *Those things aren't unheard of,* he thought as Donna started to sob.

"Hey, now," he said, while gently caressing her clenched hand.

"Hey, hey," he continued in a soothing voice.

"Hey," he said as she was almost calm.

"Hey, what the heck is your name?" he blurted out, sending her into another fit of emotion.

She was howling this time. Ever since the end of the game she'd been riddled with guilt, but it was OK because her clumsy toss had brought them together. She had made plans, picked out a wedding dress, got the kids off to school, and now felt so anonymous.

Forced to regroup, Jim quickly stammered, "Look, you're beautiful. I—I don't know you, but I appreciate you waiting with me. You're right. I may not play again. I mean, I'm gonna try, but even if I never touch another football, I'd like to take you out to dinner sometime, after I get better, you know, after I can walk again."

The tears subsided as she heard the sincerity in Jim's voice. She sniffled, rubbed her eyes, gave her hair a quick shake, and in a quivering, childish voice said, "My name is Donna."

Donna was born and raised in Athens, Georgia, and it wouldn't be easy for Jim to convince her to leave, but eventually he would, because he had to.

In July of 1977, with Donna in tow, the blessing of her father, and a few bucks in his pocket, Jim went in reverse. As they drove up to his old house on Azalea Lane, a warped poster-board sign greeted the two, and suddenly Donna wasn't so sure she'd made the right choice.

Her doubt, however, was short lived. She was sitting next to Jim. His character was unquestioned, his will immeasurable. She'd seen him on the field, and there was nothing that good that could go bad. If this was where they had to start, she'd support it. She believed in him.

Jim and Donna stayed in the car for a moment relishing the remains of their brief college romance.

"We could keep driving," said Jim.

"That would be nice," replied Donna, "but there are a few people in there who really want to see you. We'd run out of gas after a while, anyway."

"Yeah, I suppose, but before everything gets started, I wanted to tell you how beautiful you look today, and every day for that matter. I promise I won't let you down."

She wanted to say that she knew he wouldn't and that she loved him, but it was too late. Jim's mother, Evelyn, had her face pressed against Donna's window, while his pesky friend Mick blurted out a harebrained business scheme.

"We'll call it Second Down Sportswear. Get a couple of cheap shirts with your ugly mug selling 'em. How can it go wrong?"

Mick Rider sold cars and, at the tender age of twenty-three, was already parched from hot parking lots and strong drinks. Most everything he said was rubbish, but every now and then he'd have a good idea, which just happened to be the case on that sunny day.

With a drink in one hand and a business card in the other, he proudly said, "Seeing as how you're all washed up in football, I thought you might be interested in a little wrestling."

Fighting the urge to punch Mick in the face, Jim took the card instead. It was a card for Joe Slick's Wrestling Academy in Apopka, Florida, which of course prompted the obvious question, "Who is Joe Slick?"

"Who is Joe Slick?" repeated Mick. "He's only the foremost authority on professional wrestling throughout the southern states!"

"What does that mean?"

"It means he teaches big people how to wrestle. He drives around in a Cadillac Eldorado and shows ex-something-or-others such as yourself how to beat their way into the finer things in life. He's a good friend of mine, I might add—got him a good deal on a car. Now here's what I'm gonna do, I mean, because you're a friend and all, down on your luck and everything else," said Mick, grinning like the Cheshire cat. "I'm going to set up a meeting between you and Joe Slick."

Jim still wasn't convinced, but it was a place to start. Like it or not, he was going to have to do something.

So, on a hot day in August, Jim sauntered into Joe Slick's Wrestling Academy. The familiar scent of combat hung in the air, and it felt good to be in the gym again. He put on some wrestling trunks, wrapped his knee, laced up his boots, and headed out to the center ring. Everyone stopped what they were doing to check out the massive former football star.

Joe Slick was all smiles as he gave Jim the lowdown.

"It's easier to show you what we do than to explain it. I'll do the best I can to prepare you for the professional ranks and to get you placed, but there are no guarantees. If you can accept those terms, then you, James Linon, will be the newest member of Joe Slick's Wrestling Academy!"

"I accept," said Jim with a handshake.

Shaking hands was the easy part, being thrown into a ring and tossed around like a ragdoll was a different story. Battered and bruised, Jim realized the training was like football practice, only worse. He worked hard, but it was fun and with Donna by his side, he was the luckiest man alive. He was lucky but unemployed, and with Donna carrying their son Steve, Jim suddenly needed a job. So with another handshake and a referral from Joe Slick, Jim joined the Southern States Wrestling League and quickly moved up the ranks.

Starting out as Gentleman Jim, he was a pillar of the community and a fan favorite. Rapidly becoming champion, Jim was on top of the wrestling world before being stripped of his championship belt and beaten by his friends. He then turned to the dark side and formed a cartel of brutality unequaled in all wrestling history. Ashamed to show his face, Jim now wore a black mask and a cape while pounding his old pals into oblivion. Things were going well for him as the villain, until he was caught vulnerable and alone. Beaten and blamed for the misery his tag team had caused, Jim took a hard blow to the head and then returned as Gentleman Jim. He wreaked havoc on the bad guys for another few years, but due to his age and waning interest, Jim was scheduled to be written out.

After fifteen long years of wrestling, Jim finally fought his last match. He went out on top, so the going-away party at his new riverfront home was full to capacity. He had done all right for his friends and family. With two bad knees, a bum back, and a million dollars in the bank, he now needed a new profession, and Mick Rider needed a new job.

Gentleman Jim Motors

J im and Mick hadn't kept in touch. They'd both seen some ups and downs, but at the moment, Mick was in the middle of a monumental drubbing. Already a couple of cocktails down, his joy at seeing Jim was still genuine.

"You look like hell, you beat-up old antique," roared Mick in the parking lot of a downtown diner.

"I still look better than you," replied Jim in his signature throaty growl.

"Very true, Big Jim, very true."

Jim moved with an air of wealth and class. With weak knees and a sore back, he used his head now rather than his fists.

"Look, Mick," began Jim in a more serious tone, "I'm going to open a car dealership, and I'd like to bring you in as one of the salesmen."

"Well, Jimmy," replied Mick.

"Of course, I could go in another direc—" Jim started to say.

"I accept! I sure do accept that kind offer, Brother Jim. Just have to put everything else on the back burner for a while."

Jim stalled and Mick squirmed. They both knew there was no back burner as Jim finally said, "Now remember, I don't need you to run a business for me. I just need you to sell cars."

"That's what I do best, Jimmy."

Gentleman Jim's opened for business in December of 1990, and the sales were incredible. Everyone wanted to buy a car from Gentleman Jim, and Mick Rider made sure they could. Required to hold a steady job, Steve serviced the lot every now and then but preferred restaurant work to detailing cars. That's where he ran into Van, at the Chowder House, Jim's favorite beachside bistro.

After a busy week on the car lot, Jim and Mick walked into the Chowder House for a well-deserved dinner. With Steve as their waiter, the food was always fresh and the service always prompt. It was by a thin margin that Jim opened a car dealership rather than a restaurant, and by the end of the night, he usually ended up in the kitchen. That's where he was as Billy's first Friday came to a close.

After a busy shift, Billy enjoyed chatting with the regulars about as much as he liked sweeping up shattered glass. And sure enough, as he drained his first beer of the night, Steve's hulking father, with Mick in tow, parted the double doors for their customary kitchen inspection. Phil flew by and tempted Jim to grab a pan, and Jim joked that he would but for an arthritic right hand. Phil then put on the brakes to introduce Jim to his newest line cook.

"Jim, come on over and meet the new addition. This is Billy."

"Hey, Billy," said Jim as Billy grasped his huge hand and began to lie.

"Hey, Jim, it's a pleasure to meet you."

"Jim is Steve's dad and an ex-professional wrestler, a champion, no less," announced Phil.

"That would have been my second guess," replied Billy.

Slightly intrigued, Jim looked down and asked, "What would have been your first?"

Billy surveyed his bland, formal look: Unimpressive but inoffensive. Flat. Worked late, hadn't been home yet. Long sleeves rolled to the elbows with a semi expensive watch; the real gold watch was at home. Not intellectual enough to be a professional. Too big to sit in a cubicle. Made money. It narrowed down to sales. Mobile, walking, tan. Car sales.

"A really big used car salesman."

The kitchen echoed with Jim's booming laughter.

"A jock, a bodyguard, a bouncer, I've heard 'em all, but no one's ever pegged me quite like you just did. I sell used cars, but I sell new cars too. I sell a lot of them."

Jim caught Phil as he went to bring Van a beer and said, "I like this new guy. He's a real straight shooter."

"Yeah," agreed Mick, "he's the type of guy who could use a flashy new car."

Billy suddenly realized that both Jim and Phil had moved on, but this new character hadn't.

"Got a new Mustang perfect for a young go-getter like yourself. Buy it now and save 20 percent off the purchase price, available only in Puerto Rico and other select US territories, of course," stated the red-faced guy.

Wanting to keep it short, Billy smiled, made eye contact, and said, "Sure, man, I'll buy the car if I can drive it over your head!"

"No can do, compadre," replied Mick, "been there, done that. Got the old noggin run over by a '74 Bug—bashed up the fender a bit, but I still got my money out of it. Anyway, good talking at ya. If you change your mind, just remember, nobody rides better than when they ride with the Rider, limited background check and immediate financing available while supplies last," he muttered as he caught up with the other guys.

Billy cautiously looked up to make sure that Mick had moved on. *Good, they're talking to Van, maybe he'll get them to leave*, he thought before the more paranoid contemplation of, *What the hell are they talking to Van about?*

As the night came to a close, Phil tallied the sales, Steve caught a ride home with Jim, and a couple of career servers stayed at the bar to drink and complain. As far as they were concerned, Billy was good. The food was on time, looked fine, no yelling, and not a single mistake. The drinks were on them. Van, of course, extorted his fair share of beverages from the remaining staff. After all, they were nothing without him.

"So, you know Steve's dad?" asked Billy as he and Van emptied the last garbage can of the night.

"Yeah, he's a good guy."

He knew better than to ask the next logical question. It wouldn't clarify anything. It could only serve to darken the already murky waters. He simply shook his head and heaved a bloated can liner into the dumpster.

With the cleanup done and Billy headed home, Van shouted, "One o'clock?" in reference to the crew's first meeting.

Unable to halt his downward spiral, Billy answered an uninspired, "Yeah."

It was too late for Rita to get motivated as she sat on the couch and fiddled with the remote. Her thoughts began to drift as she considered the handsome, successful guys who had asked her out lately, and why she hadn't gone. Some seemed genuine.

A mysterious force, she guessed: invisible items of interest. The way a pair of sparkling eyes and a simple smile could turn an otherwise ordinary night into a lifetime.

It was too late as Billy glided up to the duplex. Rita's car was in the driveway, so he knew she'd be waiting. Another dull Friday night for a beautiful, intelligent woman—it seemed a shame. He felt responsible.

"Hey, beautiful!" exclaimed Billy, expending his last drop of excitement for a day that was just about done.

"Hey, baby," she said with a yawn. "How was work?"

"Hectic, I didn't think that little restaurant got so busy. I had to get up to speed for the first hour, but after that it was business as usual. How about you? You feel like going out for a drink or something?"

"Ahh no, I was just about to fall asleep."

"Then I guess sex is out of the question?"

"Ahh yeah, and asking doesn't quite set the mood either."

"It wasn't a serious proposal, just something to make you smile."

A slight grin slid across Rita's face as she put aside her concerns. There was no way to resist Billy when he was humble and tired. As much as she tried, she couldn't stay mad.

"I promise we'll have fun tomorrow," he said. "A day at the beach, sunset over the river, and the finest snapper in town. How does that sound!"

"It sounds wonderful," she replied. "Now I'm going to bed."

"Good night, pretty. I'll be right in, just got to jot something down."

Rita dozed as Billy typed. She heard a click, then silence, then another click, and then more silence.

"Better slow down, honey, you're going to overheat the typewriter."

Typewriters don't overheat, he thought as he delved deep into the psyche of his main character, Flash.

Chapter 1
Bad Beginning

Flash met the players and should have pulled out, but too much disappointment and too much doubt had left him desperate. He'd been victimized by uneven odds before, but long shots could pay off.

His steps popped off the wet cement, and something in the night told him to stay the course. There'd be regret, but Flash wouldn't back down. This time he'd see it through.

He knew what others didn't. He felt what others couldn't. He lived where others didn't dare to live, in the creases, on the edges, with questions in places that had no answers. In the wet, windswept night, Flash thought about beginnings. He wondered if he'd begun badly, and if he had to end up that way.

Billy liked the edgy feel, although for the moment, "A Kidnapping in Paradise" seemed too soft a title for a heavy hitter like Flash.

The typing ceased. His brain didn't budge. His fingers wouldn't move. He needed Rita.

"Are you awake, honey?"

"I am now. What's going on?"

"I need a title for a book, a good book about a kidnapping."

Even in her semiconscious state, Rita doubted the two could ever go together, but at the moment she'd say pretty much anything.

"How about, 'The Kidnapping.'"

"'The Kidnapping,'" he repeated.

He liked it. It was simple and straight to the point. Billy crumpled up the old title page and quickly typed:

"The Kidnapping"

The Meeting

The crew showed up late with a bandaged leg and a lie. Van's so-called specialists had slowed the procession discussing ways to outsmart aliens. A single question concerning an imminent invasion delayed Van. Two hours later, Van, Edwin, and the young bum, intoxicated and out of breath, sped toward the pavilion.

Billy saw them first and started to leave. For a moment he sensed it wasn't right to string the guys along, to manipulate them for his financial gain, to invade their privacy for his benefit. It wasn't too late to pull the plug—now was the time.

The justification revealed itself in the form of a simple question: If given the chance, would they use him to further their agenda? As they approached the calm, reflective river, the answer came as a clear and unequivocal "Yes."

Like a company of battered soldiers, they arrived in a small, ragged formation. Van had assembled a no-nonsense unit from the backyards and beachside bars of a nearby town. Edwin Slack and the one they called the young bum were the hired hands, or the human shields, depending on how things went.

"Hey, Billy, what's going on?" asked Van.

There was no reply.

"You been out here long, Billy?"

Still without so much as a glance, Edwin hissed at Van to get out of the way. Sensing a power struggle, Billy decided to engage.

"What's up, Van?"

"Hey man, we were supposed to have a meeting today."

"We were supposed to have a meeting two hours ago. We aren't supposed to be doing anything now."

In a thin camouflage jacket with a shock of white hair tucked neatly beneath a weathered beret, Edwin got off his bike and moved forward.

"Sergeant Edwin Slack at your service, sir."

"Sergeant Edwin Slack," repeated Billy, eyeing Edwin's army surplus garb.

"Sergeant Edwin Slack," he said again, now realizing they were hinged on his every word.

It seemed like they were taking this thing seriously, or about as seriously as they could take anything, which wasn't very seriously at all, but they were counting on it. He was counting on it too.

"Now, Sergeant Slack, would your commanding officer consent to your company being two hours late for a mandatory assessment of a top secret operation?"

"No, Commander William," answered Edwin in a gritty addiction-laced growl. "A dire emergency halted our forward progress."

"Well, what happened, Slack?"

"This ought to be good," muttered Van as the young bum anxiously twitched his bandaged leg.

"Well, we were on our way with plenty of time," started Edwin, "when out of nowhere an old man, I mean a little old lady, ran slap into the young bum and knocked him clean off his bike. She just kept going like the little old lady from Pasadena. Didn't even have a license plate on the car, must have rusted off or something."

"What about a doctor? How'd you know his leg wasn't fractured, or worse?" asked Billy.

"There just so happened to be a doctor walking down the street who administered medical care right there on the spot. We got the ice and the bandage and he did the rest. Can't take the bandage off for twenty-four hours, though."

Billy paused. He'd expected a certain degree of difficulty, but not right off the bat. If they lied and it worked, they'd lie again. In most cases it's admirable to be trusting. It's kind to believe what isn't true, but not in this business. The next thing you know, it's their loot and their story. Billy couldn't let that happen. He figured they'd show up late and drunk, but this half-baked hit-and-run story was completely unanticipated. Whether utterly stupid or semisophisticated, it was dangerous either way.

Nearing the young bum to more closely examine the so-called victim, Billy knew something was up. It was three in the afternoon, and the sun gleamed aggressively off every reflective surface in sight. Billy had to shield his eyes from the glare that flashed across the steel fenders of the young bum's bike. He addressed the next question to the group as a whole.

"Why isn't his bike damaged?"

They all moved a little, each disjointed motion in unison.

"If he'd been knocked off his bike by an old man or old lady in a car with no license plate, this bike would be marked up. At least one of the rims would be bent and the young bum would have some scrapes on him. Bum, do you have any scrapes on you?"

Unshaven in a backward cap, the young bum simply shook his head. "No."

"Well, here's the deal," announced Billy, "the young bum doesn't have any scrapes on him because he wasn't hit by a car."

Billy was picking up steam. The operation was back online. He was back in charge.

"Do any of you guys still think he was hit by a car?"

"We were just testing you, Commander. You passed with flying colors," said Edwin with an outstretched hand.

Knowing that he had won the first battle, Billy took it. He then shifted into full commandant mode, circling the group like a lion stalking injured prey.

"Now give me one good reason why I should entrust my safety and the success of this mission to a group of amateurs?"

"'Cause you need our expertise," chimed Edwin.

Doubtful, thought Billy.

"'Cause we're here," offered the young bum.

Painfully true, he silently agreed.

"'Cause we're all you got," answered Van, stating the only real truth of the afternoon.

The rest was just posturing and establishing a pecking order. It had been established. They'd yield, but there weren't any other guys in town who would get into something like this, and Van knew it. The gang watching from the woods knew it too.

Keller, Randall, and Freddy had been in the bush for the past two hours getting bit by mosquitoes and watching Billy fish. A sharp crash echoed from the marsh as Randall accidentally broke a bottle, followed by more commotion as Keller quickly pitched a stick in his direction.

"Young bum," commanded Billy as the first executive order of the mission. "I need you to scout the woods."

"What?"

"He needs you to secure the perimeter," barked Edwin.

"Why don't you go?"

"'Cause he asked you to do it."

No one else spoke up or stepped forward, so the young bum began an uninspired amble toward the swamp.

"Damn kids these days want everything handed to them," muttered Edwin.

"You could have gone," said Van.

"You could have gone too," countered Edwin.

"We all could have gone, and we'll all be called upon to do things we don't want to do. This is just the beginning," said Billy as the young bum scanned the thicket.

A large alligator then slithered into his line of sight and prompted a hasty retreat. He'd heard gators were pretty fast and was in no mood to find out.

"Everything's clear in there, guys," shouted the young bum, but as it stood, everything wasn't clear in there.

Small alligators are relatively harmless, but Randall figured this one to be about eleven feet, if not larger. He was the closest, so it would be his job to get it back into the water.

While Keller and Freddy looked anxiously on, Randall snapped into action. Eyeing a jagged, colorless object, he dove frantically for a large rock, took aim, and then pegged the gator square on the nose, sending it slithering back into the depths. They then watched the young bum jog carelessly back to the gang. The next rock would have been for him.

"OK, so you're all I got," repeated Billy, picking up where he left off. "Let's substitute that phrase for, you're all I got because I don't feel like hunting around for another set of greenhorns. How does that grab you?"

"Whatever gets you through the night," answered Van, pretty sure that Billy had taken the bait. If he was going to back out, he would have done it by now, or maybe there was something else going on. It wasn't out of the question. By the end of the mission, there was sure to be a tangled web.

Ignoring the remark, Billy drew a deep breath and then asked, "Does anyone besides Van know why we're here today?"

With no audible reply he said, "We're here to initiate code name K."

"Code name K refers to a kidnapping," he continued, staring straight into the eyes of the operatives.

"Count me in," replied Edwin. "I've been waiting a long time for something like this."

"It sounds cool to me," added the young bum.

"The rest of the information will be disseminated as needed," explained Billy, as if there actually was any other information.

"For the time being, I'll be communicating through Van. Does anyone have any questions?"

"How about the cash?" asked Edwin.

"Yeah, how much money?" added the young bum, as the thrill of being chosen for such a life-changing event had already become commonplace.

Billy hadn't considered it. Their goals were different: He was writing a book. They wanted a briefcase full of bills and a hell of a story to tell.

"We haven't discussed that issue yet. We're in the process of checking liquid assets and so on," answered Billy.

Edwin had gone through enough ups and downs for the day and was getting tired. To continue, he'd have to hear something about compensation.

"Don't take this the wrong way, Billy, but when someone offers me a job and I accept, the very next thing we talk about is cash."

Deciding to keep it simple, Billy walked up to Edwin and said, "You're going to make a lot of money."

Edwin didn't move. His expression didn't change. It wasn't enough, and Billy was exhausted. *What else can I say?* he thought as both Edwin and the young bum erupted into a chorus of excited laughter, the young bum picturing himself in a new used car, while Edwin imagined a trip to Mexico, where the money was sure to go a bit further.

"You got yourself a deal there, Brother Billy," said Edwin, obviously speaking for the young bum as well.

With a handshake to make it official, Billy spoke briefly with Van, and then left behind his fishing gear and cooler as a sign of goodwill.

"Beer and bait," said Van with a congratulatory laugh.

But in their haste to celebrate, they failed to notice three dingy bug-bitten characters closing in, the most imposing of the three now dangerously close to Van. It was none other than the crew from the other side of town, the silent partners, so to speak. Big and dangerous, they all looked mad, and Edwin was instantly put on guard.

"Well, hello, Van," sneered Keller.

"Hey, Keller, whaddya doing out here?"

"It is quite an interesting question, isn't it, Randall?"

"Yeah, he's just full of wonder."

"I didn't realize you were such an inquisitive charge," continued Keller.

"I do what I can," replied Van, starting to feel like something had gone seriously wrong.

Keller then pushed his face into Van's and in a low, sinister growl said, "If you are ever two hours late for any scheduled event that has anything to do with, or remotely involves me, I will fillet you."

"As for you two," snapped Keller, resting an uneasy glare on Edwin and the young bum, "Forget, for the time being, our presence. Is that understood?"

Unsure what the problem was, they gave a cautious nod. Randall and Freddy then scooped up the cooler and the fishing gear and loaded it into an old Chevy truck. Motoring again in Van's direction, they slowed as Keller turned to Van and said, "Next Sunday at eight, and don't be late."

Left with a monumental thirst and some unanswered questions, their most compelling inquiry seemed to be, "Why in the hell did those guys walk out of the woods and take the beer, the bait, and the fishing poles?"

"Hey, Van, why in the hell did those guys walk out of the woods and take the beer, the bait, and the fishing poles?" asked Edwin.

"I don't know," answered Van. "They must have been checking us out."

"Why did he say he was going to carve you up if we were late again?" inquired the young bum with a more poignant contemplation.

Stressed and tired, Van gave the only answer that he could. "Let's just say there's more to this little excursion than meets the eye."

"Classified," announced Edwin.

"Yeah, classified," repeated Van.

The problem of tardiness had been sorted out, though. They wouldn't be late again.

Billy would be late again as he rushed to stall Rita's departure. *Real smart*, she thought, as her foot fought against what her brain wanted to do, which was to accelerate.

"Is everything OK?" asked Billy.

"Yeah, everything's fine. You're late, and I'm leaving."

"I know, and I'm sorry. This assignment's been taking a lot of my time," he said, which was a lie, but he was counting on it taking a lot of time as he rushed to chronicle the day's events.

Intrigued by Billy's haste, Rita followed.

"Writer's block?" she quipped as he sat motionless.

"Ahh no," he stammered.

"Well, that's quite a script you got going there, Hemingway. When's the deadline?"

Jolted from his fog, Billy exclaimed, "It was last week!" as he frantically typed.

Chapter 2

Flash in the Pan

Flash had his crew and they were rough.

   But not rough in a good way, rough in a stupid and dangerous way.

He'd stick with them, though, just like he'd stuck with his bad cup of coffee.
   He had no choice.
   The coffee had brewed.
   The stage was set.
   They knew too much.
   They didn't know enough, and he was out of coffee.

Billy sat back and examined the text. Both reckless and comical, he wondered how it could work.

Rita then turned on the radio, and, of course, every song just had to mimic her romantic crisis. She moved the dial but to no avail. "Don't Look Back" popped up as an instructional of how to move on. "Accidents Will Happen" seemed to sum up their time together. "Fifty Ways to Leave Your Lover," offered an easy listening solution as Billy yelled, "What's a good name for a zany kidnapping story?"

Considering the perennial song of flight, Rita answered, "How about 'Fifty Ways to Botch a Perfectly Good Kidnapping.'"

"Fifty ways to botch a perfectly good kidnapping." *Kind of reminds me of that song—it's the same but different.*

"Nice work, Rita. Kind of reminds me of that song."

He could have at least dragged his ass out of the bedroom to say thanks, she thought, as fifty ways out seemed to be forty-nine more than she'd need.

Back in form, Billy typed:

"Fifty Ways to Botch a Perfectly Good Kidnapping"

The End

The End was the place Keller called home: the trailer at the end of the park.

There was no formal designation other than a weathered black mailbox with the words *The End* scraped into it. Appropriately damaged, it was a grim reminder of what to expect.

More prone to intimidation than violence, at times, Keller could operate. Most of his petty schemes worked out. Most of the time he could settle a grudge. He mostly stayed on the right side of the law, but he'd never gotten the best of Billy Winslow. On the contrary, when dealing with his former friend, Keller always seemed to get the short end of the stick.

It was an unhealthy fixation at best, but he was determined to destroy Billy even if it meant his own demise. An end to his torment would be the end result of an endless pursuit to eliminate the man he had once called a friend.

An end to a life of poverty was on Van's mind as he hiked the dirt road to Keller's.

The sun set into a tattered fluorescent smear as Van traveled the broken path with confidence. His posture was solid and his mind clear. He wouldn't be intimidated today. After all, no real commitment had been made. There was no incriminating evidence. If Keller wanted Billy in jail, that was fine. If he wanted to strut around like a big shot in front of his goons, that was fine too. As long as Van was treated like an equal, everything would be fine. Everything would be fine, that is, until he noticed a body being loaded into the trunk of a black Lincoln Continental. Randall and Freddy, Keller's closest assistants, had lost their grip on the limp figure swathed in soiled bedding.

"Watch the arm, watch the arm, you damn idiot!" yelled Randall, as a heavy white arm dove hideously from the sheet.

"Easy, bud," answered Freddy, "I haven't had as much practice doin' this kind of thing as you have!"

"It ain't something you need to practice," replied Randall as he scrambled to secure the wayward appendage.

With the crisis averted, the pair then turned to see Van. He didn't have time to split. They could chase him. He couldn't talk his way out of it, because he didn't know what he'd gotten into.

"Give us a hand," called Freddy from the back of the car.

What if he said no? They'd be loading him up next. They'd be letting his limp body fall all over the place before shoving it into the dirty trunk of a late-model gas guzzler.

He couldn't think it through. He'd do it, but then that was it. *I'm going to end it with these clowns*, thought Van, as his final heave coasted the lifeless load into the trunk.

The cargo fumed with an overpowering odor of mothballs as Van turned to be blinded by a sharp flash of light. He then spun back to the car but saw only a bloated white heap.

"So what? You got my picture in front of an old sheet, big deal."

"Look closer, my ignorant friend," replied Keller. "Is it common for the deceased to be haphazardly piled into suspicious automobiles?"

Upon closer inspection Van noticed a pale wrinkled face protruding from a crease in the sheet. He hadn't seen it before, but it looked larger than life now and he felt like he was going to puke.

Who was it?

How did it happen?

And was he guilty of whatever happened?

He felt numb and violated, confused and frightened, sad that he'd been thrust into a life divided by one tragic event.

He was wrong. His innocence hadn't vanished long ago, but it was gone now.

Van trembled as he fought the urge to attack.

"What the heck is your major malfunction?" he hissed, deciding not to rush into a second homicide. It was all too new.

"There is no problem here. On occasion I've found it helpful to provide my operatives with an added incentive. Call it an insurance policy of sorts, a measure against deceit."

As Van scanned the dimly lit yard, Keller stood in the center with Randall to his right and Freddy on his left. Their faces collected just enough light to show the previous afternoon's mosquito bites. Freddy had gotten hit the worst. Freddy always took the most punishment. He was big and slow. Among a crowd with limited potential, his was the most limited. That's probably why they kept him around: he could handle the beating. He could do the time. Freddy was tall and—most of the time—shirtless, kind of a deterrent to things getting physical.

Randall was a bit more refined. With rugged good looks beneath a wiry beard, he had the potential to polish up. Semiskilled and not completely ignorant, he'd once had a plan, one without Keller in it.

Both Randall and Freddy worked the shrimp trawlers that ran out of the port, not the easiest bunch to intimidate. They were tarnished, but so was Van. Maybe he was in the wrong place, but then again, maybe things were all going according to some kind of a deranged plan.

Van slowly embraced his new status as an outlaw. Forget the dead guy. He hadn't killed him. Whether in the trunk of a car or a hole in the ground, everyone would eventually be loaded into something. He wouldn't do it again, but he could live with the fact that he had and because of it, he'd have to do something else. If things went wrong, he had only himself to blame. He guessed he could live with that as well.

So as Keller knew it would, the momentary standoff ended, and the trio commenced a second meeting. Van obviously wouldn't make waves, but he'd have no loyalty to this bunch. When it was time to split, he'd do just that, picture or no picture.

"I think you know Randall and Freddy," stated Keller, "and I believe you've met my beautiful girlfriend, Emily."

Van cautiously moved his head, grasping for confidence in a room where he was severely outnumbered.

"Do you know why I requested your presence this evening?"

"To load a stiff into a crappy car, I guess," answered Van.

"No," Keller calmly replied. "We are here to discuss an enterprise, you miscreant."

"Well, excuse me for not being thrilled about shoving dead bodies into ugly automobiles."

"I am beginning to get insulted by your criticism of my vehicle. Perhaps a German sedan or a sleek Italian roadster would have been better?"

"It wouldn't have been in front of your house."

"I choose not to make poor investments."

"You have no style."

"If you're not pleased with the way things are going"—paused Keller to extend a bony finger—"there's the door."

"But it's my idea," snarled Van.

"It *was* your idea," growled Keller. "This isn't the first time you've been to my house, is it, Van?"

"Uh, no."

"You came here to borrow five dollars, which you've never repaid. A cold beer has always been available, yet I don't believe you've ever brought any. You were two hours late to a meeting in which we were involved, and now you have the audacity to question my leadership and insult my ride?"

Keller then lowered his voice and said, "I should let Randall and Freddy feed you to the fish. I'm doing you a service by allowing you to continue. You could be replaced. It happens all of the time, so get it together."

All eyes were again on Van as he sat motionless. He still wasn't going to tell them that Steve's dad was a professional wrestler. If the subject came up, he'd say that he owned a car dealership, simple as that.

Sensing that order had been restored, and realizing he needed Van to get Billy, Keller again asked, "So, Van, do you know why I requested your presence tonight?"

"To discuss the plan," answered Van in a childish monotone.

"What else are we covering?"

He wasn't sure. "To talk about me not being such a good houseguest?"

"No, imbecile, we are here to discuss the destruction of Billy Winslow."

The words sank in. It was something Van would have to get comfortable with, dead bodies and destruction. He'd have to play it cool.

"So, what does Steve's dad do for a living?"

"He owns a car dealership."

"He owns a car dealership," repeated Keller.

"Car dealerships make a lot of money," affirmed Freddy.

"They do if they sell a lot of cars," cautioned Randall.

"So," Keller menacingly asked, "does his car dealership sell a lot of cars?"

It was a valid question. Lack of funds would make a kidnapping useless. No payoff, no point. Van assumed that Steve's dad was loaded, but when faced with a question of full financial disclosure, he wasn't sure. The guy could be carrying a lot of debt. He could be mortgaged to the gills.

All three criminals were once again staring a hole in him as he concocted the masterful answer, "Yeah, sure."

"'Yeah, sure' isn't quite a phrase to inspire an act of bravery and dedication, now is it, Van?"

With slight resignation, Van replied, "What do you want me to say? He drives a nice car. He's got a pretty wife and a big house. He's got an expensive watch and about twenty or so guys working for him. He doesn't exactly discuss his finances with me. I'm the dishwasher at the restaurant where his son, Steve, works."

"I realize what you do," snapped Keller. "I'm trying to ascertain, through the limited scope of your knowledge, if this thing is worth getting into. OK, he's got a nice car and a nice watch, but is there anything else we might want to know?"

"Yeah," said Freddy, "is he a cop?"

"Not that I know of," answered Van, pretty sure he didn't have a shield.

"How 'bout a Green Beret?" asked Randall.

"Doubt it," replied Van, quite certain he wasn't special forces.

"Maybe he's a secret agent," chimed Keller's girlfriend, Emily.

"If he is, who'd know? They don't exactly share that kind of information."

"What information has he shared?" inquired Keller, his outlaw instinct sensing something more.

Van almost cracked. He almost got himself into hot water. He almost admitted the guy was a local hero, recognizable. Billy hadn't taken the news too well, so Van figured it could be somewhat of a deterrent, or possibly grounds for an ass whipping. He quickly decided to use ignorance as a buffer between what he knew and what he wanted them to know.

"Not a whole lot," continued Van. "He could be a pilot, or maybe even jumps out of airplanes."

"Skydives," corrected Freddy as Keller glared.

"Yeah, skydives," nodded Van.

"Maybe he sings karaoke after a few too many beers. I wouldn't be able to tell you. He could dress up like a woman, how would I know? He might even have his own damn makeup, who's gonna tell me that?" he continued as the eyes of Keller's cronies widened a bit.

"He brings me a beer every now and then, and tells me I'm doing a good job. He's real tight with the owner of the joint and a big tipper."

And after Van had completely misdirected the crew and utterly obliterated the point of discussion, he closed with the ultimate disclaimer of,. "You check it out. You do the math."

They all sat there stone faced, each waiting for the other to react.

Van figured that might be it, the end of a risky plan that was getting way out of hand. It wouldn't break his heart. He had a few more pokers in the fire.

"I'll have Randall and Freddy look into it," ordered Keller, "and of course we'll also need an address."

Van froze at the first mention of anything real. The pen was heavy and the paper a pale, institutional white. He couldn't write anything on it, and he couldn't not write anything on it. It would make him irrelevant. It could document his involvement.

Maybe Keller knew more than he was letting on. How did he know that Van knew where Steve lived? The request wasn't posed as a question—it was a command. A litany of uncertainties materialized, the main one being, did Keller know that Van was lying? Maybe he was being set up, less baggage.

In the lucid moment he expected prior to his undoing, Van grudgingly scrawled, *James Linon, 1289 Harbor Street Blvd, Melbourne, FL 32930.*

"Umm," muttered Keller, "nice neighborhood."

"Some nice boats around there," added Randall.

Great, thought Van, *these guys are nominating the place for a beautification award while my life hangs in the balance.* He needed to get out of there and now.

Van rose from the floor and said, "Ahh, looks like we covered just about everything."

Nearing the door, he heard a jovial voice proclaim, "Oh, and Van, I may be getting a new car soon, one with even more trunk space." The tone then changed to one of severity as Keller added, "So don't screw up, and stay available."

Safely out, Van looked back to make sure that no one had followed. Maybe he wasn't such a natural outlaw after all. A dim light radiated through the cheap living room blinds as a quick walk turned into a run. His thin legs stretched through the warm evening air, creating safety and distance with each powerful stride.

Van continued to run long after he left the park. It felt good. He felt like a kid again. He felt free. He felt sick as a powerful cramp paralyzed his speedy exodus. It reminded him of why he so rarely ran—it was painful.

As he doubled over on the tepid blacktop, fragrance from a night-blooming jasmine coiled through his senses. He had picked a quiet spot. Some of the best places to sit weren't on a bench or in a park. They were hidden. There was no invitation other than a feeling, a call for the weary to rest, a secret spot. Van had found one, and he needed it.

So, three villains and a lovely lady stayed in the trailer to discuss other crimes and to laugh at Van. Every day was the same. All they did was feed on one another—it's all they knew. Most conversations were in the form of accusations, but when Emily spoke, Keller became cordial, maybe even friendly. And when no one else was around, he could be sensitive, even loving.

She was insulated from their petty dealings. As far as Emily was concerned, scheming is what men did and that wouldn't change. She wasn't quite so lenient with regard to Keller's other obligations, though. Friendly with a few of the elderly neighbors, Emily helped out from time to time. She didn't demand Keller get involved, but if he did, she made sure that he followed through.

He first scoffed at the notion of helping anyone at all, but after noticing a steady stream of trucks and churches carting off donations, Keller instantly became a pillar of the community. Slightly dependable and about as trustworthy as possible for a crook, he now sold estate sale items and garaged treasures of all sorts. It was a good moneymaker and perfectly legal. He bought a new truck and trailer and had just inherited a car with enough trunk space for a bag of old clothes and a dead body. As far as Keller was concerned, the future looked bright.

With the body secured and the gang on the move, Keller and Emily finally had the place to themselves. Emily wouldn't challenge Keller in front of his goons, but she wasn't about to sit back and let a good man be desecrated for the benefit of a worthless enterprise.

"So, was it completely necessary to dump Mr. Crawford into the trunk of his own car?"

"Would it have made a difference if it were in someone else's car?"

"Maybe."

"Maybe isn't the type of answer I would expect from someone who is getting into my business."

She knew that Keller was going to take a serious ass kicking one of these days, and when he did, she wouldn't step in.

Flash Smells a Rat

In a shadowy corner of the trailer park, falling into the same holes, kicking the same rocks, and arguing about ways to fix the road, Randall and Freddy followed the broken trail out. Nearing their favorite convenience store, the topic naturally changed from bad roads, to beer as Freddy said, "I could sure use a cold one."

"You and me both," replied Randall, as he reached for the door handle and pulled.

Weaving slowly through the cluttered aisles, he heard a familiar voice and stalled. Prompting Freddy to do the same, Randall spied the one and only Billy Winslow and muttered, "Well, lookee there."

"Yeah, lookee there," repeated Freddy. "What should we do?"

They should have done nothing. They should have hidden, or as usual, pretended they didn't see him, but tonight was different. Tonight something was brewing.

"Let's talk to him."

"Yeah."

Getting closer to their unsuspecting target, Randall cleared his throat as both Billy and his stunning girlfriend, Rita, did an about-face.

"Randall, Freddy, how you guys been?" asked Billy while Rita, prompted by a slight nudge, cut for the parking lot.

"Wow, Freddy, you're looking good. Have you lost a few pounds? And Randall, how is it that we get older, but you stay the same? What's your secret, man? Sign me up."

The two just stood there dumbfounded. They had expected some nerves, or at least a snub, but this was the complete opposite.

"So, how are things going at the Chowder House?" asked Randall.

Encouraged by Randall's inquiry, Freddy added, "Yeah, how's the kidnapping going?"

Both Randall and Billy immediately turned to Freddy. No one wanted to seem overly tense, but it was a hell of a surprise. After all the years of self-sabotage, Randall still couldn't anticipate the stupidity of others. He was still being blindsided.

No one spoke. Randall's expression didn't change. It couldn't— Billy was watching. Freddy didn't mean to say kidnapping. He meant to say *cooking*. "How's the cooking going?" is what he meant to say.

Numb with rage, Randall paused. He wanted to just walk away, but a blunder of that magnitude had to be addressed. Billy couldn't speak. What did they know and how did they know it? If the silence continued, he'd have to find out.

Just as things were about to get really awkward, Freddy miraculously said, "I meant to say cooking. Don't know where that kidnapping thing came from, just got done watching a movie about it. The old brain gets stuck in a rut every now and then."

Billy sensed a deeper purpose to the encounter. He knew the question was more than just an innocent slip. These guys hadn't talked to him in years, and now out of nowhere they decide to ask him about his job? Billy wasn't buying it, and he also had a question. Depending on their answer, he'd have his. He wanted to know what they knew.

Still playing the part of an old buddy, Billy said, "Oh really, must have been a good flick, Freddy. What was the name of it?"

Randall couldn't tolerate any more slipups. Too much had been said. The plan was already compromised. Given enough time, there was no telling what Freddy might do. As Randall yanked Freddy toward the door, he said over his shoulder, "Ah, it was an old made-for-TV thing, what not to do and such. Had a couple of famous actors in it, ahh, before they got famous. You should check it out sometime."

As they made a hasty retreat, Billy stood beneath the bright lights of the cold little store and wondered what Flash Shackelford might think.

Flash smells a rat.

A stern double beep reminded him of the need to drive a pretty lady home. Warm, heavy air replaced the chilled confines of the store as Billy raced across the parking lot. He knew it was coming. Rita waited until he eased onto the highway.

"You know, Billy, I don't ask for much, but if you want to leave me waiting around in a hot car next to a stinky gas pump, just leave. If that's how much you value my companionship, just call it quits."

Billy was used to it. Things always took longer than they should have. He was always running into someone. It was hard to get away with a simple "hello" or "how ya doin'?" She knew that.

In a way, he'd lost his patience for always having to explain it.

"You could have moved the truck."

"You had the keys."

"That's right, I did have the keys," he mumbled.

Rita was cute when she got mad. Billy knew she'd never truly be happy in the sense of surrendering to petty grievances with a smile. There would always be a pair of jeans that didn't fit just right. The traffic would always be moving too slow. The mountains wouldn't be high enough, and the sky would be too low. Rita was quality.

She'd make it. He knew it. She didn't. That's why he could laugh when she got mad and smile when she was irritated. It made her furious, but he thought it was hilarious. Eventually she'd leave and be better off.

"I'm sorry. I just got hung up with those guys."

"Why did they leave in such a hurry?"

"Because they're idiots."

"Idiots do things quickly?"

She'd known idiots to move at pretty much any speed, most of the time too slow.

"If they're in a hurry, they do."

"I could have figured that out," she snapped. "It just seemed like an odd meeting, and for them to leave the store without buying anything?"

Billy should have acted like a concerned boyfriend. Maybe goof on their looks, give her something to laugh about. He loved to hear her laugh. But he couldn't. He had something to hide, and the best way to make her forget was to piss her off. She'd find out when the time was right, then they could both laugh.

"Like I said, they're idiots."

"You're an idiot," she said, viciously lumping him straight into their category.

Farther down the road, Randall got into Freddy's face and in an utterly confused, half-crazed tone, asked, "What in the hell was that all about?"

Instead of pushing out his chest, Freddy decided to apologize and hope that Randall wouldn't tell Keller.

"I don't know, man, it slipped out. I messed up—cooking sounds kind of like kidnapping."

"Cooking sounds nothing like kidnapping," snapped Randall, as he contemplated a couple of worst-case scenarios.

Worst-case scenario number one: Billy tells Van; Van in turn tells Keller; Keller kills Freddy. Worst-case scenario number two: Van tells Keller; Keller kills them both. Like it or not, what happened to one would happen to the other.

In the darkness, Freddy was pensive. He was too old to start over and too vulnerable to go straight to the bottom. Randall would figure something out, he always had. Freddy silently waited as Randall pursed his lips, kicked the dirt, and took the blame. In the greater sense, it was his fault. He was in charge. It was his stupid idea to approach the enemy, but he wouldn't let Freddy know.

"I'm not gonna tell Keller, but Van might."

After all, there were only two ways that Keller would find out. They could tell him, or Van could. Van may not even know. Billy might not even mention it. No need to panic.

"I'll handle Van," said Freddy.

Following a solemn ride home, Billy and Rita clattered down the drive. A warm evening had turned her sear into a burn as she quickly exited the truck. Accessories jangling, hair bouncing, and tanned legs moving swiftly toward the porch, Rita opened the door and then slammed it shut. She popped a soda, turned the air conditioner to high, and plopped down on the couch. She'd make it a point to inconvenience him as much as he had inconvenienced her. *It must be love*, she thought.

After a brief conversation with the front door, Billy let himself in.

"Look, Rita, those guys just aren't worth discussing."

She didn't answer. She wasn't mad. She just didn't care. His words were gibberish. His face looked like a rock, and his house resembled a cave, a hot cave. Hopefully the AC would hurry up and cool the place down. Amused with her foray into fantasy, Rita looked at Billy and laughed. He wasn't a brash modern-day swashbuckler or a Renaissance man—he was a caveman.

Be careful, Flash, thought Billy, as he wrote.

Chapter 3
Deadly Game of Deceit

Flash couldn't believe it: a crease had formed, a slight wrinkle. There were new characters, but it was the same old story. He got the picture, episode 12, Deep Water. The hero takes a plunge. Old friends become new enemies.

His crooked index finger traced the scar tissue that pulsed whenever he was reminded of the rerun; intro to blunt force, all lemons, never any lemonade.

The sun cooked his pale skin as the scantily clad waitress continued delivering strong drinks. For the first time, Flash noticed the second look he'd been getting from the stunning server.

"Can I help you?" asked Flash in a less than flattering tone, as he knew that a nice guy was the last thing on this chick's mind.

"Maybe," she answered in a seductive hiss.

Knowing that he could usually rely on truth from strangers, Flash thought and then spoke, "Before we get on to bigger and better things, can I ask you a question?"

"Shoot, Tex," she said without missing a beat.

"Do I look stupid to you?"

"Not at all," she answered in a deep, lusty tone.

Flash sank back into his chair ready to take on the world. If he didn't look stupid, odds were he wasn't stupid, and these cats who were on the prowl were about to step into a trap. He slipped the beach beauty his room key and headed out. She'd be by later.

Nice work, thought Billy. Romance and danger, or was it danger and romance? Anyway, it was a good mix, like salt and sugar, or sugar and salt. He took a break as gunshots rang out from the living room.

"What's going on out there, Rita?"

Stupid questions annoyed her, especially when she was asleep. "Someone is shooting a gun."

"Well, can you shoot me a name for an exciting new novel?"

"What's it about again?"

"A kidnapping."

She drearily raised her head as the credits for *The Outlaw Josey Wales* ran. If anything, Rita liked to be resourceful.

It was a bore. She was too good.

"Outlaw Kidnapping Tales," she yelled from the living room.

Kind of good, he thought, *I can definitely use that.*

"Yeah, that's kind of good, I might use it," he said, not wanting to compromise his intellectual property.

"Do as you wish," she offered, again descending into the soft pillows.

Billy then typed a quick page and stuck it on the refrigerator for all to see. The title simply read:

"Outlaw Kidnapping Tales"

Rita

Heat dissipates in the darkness. It escapes and heads back to the sun. The concrete cools and becomes part of the landscape instead of something opposed to it. Lately the nights didn't last long enough—not enough time to sleep and too much time to think. It was morning, but to Rita it seemed like the sun was setting.

She yawned, gave the covers a sharp tug, and wondered why she was always up first. Why did she always have to make the coffee? Why did she always have to give him a light nudge and a soft "Good morning"? It should have been other way around. It was in the beginning, when they both worked days.

At the time, he was a breakfast cook and she'd rise every morning to a different pastry and the best hot coffee she'd ever tasted. On occasion they even had sex before his shift. It was early and she was tired, but she enjoyed it anyway. That's when there had been hope for the future, when she thought he might turn into something other than what he was, if that were at all possible.

But it was her needs that kept them at odds, her lofty goals that complicated the two, and Rita was OK with that because maybe it was her time and his had come and gone. Maybe he didn't need a time, but she did. Moving from one small, gritty apartment to the next might work for some, but it wouldn't do for her. Rita didn't know where she'd end up, but she knew for sure that it wouldn't be in a one-bedroom across the street from the beach. That was a summer vacation, not a life.

Billy was beautifully uncommon but tragically unmotivated. Either that or his enthusiasm had been sapped by putting too much into too little. Rita believed the road was less traveled for a reason, that it was overgrown because it didn't lead anywhere, only to other desolate paths.

His potential kept her around. His words made her laugh, his kindness gave her inspiration, but it was two years to the day they'd met and there was still no real commitment. He was still in bed and there were no cards on the table. Nothing was on the table besides a couple of magazines and an old Sunday paper. Looking around, nothing had changed, everything was old and it was starting to take a toll.

New to Florida and in need of some quick cash, she eventually found work at Rocco's Italian Eatery. Not sure how long she'd be able to stay, Rita submitted another application with mixed feelings.

"No experience, no problem," they said.

Rita started on a Friday and was instantly in the weeds. Everyone was yelling, and after a while, even she was yelling—that's an instant before she brought a check to table one, took an order from table two, got appetizers for table ten, and then recited the specials for a few more tables still waiting on water.

"Could we possibly have a lemon wedge with the water? It makes it taste a little better," asked the date, who was obviously trying to be a little less demanding.

"Sure," answered Rita, trying to stay calm while juggling a tray of whiskey sours to the early bird crew.

Tall, wild-eyed, and attractive, Billy caught her eye, not as a potential suitor but just as a guy who wasn't bad to look at.

"Uh, that's Billy," they said.

It spoke volumes, she remembered. All the other cooks had asked her out, but Billy was the only one to offer an aspirin while she sat visibly rattled after another sleepless night. Vicious migraines had appeared as her father lay motionless, losing a long bout with cancer.

With a few loose ends to tie up, Rita took leave and Billy also left. There were plenty of jobs out there, but not a lot of girls like Rita.

With slow sauntering steps they traveled into uncertainty, unraveling at the same time. *Great, my knight in shining armor is a bum*, thought Rita, before pulling her last cigarette from a collapsed pack.

After a cupped light and quick puff, she said, "OK, genius, now what?"

"Now, we drink," he answered, which seemed to be his remedy for pretty much everything. "That's just the way it is at the beach," he said.

Maybe at Brewski Beach, she thought.

Billy's house was quaint with a nice front porch. It was a cool November night, so he lit a pile of dry kindling and gave a satisfied nod. He was cute, and what he'd done was charming. It was also ignorant. What were their chances? She needed to quit sizing it up and get back to the grief.

Billy then brought out some drinks, and Rita let her hair down.

"I could really use a cigarette," she said in a rueful moan.

"The store's right down the road."

She gave it a thought until he added, "Although you're more beautiful just being yourself."

How did he know who she was?

Where she came from, looks were everything. The apartments were huge, and the fires were always inside. It was always, "Let's go have a smoke." She wouldn't have dreamed of having a drink without a cigarette. She would have had three by now and definitely wouldn't be listening to the guy who pulled out a couple of snappy lines. But at the moment, she felt flawed, and maybe this guy wasn't just stringing her along. She needed to soften up, to let her guard down. And as the liquor lowered her inhibitions, she thought that maybe she needed to get closer to the handsome gentleman on her right.

"Well," whispered Rita, "if I don't smoke, I'm going to have to do something."

Oblivious to the innuendo, Billy flatly replied, "Start riding a bike. Ride on the beach, better scenery."

Rita moved her shapely figure into view. She eclipsed the flames. She took their place.

"What I'm trying to say is that I'm going to have to replace my nicotine cravings with something else."

As much as he wanted to, and as much as he thought he should, Billy couldn't object. He wanted to say something else, but all that came out was, "You couldn't be more correct!"

Then they kissed. It was a long kiss, one that lasted all the way to the bedroom. A rather small bedroom, she remembered, but it didn't matter at the time.

Rita woke too early again. The unemployed lump next to her probably wouldn't be up before noon, so she searched for a phone book. Besides, who knew if she'd ever see him again. One-night stands weren't part of her MO, but they happened. She cringed to think that most of the time alcohol was involved. With a cab on the way, she left a note that simply read, "Call when you get the chance" with her phone number in parentheses.

After all, they hadn't exchanged any information besides the most pleasantly damning and awkwardly revealing. She caught herself wondering how they'd act. Would he be timid, would she get nervous, and most important, would they do it again? All good questions, but right now she had to get to the hospital. It would be one of her last visits.

Rita hoped the cab would arrive quickly, before the morning after, but she really did have to leave. It wasn't just a fight-or-flight response, although that would have made sense: Abandon ship; this one seemed to be sinking. *Going nowhere fast*, she thought as a bearded cabby pulled up the driveway.

Tucked neatly into the taxi, Rita turned to see if the door opened. Maybe it happened. Maybe she had a crush on him. Her preoccupation was a good buffer between insecurity and rejection, but neither mattered.

As they accelerated through traffic, the license plates on the passing cars all gleefully advertised the Sunshine State. She was a hell of a long way from the Land of Lincoln.

Her parents were the first to leave. Gene and Jillian Polli moved south to manage an illness in remission. Gene walked the beach every morning until the cancer returned. Inoperable and spreading. Rita was told that if she wanted to spend any more time with him, she needed to do it soon. Now, riding around with a stranger, moving wearily through another day, she found the landscape quite unfamiliar.

In Florida, the seasons changed but only slightly. The leaves stayed the same but more importantly, so did the sidewalks; they never got icy. Instead of Lake Michigan, she now had the Atlantic. Warm and inviting, there was substance in the way the ocean water slid from her skin. It left something behind as she walked to her towel. It turned into something solid as she baked in the sun. It left her feeling crisp at the end of the day but extra soft after an extended shower. The sun still felt the same, but in Chicago there just wasn't as much of it.

Perhaps due to the changes, Rita was still out of sorts. It just didn't make sense to go from Evanston Township on to Northwestern only to become a professional beach bum. Signed early on to an upscale modeling agency, in Chicago Rita was both smart and beautiful. In Florida she always seemed to be hot, and now that she was going out with Billy, most of the time bothered.

So, Billy was jobless with Rita fatherless and free to go. She thought about the sand between her toes and the ragged orange sunsets. School didn't start for another few months, and with a new guy around, Rita decided to stay. She hadn't planned on falling in love.

The sound of Billy's truck rattling down the driveway returned her to sanity, or to what she thought was sanity. Maybe she was insane. Watching him hoist an oversized bag made her think he'd been somewhere, somewhere a cheapskate goes to buy a bunch of junk.

"I've been to the thrift shop again, babe."

"I can see that," said Rita as she grabbed the sack and stuffed it straight into a garbage can. *Oh, I'll save the boomerang*, she thought. *Pretty cool.*

It was her way of saying they had too much trash already—a houseful, to be exact.

Billy stood in the door, certain she'd have to do better than that. There were treasures in there, things he really needed.

"Hold on. I need some of that stuff."

"You need none of that stuff."

"Look, hon," he said with a grin, "I know you've been feeling overwhelmed by what you call the copious amounts of clutter. While I generally disagree with your designation of my personal items as clutter, I'm willing to negotiate for the release of some of my stuff."

She got a kick out of Billy when he tried to be manipulative—it wasn't his strong suit.

"I called it junk," she replied. "I took a piece, so I guess it's only fair for you to get something."

"OK," he said, snapping back into form. He wanted her out of the room so he could get more. One wasn't enough.

"Ahh, I put the mail on the coffee table. It looked like there were a couple of things for you, maybe a check or something."

A check? Wow, she thought. She'd been waiting for one, but all that seemed to be in the stack were bills and stupid credit card offers. *Wait a second*, thought Rita. *That little sneak!* She bolted back into the kitchen only to find Billy stashing even more contraband. In a fit of rage, she stomped the remaining crap as he fell to the floor trying to save it.

"This stuff is worth something," he screeched.

"It *was* worth something," she roared.

"Stop it," he said.

"No," she answered, suddenly aroused among a set of watermelon-print cups and an old Polaroid camera. Then came the battle to disrobe, with Rita on top staring into the flushed face of her captive. A couple of loud and final heaves ended the spontaneous tryst as Billy slithered away to toy with the old camera.

"Let's see if this sucker works," he said, snapping a film cartridge into place.

With shadowy eyes surrounded by elements of other people's lives, Rita turned to hear the old Polaroid click. She was one of the things on the floor destined to travel, to change hands, and to finally find a home. Hopefully it wouldn't be broken up in a strange place.

"I've never seen you look so beautiful," said Billy as the exposure came to life.

"Maybe I've never been so beautiful," she sighed. "Maybe I won't ever look like this again."

"I doubt it," replied Billy. "Beauty like yours doesn't come from the outside."

"Ahh, you're just saying that because we did it."

"I'm just saying that because it's true. You make me want to do things," he added with a renewed vigor. "Right now you make me want to clean this house. You're right. I don't need more. I need less."

"Hold on," chimed Rita, "do you possibly need to cook?"

"Oh, you're hungry? So am I," he said, motioning frantically toward the refrigerator. "Fish, I've got some fish! Let's have it with red bliss potatoes and steamed cabbage. Lay on the couch, princess. I'll do the rest."

It was a fine afternoon. They had the day off. They had a little extra money, and they'd just finished having sex. The dinner wasn't bad either.

With the day heading into dusk, Rita commandeered the couch as Billy slithered off to begin his next chapter.

Chapter 4: Along for the Ride

Flash wasn't the beast he'd once thought. He had a softer side. It only took a barmaid and a few strong drinks to bring it out. He slipped her his key, and she used it. They woke up together in a dark room. The room was still dark even though it was well past noon, and he liked that. He also liked that he could have another beer. The refrigerator was cold, and the light beer tasted like cold carbonated water. He quickly downed two more, jumped back into bed, and pounded the creaky springs into oblivion.

She reopened the gashes on his back from the night before, and he liked that too. Flash liked it all. This girl was a keeper. He was going to bring her along for the ride.

Hope it's not too hectic, thought Billy. *This guy can't be a romantic. He's gotta have an edge.*

He needed a new title. He needed Rita, but she was fast asleep. The day was just about done, so he left her alone, serene and dangerously beautiful.

Mistake Number Ten

Of course, Keller didn't count his mistakes. Most people don't. They just keep bumbling along, stubbing toes and putting too much salt in the soup. Most mistakes can't really be measured, but the big ones can.

For starters, Keller was first expelled for stealing the high school principal's car. Then he was evicted for setting his parents' house on fire. He was fired from his one and only job for stealing booze. Then he was incarcerated for driving drunk. He bought a stolen stereo. He stole a stereo. He beat up a nosy neighbor. Billy beat him up and then somewhere along the line, Keller decided to become a career criminal.

So, with a nasty temper and a score to settle, he committed mistake number ten and ordered Randall and Freddy to case Steve's dad's car dealership.

The neighbors stared carelessly in their direction as Randall and Freddy trudged the dusty road to Keller's. Oddly enough, they weren't out of place. They seemed to fit in amongst the gracefully decayed backdrop of temporary things, stuff that wasn't anchored, items destined for the scrap heap.

Finally at Keller's trailer, Randall knocked as a sinister voice said, "Enter."

Weary of the theatrics, Randall opened the door as Keller motioned the two operatives in.

Following a brief silence, he said, "After much soul searching and prayer, I have decided to bequeath my two most trusted associates with the task of casing Gentleman Jim Motors, the car dealership owned by Steve's father. Steve being our primary target."

Freddy was jazzed.

To Randall it meant something different. It was a lie. Keller didn't trust them, and he'd never said anything even close to a prayer, unless it was a prayer to save his own ass. Keller didn't want to be seen. He wasn't planning on doing anything besides running his mouth and collecting a ransom. That was OK, though, because Randall had his own agenda—to get the money and the girl, thank you. He figured with a nice set of clothes and a shave, he might be able to pull it off. He was sick of Keller. Their relationship was strained, and it seemed to be the perfect time to go out with a bang. A sly grin slid across his face as he replied, "Sure thing, pal."

"Yeah, Keller, count us in," added Freddy.

"Are you familiar with the establishment?"

"We can find it," answered Randall.

"Yeah, piece of cake," said Freddy as Randall cringed.

Keller used to talk only to Randall, but it now seemed like he was talking to both of them, and they were both answering. It wasn't supposed to be that way.

As they left the trailer, something felt different. Randall glanced at Emily as she quickly looked away. Keller also caught the exchange but didn't care. He wasn't worried about Randall.

They walked out as they walked in, with one talking and the other not listening. Only this time, the other one received a sharp poke.

"Listen, bud," said Randall, "when he's talking, he's talking to me."

"Seemed like he was talking to both of us."

"He was talking to both of us, but he was more talking to me. I'm the field general. I'm in charge out here!"

They had all started out as friends, surfing, drinking beer, and lifting a bit of fishing gear here and there, but things had changed, and they were about to change more. Randall knew the end was near, but they were all locked into this one last thing and he couldn't let Freddy screw it up.

"Why can't we both be in charge?"

"Because we can't, and don't forget that you blew our cover the other night. I didn't tell Keller, but I can—he may still find out."

"Oh," said Freddy.

"You're gonna get your chance, so just keep it together and don't do anything else stupid. What you can do in the meantime is figure out where the heck Gentleman Jim Motors is. We'll check it out tomorrow after lunchtime. Give everything a chance to heat up."

"Sure thing, boss," Freddy dutifully answered, suddenly remembering that Randall was older than him and that he'd take care of him. He always had.

Everything was good for the moment. They had their mission, and Freddy had been put in check. All they needed now was a reliable car.

Randall carefully stroked the flawless curves of the Chevy they'd drive to the mainland. The car had belonged to Randall's father and was religiously maintained. His father was dead, but the car wasn't, so on occasion he'd borrow it and then promptly return it to the garage. Some things were sacred.

The convertible Caprice sped effortlessly along, covering every spare inch of blacktop available. Randall knew the car better than most anything, understanding exactly when to adjust the wheel, knowing precisely how to compensate for the drift of a real car.

Over a long, narrow bridge, the river below looked like the sky, gray and still. Unnaturally neutral, it was like the water had been frozen and the color erased. It all blended with the horizon, the sky, the river, the car, and all of the other cars. It was just that kind of a day.

All the large car dealerships were across the causeway, and Gentleman Jim's was the largest. All the big car dealerships were shiny, and his was the shiniest. Not the type to attract much attention from the sales staff, Randall and Freddy parked the car and made it past the group without even a "howdy" or a "hey, captain." It was encouraging, and Randall thought they could operate unnoticed until a sunburned salesman exclaimed, "Welcome to Gentleman Jim's!"

They'd been ambushed. He was too close, and Randall thought that he might have to fight.

"Mick Rider here, selling buggies, rollers, and strollers. Selling trolleys, trucks, and cars. Hell, we'd sell stars for thar's if we could get our hands on them."

Freddy was hooked, but Randall kept his distance.

"Ya see, I saw you guys from the other side of the door and knew right away we'd click. We get all types in here: the heavy hitters, the happy families, the first-time buyers, the single ladies, and the up-and-comers. Everyone comes in here trying to be somebody, trying to look like somebody, but not you guys. You're stripped down, no nonsense. You're like me at heart, honest, no frills. I just gotta put this on for work," he said motioning inward. "So just let me know how I can help."

That was it. That was his spiel, and he was done. Now it was their turn. Randall was patient while Freddy looked left, gave a nod, made a slight "hmm," and then asked, "Is that the new Cavalier?"

"Thought you'd never ask," answered Mick as he grabbed Freddy and then said to Randall, "You don't mind do you, compadre? You're sure welcome to come along."

"No, no, I'm not really a Cavalier kind of guy."

"Don't worry, partner, we got a new 4x4 that'd do ya just right."

Not today, thought Randall. What he said was, "Sounds good."

As they motored carefully away, Randall could now do his job.

The sales floor shimmered beneath a life-size portrait of Gentleman Jim wearing a huge golden belt. In the picture he was bloody and ecstatic, forcefully celebrating another hard-fought win. Not being a wrestling fan, Randall wondered about the tights and the weird belt, but the football pictures made a little more sense. *This guy's a freaking local hero,* he thought. *A really big local hero.*

To Randall's left, a hotshot haggled over an upgrade while the man in the picture stood to his right. Every bit as tall as Randall, Jim was a lot thicker. With deep facial lines and an even deeper voice, he appeared to be formidable.

These things were a problem. The other problem was that he seemed to be chatting with a plainclothes cop. This guy wasn't just a rent-a-cop, he was a detective.

Wouldn't surprise me if he was the sheriff, thought Randall as a thin youngster entered the picture. Randall then edged forward to get a better view. What the heck, he wasn't breaking any laws. He had no reason to be nervous. He wasn't making any trouble, just a normal citizen casing a car dealership; just a regular guy planning a kidnapping.

The thought of it made Randall cringe, but he advanced anyway, trying to pick up some info. With a nasally voice, the kid asked for something as Jim's right hand, laden with expensive reflective items, peeled off a few twenties and sent him on his way. That was a good sign. The place reeked of money. People weren't just kicking tires, they were buying.

"What can I do for you today, friend?" asked a voice in the near distance.

Thinking the voice might go away, Randall stayed quiet.

"How can we help you today?" it said again, this time with a little more force.

"Uh, here with a friend, looking at a car," Randall cryptically replied.

"Oh great, what are they looking at?" asked Jim, half wondering and half probing.

"A Cavalier," sneered Randall.

"Oh yeah, the new Cavalier, great economy with that one, should hold its value pretty well."

That's a lie, thought Randall. But Randall had lied to him, so the two lies canceled each other out and they were even.

Just as things were about to get dicey, Freddy and Mick Rider walked up raving about the smooth ride and the low, low introductory rate.

Mick grabbed Jim by the sleeve and motioned to Freddy. "Guy's a real live fisherman, an American hero."

Jim's eyes widened a bit.

"You guys do any business with the Chowder House?" asked Jim. "My son, Steve, works there."

That was it: the smoking gun. The kid was Steve, and Jim was his gargantuan father. Jim would gladly pay a ransom, but he would also kill whoever collected it.

"We don't really get involved in the wholesale, Mr. Jim," said Freddy with a measure of respect.

Randall was impressed. Whether Freddy meant to or not, he was doing a hell of a job.

"So, where do you want to sign, compadre?" asked Mick, tightening the screws a bit.

"I guess wherever you want to," answered Freddy.

Sure, Freddy could sign. He could get it with no money down, but to do that he'd have to have credit, which was something the great American hero severely lacked. Randall was going to have to intervene. If they started to crunch numbers, he'd to have to sit there with Jim for the next two hours. By now they'd most likely been committed to memory, which wasn't part of the plan. They needed to leave, and they needed to leave now.

Randall pulled Freddy aside and said as much, as Mick strained to listen. He needed this cat to relax its bite because right now he was choking Freddy out; he was toying with him.

"Thanks for your attention, Mick, but we can't buy today. We're fishermen, not bankers. I'm ashamed to say, we don't always make sound financial decisions."

Randall again went into his cryptic phrasing. "Boats sink, bills unpaid, ahh, debts pile up, and that sort of thing."

Mick stood strong, smelling the hustle from a mile away. He didn't speak. He was going to make them squirm or sign. Some signed, others ran, but they couldn't run; Mick stood between them and the door. They had to face him down.

This sucks, thought Randall. If he caused a commotion, they were as good as dead. They'd stick out like a sore thumb. They'd be calling the law firm of Jenson and Jenson as soon as the bail cleared. He could see it now. *Hmmm*, thought Randall, *a class action lawsuit, makes perfect sense.*

"You see, what I'm trying to say is that Freddy doesn't have any money right now. Freddy doesn't have any credit right now."

That damn Rider wouldn't move, not even a nod. This thing was going to have to go all the way.

"I'm not really comfortable discussing Freddy's finances, but he's about to come into some money."

Mick stepped back. That's what he'd hoped for, the big fish. Boy, he really knew how to read 'em.

It still wasn't enough, but Randall was ready. "See, Freddy's part of a class action lawsuit that's just been settled. Due to defective fishing hooks, Freddy's got no sight in his left eye."

Mick Rider then flashed a hand toward the left side of Freddy's face, and miraculously, Freddy didn't flinch.

"Heh, heh," laughed Mick. "Them damn hooks, got one through the thumb last year and ended up in the ER. Had to drink a bottle of whiskey just to ease the pain."

"Yeah," replied Freddy, "the pain was bad."

Mick was satisfied. He'd spent enough time with the two, and there were still cars to sell.

"Here's my card. Come see me when you get the money, compadre. I hang at the Easy Street Bar and Grill—the drinks are on me."

"Sounds good," said Freddy.

Randall then dragged him out of the dealership without even a courtesy wave. "Let's get the hell out of here," he ordered, with Freddy practically running to catch up.

"What's the problem?"

"Too much interaction. I didn't want to talk to anyone. If we end up running into those guys again, I don't want to be recognized."

Freddy was disappointed that he couldn't buy a car, or hang out with Mick. Maybe later, though.

As they drove off in silence, Freddy asked, "You're not saying much, Randall. What did I do this time?"

"Nothing, Freddy, you did a real good job. You got that guy out of my face so I could do what I needed to do."

Randall was concerned with the greater issue of what to tell the boss. He'd tell him the truth: they should stay away from it. Stick to the nickel-and-dime stuff, let Billy and Van make fools of themselves. Billy wasn't going to kidnap anyone, and Randall knew it. It was just another one of his half-baked schemes.

Another Bad Deal

After Randall topped off the tank and returned the car, he and Freddy walked the distance to Keller's. While they walked, they talked.

"What do you think about the whole thing now?" asked Freddy, sensing that Randall wasn't exactly thrilled.

Who would have been? Lately, things just hadn't been going his way. It was becoming more and more obvious that this wasn't the life for him. Instead of an easy job or a quick score, he was being pushed headlong into another bad deal. It was actually the worst deal yet, but for now, he'd yield.

"It looked all right, should be an easy gig."

"Yeah," agreed Freddy, "I was kind of thinking the same thing. They probably won't even call the cops, probably don't even know the number."

There was a cop right there, thought Randall, shaking his head. Freddy didn't catch it, though, and on they walked. By the time they got to Keller's, it was dark and there was a guest. The guest was Van.

Not sure what to do, they waited. This was unexpected. Billy could have told Van about the risky confrontation, and Van could have told Keller. Randall finally gave a quick triple knock and the door slowly swung open. Van sat on the floor while Keller took up most of the couch. They both stared at the television as a red Ferrari sped furiously along the jagged cliffs of Honolulu. The car then screeched to a halt as a fake moving truck blocked its run. Already beaten, the handsome protagonist exited the automobile only to face a loaded revolver.

"Compelling, don't you think, Randall?" was the question deviously posed by Keller to his top lieutenant.

"Same old story," answered Randall. "A chopper's about to fly in and save his ass."

And then, right on cue, a helicopter buzzed the goons who were about to lay into the PI for a second time.

"How'd you know that?" asked Van.

"Lucky guess," shot Randall, which was a lie.

"Yes, of course," said Keller. "Anyone could have seen it coming."

"Did you?"

Keller paused as he so often did and then answered, "Yes, I saw the rerun about a year ago. But you couldn't have seen it, right, Randall? A man of your stature would have most certainly shared such a detail with us."

"Yeah, these shows are all the same. Like I said, it was a lucky guess."

"Well, perhaps some clairvoyance can aid this mission," stated Keller, although he knew Randall had seen the damn show.

After settling himself with a quick Buddhist prayer, Keller said to his pretty girlfriend, Emily, "Dear princess, please furnish these two gentlemen with a cold beverage."

They all watched her walk away, as if they were on a boat and the boat was in the middle of the ocean and she was the only woman on the boat but she belonged to the captain so he allowed them to look because if he didn't they might throw him off the boat. After this big score, they wouldn't be leering anymore. They wouldn't be around.

As Emily returned with a fresh round, Keller cleared his throat and began what was to be his crowning achievement: a kidnapping along with the incarceration of Billy Winslow.

"I've requested Van's presence tonight because he is going to fulfill an important aspect of this mission. He's operating as a double agent, so to speak."

It sounded good so far, no mention of any malfeasance. Either that or Van had kept his mouth shut.

"So, let's get down to business," said Keller, unusually terse. "What did you find out?"

This was sure to be a telling part of the mission. Lights flickered and numbers clattered as a shiny metal ball rolled helplessly in between two flippers, game over. He was convinced the group wouldn't listen to reason, that they'd do it regardless. But maybe he could change the course of events, turn it into a conversation, make it something to laugh about. A "Wow, were we actually thinking about doing that?" moment.

He could try, but then he looked at Emily. A maniac like Keller didn't deserve her. Keller didn't deserve anything other than what he was going to get, which was a bad time. Randall would save her in the end. He'd watch out for her. This could be a means to get Keller out of the way. Risky as it was, it would be absolute, no loose ends. He just needed to stay far enough away to split when things got dicey.

"There's money there," he said.

The crew wanted more. Like prospectors gazing into a sack of gold, they were hooked.

"The place was shiny," added Freddy.

"It's a car dealership. They're all shiny," sneered Van.

At this point, Randall had no interest in changing the game. It was final. He'd go one way, and they'd go another.

"I saw the kid," said Randall.

"You did, eh?" replied Keller in an eerily sadistic tone. "Was he big?"

"No, he was thin, didn't look like much."

"That's a bonus," said Keller. Not really an authority on kidnapping, he felt like a smaller subject would be easier to control.

"He had expensive boat shoes and wore a shirt from the marina," added Randall.

"His father, what was his father like?" asked Keller.

That seemed to be the million-dollar question. *Big and scary is what he should have said. He was hanging out with the sheriff.* He probably could have mentioned that. *There was a life-size picture of the guy covered in blood.* That might have been good to know. But rather than delve into his concerns, Randall sugarcoated it. Hell, Freddy was about to go to lunch with the salesman, he wasn't going to speak up. Van already told what he knew.

"I ain't gonna lie, Keller," cautioned Randall, "the guy's big and he's got ties to the community."

"That much can be expected," replied Keller. "He probably hosts car washes and cookie sales for the local high school. He'll be extra ready to pay a bloated ransom for his whiny son."

It was designed to be a warning and Keller blew it off. So be it.

"Van, you're in deep cover. Keep an eye out and make sure to report anything out of the ordinary. Randall and Freddy, remember the shipment coming in from Jamaica, we'll need all hands on deck. This meeting is now adjourned, thank you all," said Keller in his usual arrogant tone.

With a parting gaze they all said good-bye to Emily before piling into the darkness. In need of sustenance, they ambled up to the same luminous store where Randall and Freddy had confronted Billy.

Moving deliberately through the shrubs and rutted pavement, Randall slowed. While his eyes adjusted to the glowing structure, it seemed to be none other than Billy Winslow at that same damn gas pump with the same girl.

"Van, is that Billy?"

"Looks like him."

"Yeah," said Freddy with a sneer.

"We can't be seen together!"

"I'll second that," answered Randall.

Drawn toward the glow, the three continued on. He was in the light, and they were in the darkness. They could see him clearly, but he couldn't see them. Then as a gorgeous brunette moved swiftly in their direction, they panicked. Randall and Van flew headlong into a repulsive pile of convenience store trash while Freddy stood firm. Rita looked up in surprise to see a guy standing by the dumpster and then quickly returned to the store.

"What the hell are you doing, Freddy?" exclaimed Van, wiping some rancid chili from his face.

"Come on, man, we gotta get out of here," added Randall, shaking a wavy potato chip out of his hair.

Still wary of Van, Freddy listened to Randall as they naturally set out for the next store.

Meeting Billy back at the truck, Rita said, "That was strange."

"What was strange?"

"Someone was standing behind the dumpster."

"Was it a bum?"

"What do you mean by 'a bum'?" she asked.

"I meant a homeless man, one who might be looking for food in a trash can, a guy down on his luck."

Rita gave a coy smile and continued, "So, there was this guy behind the dumpster, and I could have sworn I saw a couple of other guys jump into a pile of trash."

"Two others?" asked Billy.

"Yeah, like I said, a couple," answered Rita.

"The funniest thing is that he looked familiar, like I had seen him before, like I had seen him here before."

Billy instantly knew the deal. He knew who they were.

"Was the guy big and blond?"

"Yeah."

"Did he look stupid?"

"I suppose, I mean sometimes you look stupid."

"I guess we all do at times."

"Ahh, some more than others," she said, feeling as if there were still some unanswered questions.

Strangest thing was that Billy felt the same way.

Now safely home, Rita snored as Billy examined the new set of circumstances. The same trailer park, the same gas station, the same guys except with an addition. What did it mean? For one, it meant that he needed to go to a different gas station. But in a broader sense, he felt like things were about to get serious. Something was up. He was pretty sure that the two were Randall and Freddy. It was their turf, but who was the third? Billy sensed a kinky-haired turncoat, a sunburned scoundrel. He thought of a name, and it was the name of the man who had first asked him for a hand. The man's name was Van.

He had actually counted on it, but that was in theory. This was real. It was all going according to plan. He was completely stunned, if not disheartened, that nothing but this foolish scheme had ever gone according to plan. It was insane, but the material was good.

What's Flash going to do? thought Billy as he glanced toward his bookshelf. A handful of Westerns stared back. The name on the books read Louis L'Amour, and the titles spelled danger: *The First Fast Draw, Mohave Crossing, The Quick and the Dead.* In the spirit of the old West, Billy began the next chapter.

Chapter 5

Turncoat Junction

Flash looked at his boots and they were worn. His face was worn too, but he'd found a woman who liked it. She was the kind of woman that a man built something around. He hadn't planned on falling in love, but it was nice to feel good for a change.

He took a long swig from a cold beer and set down the paperback he'd been reading, High Lonesome. *He thought about Considine, and what he had been owed and what he would take. Cut from the same cloth, he and Considine were both surrounded by enemies and deeply in love. It wasn't the first time he'd fought his way out of a jam, but it would be the last. Just as the lone gunman had done, he was going to do. He'd ride out of Turncoat Junction alive.*

Billy liked the Western twist. Instead of backing up, move forward; instead of running away, stay and fight.

Jolted awake by an uncommonly loud snort, Rita thought, *Maybe I do snore.*

As she fell back asleep a sound came, muffled and then louder.

"Rita," hissed Billy.

She opened her eyes to those of a madman and asked, "Why are you waking me up in a freaky whisper?"

"I'm trying to cushion the blow. I know you don't like being woken up."

"Do you?"

He was slow to reply as she hesitantly asked, "But I'm up now so what do you need, sweetie? How can I help?"

"You know the book I've been working on?"

"That kidnapping blockbuster?"

"Yeah," answered Billy. "I'm hung up on a name for the thing."

"I've already named it three or four times. Why don't you just name the book when you finish?"

"That's not part of the process. I want it to be fresh, in the moment."

"Does the moment include someone else naming your book?"

"I'm not saying I'll use it, but if I do, I'll give you credit."

Rita wasn't sure she wanted credit, but she was tired and he didn't seem to be leaving.

"OK, well, give me something to work with."

"It's going to be like a Western, maybe a modern-day Western, but the bad guys are kind of like the good guys."

Prompted by Billy's creative deadlock, Rita's nighttime wanderings returned to a time of sepia-toned warriors and hardened, expressionless settlers. The legends of the West were real, carved and blasted into submission by a force more stubborn than nature. The land would eventually yield to so-called progress, strip malls, and parking garages. Hopefully some wild places would remain, within her, and in the tiny spaces where things could still be free.

An image of a fresh-faced kid with a short-lived look of destiny came to mind. Wearing a top hat at a tilt armed with a shotgun and a six-shooter, the caption read, "Billy the Kid."

"How about 'The Kidnap Kid,'" she said as she sank back into the couch.

"Not bad," muttered Billy as he produced a fresh piece of paper, centered the text, and typed:

"The Kidnap Kid"

The Plan

The two baked beneath the sun like ancient sections of parched earth. Like weathered structures, their color had changed. In the caustic glow, they resembled something prehistoric. In the light of a new day, they looked like something old.

Drawn together like battered magnets, Edwin and the young bum had history. Before the rusty bikes and beachside apartments, there was a house, on a lane, with a white picket fence. Edwin Slack, Samantha Lee, and the young bum had been a family.

Jack Lee was the young bum's given name. But when his mother left Edwin, and then left for LA with a fake, drunk movie producer, things changed. Too young to go it alone and too old to listen, Jack's issues increased. With a recent lapse in hygiene, a backward cap, and scraggly blond hair, he became known only as the young bum.

In a sleeveless flannel with his signature beret, Edwin, on the other hand, wore a look of purpose rather than missed opportunities. Constantly on the move, his only concern was the next job or the next score, no change and no regrets. At this point, they also had no refreshments.

"It looks like we need to get a few more beers," said Edwin, knowing full well that the cooler was empty and that the young bum had money.

"Yeah, maybe," offered the young bum, in no real hurry to do anything.

Edwin knew the deal. On most days he could wait him out, but today was different. Today he had a plan.

"Come on, bum," started Edwin, "I know you got money. I also know that you know that I don't have any."

"That's about the size of it."

"Well, that's a shame 'cause I got a plan, but to carry it out, we gotta get mobile."

"Mobile, huh?"

"Yeah, we need to move. We need to go in the direction of the store, so I figured we ought to get a few more beers if we were headed that way."

It was uncanny logic, spot on. He could get the beer and drink it later, maybe even tomorrow. He'd give Edwin a few for the road and then part ways for a while, maybe forever.

"OK," said the young bum, "but what about the plan?"

Even by the young bum's standards, Edwin had a habit of coming up with some pretty hazardous schemes. In an attempt to limit the damage, the young bum wanted some answers up front. Edwin, of course, was too slick.

"I'll brief you on the way."

The young bum waited. Wearing a startled expression, he couldn't do anything but grab a bike, at least to get some answers.

They regrouped in the parking lot of a quickie mart as Edwin carefully scanned the road. The young bum followed suit before fixing an angry stare on his mentor. Oblivious to the negativity, Edwin just kept looking from side to side.

"It's a convertible Rolls," he mumbled as the car got closer. "OK, here's the plan, you flop in front of this car!"

"I what?" exclaimed the young bum before being pushed to the pavement in front of the slow-moving vehicle.

The car then slammed into his ribs with a dull thud before coming to an abrupt stop. *Darn thing's got some brakes on it*, thought Edwin before rushing to his aid.

"Man down, man down, we need a medic!" he shouted as the young bum writhed in pain. He'd hoped to see someone frail with a bit of age exit the car, but what he actually saw changed everything.

It was a businessman, a big businessman wearing boots, a guy who no doubt went to one of those fancy indoor exercise places.

"Look what you did!" yelled Edwin.

"Look what I'm gonna do!" said the big dude before kicking Edwin straight in the stomach with a big black boot.

Edwin hit the ground next to the young bum, but the businessman wasn't done. He got close to Edwin, so close that the stench of cologne mixed with body odor nearly caused him to vomit.

"You think you can scam me with that sorry excuse for a flop? I ought to beat you into next week. I ought to tie you up and throw you into the river."

"Look to your left," he said, as Edwin craned his neck. "I own that bank over there. I rip people off legally."

"People don't own banks," wheezed Edwin, "banks own banks."

"Well, people own banks that own banks, and it's best not to hustle people who travel in those circles. Do you get it, man?" said the big guy as he glared down at Edwin.

"Yeah," groaned Edwin.

"And another thing," added the big businessman, "you owe your buddy there an apology."

"Check," answered Edwin as the stranger drove off while giving the two would-be scammers the finger.

"Hey, bum," said Edwin.

The young bum didn't respond.

"I'm sorry, bum, it was a bad idea, needs more logistics. This was a dry run. We'll get 'em next time."

"There ain't gonna be a next time," gasped the young bum. "And if you ever try anything like that again, I'll call the law on you myself."

"Fair enough," agreed Edwin.

As they lay on the ground waiting for the pain to subside, a lady ran over and exclaimed, "I saw what just happened, saw the whole thing. The nerve of that guy to run the poor kid over and then kick you in the stomach. He should go to jail, that's what should happen to him!"

Edwin didn't know what to think. He certainly didn't ever want to see the guy again, but this had to be good for something.

"Uh, I know, ma'am. I've never been assaulted in such a manner, and just when I was supposed to meet a friend who owed me some money, ten dollars to be exact. Looks like me and the kid will have to go hungry again."

She was quick to her pocketbook. "I just can't believe I witnessed an event like that," she declared while placing a twenty in Edwin's out-stretched hand.

"I can't believe I was involved in it. Sure wish I had gotten the plate number."

"I got it—committed the whole thing to memory and wrote it down. I'm sure this was it," she said, handing a piece of paper to Edwin as the young bum chuckled.

"And what's your name, sir, so we can be on a first-name basis when the officers do their investigation."

Edwin looked her over. He hadn't been with a lady in a while, but this one looked crazy, and the whole talk of officers and investigations had him spooked. He'd give her a fake name—if he could think of one.

"Tell the nice lady your name," pressed the young bum through a snicker.

"Shut up, you invalid," snarled Edwin.

He then turned to the lady with a smile and said, "It's Clark, Clark Gable, ma'am."

"Just like the actor!" she exclaimed.

Edwin wondered where he'd pulled the name from, and now it made sense.

"Yeah, it's been more of a curse than a blessing. But anyway, we gotta go. Thanks for your kindness and someone should be calling you soon. Hopefully we can count on your cooperation," added Edwin as they sped off with the young bum now completely convinced of Edwin's incompetence.

Van ran into the two at a beachside bar as they stumbled down the boardwalk.

"You guys trashed already?"

"You could say that," said Edwin, giving as little information as possible.

The eventful morning had given way to a quiet afternoon—too quiet for the likes of Edwin. He would have preferred the young bum to speak his piece and be done with it, but he hadn't. He was giving Edwin a bit of his own medicine. Van gave them the once-over and noticed a tear in the young bum's shirt. Edwin also seemed to be breathing heavier than usual.

"Did you guys get into a fight or something?"

"The young bum got hit by a car."

"Nice try, bonehead!" yelled the young bum.

He then faced Van and snarled, "Your brainless buddy here pushed me in front of a Rolls Royce."

"It was a way to get money," countered Edwin, hoping to add reason to something quite unreasonable.

"Someone paid you to kill the young bum?"

"No, it was supposed to be a flop."

"What the hell's a flop?"

"It's where you flop in front of a nice car. You get hit and then sue the driver. It's a simple plan when correctly executed," explained Edwin.

It was odd that Van had the only logical question of the day when he asked, "So why didn't you flop yourself?"

"I got hit too. The guy who got out of the car kicked me in the stomach. We made twenty bucks off the deal anyway. A little old lady took pity on the young bum and floated us some bills."

"So, you pushed the young bum in front of a car, got yourself kicked in the stomach, and swindled twenty bucks from a nice old lady. What you got planned for tomorrow, a slip and fall or a smash and grab? Watch it, they got cameras these days, although you probably know that, being a criminal genius and all."

"Real funny. I don't see you coming up with any bright ideas."

"Wouldn't take much to top that one, amigo. Anyway, we've got a meeting today. You guys gonna be able to make it?"

"I'm in," said Edwin, "but I can't vouch for the guy over there."

"What about you, bum? You gonna be able to continue?"

"As long as Edwin isn't doing any of the planning."

"Everything's going to be done by committee," said Van, which was a lie. But he needed the two, preferably intact.

"It wasn't a bad plan," grumbled Edwin as they moved along. They'd be on time today. After all, today was the day.

Billy watched the group amble up. He'd almost forgotten how they looked and what they represented. His art, his work. He was the master, and they were crude and bitter amateurs. He couldn't help but notice the two hobbled ones, both sunburned and unshaven with an odd mix of apparel—paramilitary for one, while the other donned a backward cap and a torn promotional T-shirt for a 5K run. Van's hat rode low on his forehead, and his clothes were clean. Today they walked with a purpose. It was like an old movie, and they were the specialists. Raw and unskilled, they were also incompetent, but it didn't matter. This was a new movie, a different movie. It was their movie.

"Greetings, Commander William, Edwin Slack at your service," said Edwin.

Billy stood idly by, immersed in reflection. His eyes were blank. He didn't return the greeting. He'd become acutely aware that depending on what he said, his life could very easily change but theirs wouldn't.

"Hey, hotshot, we didn't come all this way to watch you stand there and meditate!" sounded Van's gravelly bark.

Without a plan, and some serious questions regarding old acquaintances and strange sightings, he'd let them take the reins.

"Hopefully we all know why we're here," started Billy. "We can speak vaguely on the subject, but it involves the removal and compensation for the return of a specified item. We should be clear on that."

He scanned the group as they nodded. It sounded good so far.

"Ventures of this nature are rarely successful with too much management, too much structure, so to speak."

They waited.

"All too often the smaller voices are ignored. The people who are actually doing the work have little to no say on how it should be done!"

They were almost ready to applaud.

"Well, today I'm going to change all that. Today I'm giving the voice back to the people!"

Finally, thought Edwin.

"I don't think that's a very good idea," warned the young bum.

"Nice try, slick," said Van. "It's your party, so you make the plan."

He sensed Billy was getting cold feet and wasn't about to cut him any slack. Billy felt the pressure, the weight of the unknown. He felt the fear, the fear of things to come. He couldn't get out, so he was going to have to get in.

"I thought you guys were a tight-knit group, the dirty dozen minus a few," declared Billy. "I guess we're going to have to start from square one."

Edwin moved forward but was thwarted with a quick thump to the chest as Van growled, "I guess so."

The words dug into Billy's flesh and he knew that he was attached to something dangerous. Vague was his memory of the afternoon. Conflicted were the thoughts that all ended in doubt. Still was the wind when they decided it should happen at the restaurant, out back by the dumpster. A date was set, and a safe house established. It would have to happen in the middle of his shift so they wouldn't look for him. He'd simply disappear.

Odd was the way that it would end, happily ever after. At least that's what they thought. Billy didn't think so, but it didn't matter. The meeting broke, and the crew drifted off as Billy wondered what to do.

At the house, behind the typewriter Billy was tentative. He'd planned a kidnapping. He wouldn't do it, *But Flash might*, he thought as he launched into the next chapter.

Chapter 6

Out on Top

The rubber had hit the road. Cheap talk rang out with the chime of a sinister clock. The game was on and far from complete. Flash didn't care for games, but he liked to compete.

They'd push and he'd pull, they'd stick and he'd move, they'd rock and he'd eventually roll.

Headed down a ramshackle road to meet a man at a certain spot, they'd surely conspire and plot, but Flash had no other choice but to come out on top.

Heels clicked and the door clapped shut as Billy finished his last desperate sentence.

"Working late again, honey?" asked Rita.

She was happy, and he wondered why. Like a wounded beast or a disfigured outcast, Billy slowly turned to face his salvation.

"What's gotten into you?" she asked.

"Things just got real," he answered.

"That sounds good. You know what you need?"

He knew, but didn't think that she did.

"You need a spectacular title for a fantastic new book!"

Slowly being revived, Billy laughed and shook his head.

"So, what's going on?" asked Rita without a hint of fear.

"Something bad happened, something that could forever change the course of our lives."

Rita felt deviously empowered. The feeling wouldn't last, but as long as it was there, she'd use it.

"It's simple," she said, "Something Happened on the Way to a Kidnapping."

Billy groaned. He couldn't feel distorted when she was so chipper. Instead of feeling like the phantom of the opera, he went back to being himself as he typed:

"Something Happened on the Way to a Kidnapping"

The Other Plan

Darkness descended on the group as they traveled into uncharted territory. Van knew where they were going, but Edwin and the young bum had only been given a name. All they knew is that they were going to The End.

In a deserted corner of a darkened trailer park, Randall and Freddy unloaded some cargo. They both showed signs of a hard day's work while Keller was fresh as a daisy. He believed in working smarter, not harder.

Keller's sharp gaze followed the trio as they made their way into the compound. The goods that Randall and Freddy were handling appeared to be long, shiny object, and as the crew got closer, a truck-load of brand-new surfboards gleamed into view.

"Give us a hand," growled one of the guys.

Instead of moving forward, Van stalled. He recognized the setup. Edwin and the young bum, on the other hand, were only too happy to oblige. They jumped in but quickly realized that the others had moved aside. A bright light then fractured the night, and, in an instant, their good deed was preserved for posterity. The young bum held up another board, there was another flash, and then Van stepped in.

"Enough with the camera, Keller."

Keller then leaped off the porch with an evil grin and said, "And why would a man who so enjoyed his last photo opportunity spoil it for such willing subjects?"

"'Cause they don't know you," answered Van.

"And what better way to get acquainted than through a photography session?" snapped Keller, throwing the two an innocent glance.

"So, what are they supposed to learn from a stranger taking trick pictures of them?"

"It's a lesson on who not to mess with," growled Keller.

Whoa, thought Edwin, *that doesn't sound good.* The young bum didn't care either way, but he liked the boards.

"You both should know that those boards were stolen from a local surf shop this morning."

"What?" exclaimed the two in unison.

Edwin lunged for the camera as Van held him back while Randall and Freddy edged forward.

"What kind of a low-down dirty trick is that?" exclaimed Edwin.

"Look, guy, if you're planning to blackmail us, we don't have a whole lot," added the young bum, a bit more refined in his fury.

"I don't want what little you possess. I want your undivided attention. I simply want your cooperation."

"All you had to do is ask," said Edwin, not really sure what this was all about.

"I'm certain you'd tell me that your word is your bond, and that you'd favor death before dishonor and all of that other hogwash. But you are here, and more importantly, you are here with Van. Van, as you know, is not trustworthy, so I'd assume that neither are you."

"Neither are you, pal," snapped Van.

"No one here is really trustworthy," added Freddy.

"I am," asserted Randall.

"You guys can trust me," chimed the young bum.

"Rule number one: never trust anyone who declares themselves trustworthy," offered Edwin.

"Hey, whose side are you on?" snarled the young bum.

"Obviously not yours," answered Freddy

"Don't worry about it, Stretch, the kid's just learning," countered Edwin.

"Silence!" yelled Keller. "My point is that we all now have a vested interest in the success of this mission."

Thoroughly confused, Edwin turned to Van and asked, "What's he talking about?"

Van found no comfort in the fact that he was double-crossing Billy, but it wasn't his choice. Billy had been acting kind of strange anyway, almost like he was setting them up, and what had been said was true—there was no honor among thieves.

Van remained silent and deferred to Keller. Keller cut right to the chase.

"Billy's not taking Steve. We are."

Quiet followed the announcement. Edwin was silent. He recognized it as a hostile takeover and knew better than to voice any immediate dissatisfaction. It didn't change anything for the young bum. As of this afternoon, his allegiance was to himself.

Smooth was the way in which the new plan was formed. Altered was the day that it would happen. Changed was the place where the kid would be kept. The end result was assumed to be the same, although with an added bonus—the great Billy Winslow would be jailed for the crime. Case closed!

As they left the park, Edwin turned to Van and said, "You got some explaining to do."

"What's to explain? We're setting Billy up. He'll take the fall and we'll get the money."

"I don't know if that's such a good idea."

"Why not?"

"Yeah, why not?" repeated the young bum.

"Because he's got that look in his eye," said Edwin, "that faraway stare. I've seen it in the eyes of a soldier carrying a couple of his buddies out of the muck. That same guy went back into the jungle with a machine gun and cleared it out, if you know what I mean."

Both Van and the young bum cringed before Van finally asked, "So, what were you doing while he dragged the guys out? Couldn't you have at least grabbed one of them?"

"Yeah, instead of admiring his form, you should have helped him out."

"I had taken a shot to the gut," hissed Edwin.

"Well, let's see the scar," said Van.

"It wasn't by a bullet," snarled Edwin, "I got smacked with the blunt end of an AK-47."

"So, you couldn't help the guy out because you had a stomach-ache?" chuckled the young bum.

"I couldn't help the guy out because I was on the ground!" yelled Edwin, red-faced and furious.

"OK, OK, you were there, man," said Van.

"Yeah, ahh, thanks for your service," added the young bum.

A stern "Hmph" was about all Edwin could muster after the heated exchange.

"So, what company were you with again?" asked the young bum as a parting jab.

Van got to Edwin before he blew a gasket and said, "Don't worry about the kid. We've got bigger fish to fry."

"Yeah," muttered Edwin.

Attempting to add some clarity to the murky nature of the mission, Van decided to be as candid as he could.

"The bottom line is this: he's got you guys lock, stock, and barrel. If you leave, he'll turn those pictures in to the police. He'll stick you with the boards, trust me."

"Well, what about you? Why are you hanging around?" asked Edwin. "Seems to me that you could opt out without too much trouble."

Van took a deep breath and sadly recalled why he was now on the other side. A hitch was there: a crease in his sanity, something to feel bad about any time of day, but mostly at night.

Wearing a blank gaze, he faced the two and said, "I can't get into it right now."

Back on Cedar Avenue as Billy made his usual entrance, Rita didn't turn to see who it was. She knew from the slam of the screen door that it was the inconsiderate one. Billy thought it strange to see his gorgeous girlfriend toiling in a hot kitchen.

"Hey sexy, you got time for a back massage in between all that slicing and dicing?"

"Oh, that's just what I need. I've been on my feet all day long."

"I was thinking you might be able to give me one."

"I'll give you a punch in the head," she said, turning back to the stove.

Billy then started to rub her shoulders as Rita turned off the burner and walked into the bedroom. With their dinner plans on hold, they spent the rest of the evening doing something more interesting.

As sunlight broke through the cheap bedroom blinds, Billy woke to an immediate hunger. He had again escaped eating one of Rita's creations. At least this time he had a decent excuse. After a lazy breakfast and a short nap, Rita went for a run, and he started to write.

Things had changed. The book had changed. Starting out as an all-access thriller, it now seemed to be one of survival and introspection. Billy wasn't much for reflection, but it was good for getting into character. Flash Shackelford, the all-time baddest dude on the planet, getting double-crossed and determined to be the last man standing.

Billy liked it.

Chapter 7
The Last Man Standing

Flash had worn a scowl for far too long. With the right woman he could relax and remember what it was like to be a man without a weakness.

The scowl had served him well, and his weaknesses were few, but at the moment they were all he had. She had put a smile on his face, and for that he gave thanks, but now she'd laid claim to something that wasn't hers and revealed his true weakness: women.

"You don't have to do it, Flash. Let's run away together."

Yeah, turn tail and run, *he thought.*

"You don't owe those guys nothing, Flash. They're getting you to do all the dirty work."

"That's the kind of work I do," he said.

Her words could help, but they could also do him harm. They could change him, and he didn't want to change. At this point, he knew he was being taken for a ride, but he liked rides. At least now he felt like he was at the wheel, controlling his own destiny, determined to be the last man standing.

Rita returned from her run as Billy was about to wrap it up. She appeared in the door like an angelic fitness model. Light from the living room framed her damp bronze body, giving it the look of something divine. Billy stared as she bent over to see what he was writing.

"Not so fast, it's not ready yet."

"I can't read the stupid thing, but every other week I have to name it?"

"That's the way it goes. It's even hard for me to understand."

"I didn't realize you were so advanced. It sounds scientific," she said, chuckling at the thought of him in a lab coat.

"It is. Anyway, sugar plum, I find myself once again in need of your services. It seems like my mind goes blank whenever the time comes to title this complicated manuscript."

"All right," she halfheartedly agreed. "I'll, of course, need a synopsis of this great work."

"A synopsis?"

"A summary, genius."

"OK," agreed Billy. "It's a story about a guy walking into a trap. He knows it's a trap but continues on. He wants to destroy the trap—to destroy himself and to be reborn."

A single word came to mind: *redemption*. Rita then reflected on their romance and wondered if it was ending. She then added that into the title.

"Ending in Redemption," she announced.

From one artist to another he said, "Very nice, babe, very nice."

Billy then dramatically grabbed a fresh sheet of paper and with a newfound confidence typed:

"Ending in Redemption"

Home

To the young Steve Linon, home wasn't where the heart is, it was where all of the other million-dollar homes were. That's not to say that he didn't love his family, he did, but he loved them in serious comfort, which unfortunately came from his father's discomfort.

The Linon family lived on a charming riverfront cul-de-sac surrounded by salt water and fishing skiffs. Their yard was tidy, and the neighbors' yards were tidy. Everything seemed to be done because they lived in the kind of neighborhood where things got done. Across the street, a home-improvement truck slowed to a stop. Next door, the painters set up shop. When it was hot, the homes were cool. When it was cool, they'd be pleasantly warm. And if it rained, there'd be plenty of room to move the party inside.

After a long day of sales and details pertaining to car sales, Jim Linon liked to relax on his large leather couch and have a soda or two. In his huge hands, the cans looked like toys he might accidentally crush, so his lovely wife, Donna, would bring him two Cokes in a large tumbler filled with ice. Jim and Donna were still happily in love.

When they were young, things had been different. They had fewer wrinkles, but she was artful in covering hers up, and he just didn't care. They enjoyed staying home, but with a brand-new business and bills to pay, Jim and Donna had to hit the town. They smiled, shook hands, handed out business cards, gave away cars, and Christmas-caroled their young dealership all the way to the top sales spot. To Donna's dismay, a friend of Jim's named Mick Rider had also helped out. Donna and Jim did the fund raisers and the meet and greets, while Mick did the other stuff: he sold the cars.

So as Jim drank his double Coke and Donna thumbed through the newest *Southern Living*, Mick Rider took his usual place out back.

"So, when's Mick going to be allowed in the house again?" asked Jim.

"When he learns some manners, so for him, that should be about never."

"What he did wasn't all that bad."

"He needs to quit calling my son a pip-squeak."

"How do you think Steve's going to feel about his mom fighting his battles for him?"

"He'll probably feel good about it," she said.

All Jim could muster up was a slight, "Hmph."

"Make all the noise you want. I'm not going to have my son treated like any other kid off the street."

"Steve wants to be treated like a regular kid. He is a regular kid."

"He's not a regular kid—he's my son and he's far from regular. He might get the regular part from you," she said with her eyes still down.

Jim laughed. Yes, he was regular, and Mick was abrasive, and Steve was thin—all of these things were true, so he decided to surrender. It wasn't completely necessary for Mick to be in the house, but as long as he was the sales manager, there'd be times when she'd have to suffer his company. As much as Jim yielded to Donna with regard to most household decisions, he wasn't quite keen on having her decide who could or couldn't enter the house.

Donna had yet to look up, which was a sure sign that she wasn't going to give in. He loved her tenacity, her unwillingness to bend. She had showed up at the hospital and refused to leave. She forced him to make some tough decisions. She stuck by him when he decided to break his body up for a living. In the lamplight she was radiant. In all of her postures, moods, and ways, she was older but hadn't aged.

"How about if I get Mick to apologize?"

"That would be fine, and it need not happen again," she stated, finally separating her gaze from the unimportant pages.

An exhale marked Jim's entry to the screened porch, where Mick drank and pounded out "Joy to the World" on the sturdy patio furniture.

"Dang good tune, Jim. Glad you finally had the sense to join the party!"

"Look, Mick, you know that you've been banished from the house again."

"Heard something about it, Jimmy, kind of like it out here, although some grub might come in handy."

"There's not going to be any grub."

"No trouble at all. I'll just call for some takeout."

"Donna's ticked off, Mick."

"So, what's new?"

"What's new is that you need to apologize to Steve."

Mick focused his bloodshot eyes squarely on Jim and calmly said, "Never."

"Then you're fired."

Mick didn't move. He was accustomed to groveling. He had no principles.

"Just kidding, Jim. So, where's the little tyke anyway, most likely hitting the books, I'd bet. That Steve's got a dang good head on his shoulders. And I'm so sorry to have upset your lovely wife. I—I don't know what got a hold of me, Jimmy. The devil just rises up in me every now and again."

OK, so he's blaming the devil, thought Jim, *I guess that's a good sign.*

"Well, just make sure that it's the last time the devil makes you upset my wife, or I'm going to have to fire you. I mean, we're gonna stay friends."

"Oh yes, Jim, of course, of course, our friendship is something I cherish."

A steamy dusk had turned into a hot night, and Mick's drink was empty. The rest of the booze was inside.

"Well, what are we waiting on, Jim?" asked a sweaty Mick Rider, shaking the ice in his tepid glass.

"Waiting on you, my friend. Donna's in the living room, and Steve should be home soon. Start with Donna and choose your words wisely."

Man, what happened to Jim? thought Mick. *Can't believe I gotta tiptoe around these amateurs. Who sells more cars than me? That's what I should say.*

Jim heard the grumbling, shook his head, and then paused so Mick could enter first. His tall frame loomed above the repentant exile as they moved into the spacious house.

"Donna, it's been brought to my attention that I've upset you, and I'm here to make amends," said Mick.

She looked up and was silent. The booze was wearing thin, and Mick actually started to believe that maybe he did owe someone an apology.

"At times I just get carried away. You've all done a lot for me, and I need to be more appreciative. In short, Donna, I'm sorry."

He sounded sincere. He looked humble. She'd give him another chance.

"You've done a good job for us, Mick, but we'd like it if you could be more professional. And by professional, I mean not insulting my son and others."

"I know, I know, Donna, but you know how me and Jim were raised up. I mean, we had to fend for ourselves. Things are different now, and I need to understand that."

"Well, Mick," replied Donna in a sweet Southern drawl, "It sounds like you've seen the error in your ways and decided to act accordingly. I appreciate it, and I'm sure that Steve will feel the same way."

"Ahh yeah, of course, Donna. Where is good old Steve?"

"Sounds like he just drove up."

"Yeah, that's him," confirmed Jim. "Looks like Jennifer's with him too."

Damn, strike two, thought Mick. *I gotta do this in front of his cute girlfriend. Maybe my mom and my first-grade teacher will show up too.*

Steve opened the door to a horrific sight. Mick's red face strained to look inviting. His first instinct was to protect his girlfriend. His second was to pretend that Mick wasn't there, which wasn't as easy. Steve moved right, and Mick followed. He took a step back, and Mick lunged forward.

"Who broke the bottle of Jack Daniel's?" exclaimed Steve.

"Ahh!" squealed Mick, as if an arrow had pierced his shallow heart.

Steve and his girlfriend then stepped aside as Steve asked, "What's with him?"

"Steven, Mick has something to say."

"Oh, you were just kidding about the broken bottle, eh," said Mick, slapping Steve on the shoulder.

Steve recoiled as his girlfriend slipped away. Mick was now too old to be cool and too predictable to be edgy. In the living room in front of the family, he was something that didn't belong. He was a vehicle, just like the ones he sold. He wasn't driving; he was being driven.

"Look, Steve, I'm sorry for insulting you every now and again. You're my best friend's son. He's my boss, so it kind of means you're my boss, and I kind of guess I shouldn't be insulting the boss."

The words were out of place. To a guy like Steve, they didn't make sense. He was thin and smart and couldn't care less about an old drunk. Especially when the old drunk worked for his dad.

"Oh, so that's what this is all about," guessed Steve. "You actually think I care about anything you say?"

"It wasn't my first thought."

Steve loaded up. This plastered fool had been following him around for too long. His stupid gold chains, fake blond hair, and dragon-print shirts were about to go down in flames.

"I don't take drunken old prunes like you seriously. I usually just give them some spare change and send them on their way."

The words stung, and Mick was incensed. If he were a chimp, he would have ripped Steve's arms off and pounded his chest with the severed appendages. But he wasn't a chimp, so he did what a beaten man might do, which was to relent.

"Well, I'm sorry, kid. That's all I got to say."

"That's all you need to say. You didn't even need to say that," said Steve, sharing a healthy guffaw with his girlfriend.

"Actually, the less you say the better. You're not still talking, are you?"

"I think he's crying," added the girlfriend.

"I'm not crying," snapped Mick. "I'm showing restraint."

"Your brain is showing restraint," remarked Steve.

"Wait a second, how can his brain show restraint if he doesn't have one?" asked his girlfriend.

"Good question, why don't you ask the brainless one?"

"That's enough, Steve," sounded Jim. "You guys run along now."

Sufficiently wounded Mick said, "I'm bushed, Jim. Is there anything else I need to do, any other demeaning tasks that need my attention?"

"Not at the moment."

"Are we good, Donna?"

"Yes, Mick, see you next week," she answered.

So, Mick found the door and slunk off into obscurity. He'd started out the night feeling like a pretty swell guy, but now he felt like a failure. Steve was a spoiled brat and when he went down, Mick wanted to be there.

Home to Billy and Rita was a faded beige duplex on a quiet side street. She said it was small, and he said it was quaint. She said it was old, and he said it had style. She said it was yucky, and he said it was a block from the beach. She said there were a lot of nice homes a block from the beach, and he told her to go live in one. She said maybe she would, and he said maybe she should. She then stormed out of the house as Billy said, "Look, honey, I just don't make a lot of money and I'm sorry."

"Bravo," applauded Rita, "another moving declaration of the simple man."

It wasn't the money. It was the future. He didn't seem to have one. It almost seemed like he didn't want to have nice things, like he didn't want to have her.

Billy had pushed her buttons by extending a simple conversation into a "go ahead and go" match, and now he needed to defuse the situation.

Billy softened his gaze and moved closer. He gently cupped Rita's shoulders and said, "It's not that I don't care, that's just not my style."

She was listening. There seemed to be more.

"Look," he said in a hushed voice, "I'm going to write a book that's going to fix everything. I'm going to write it, you're going to name it, and we're going to sell it!"

Oh, she thought, *Why didn't I think of that? Just write a best seller.*

Of all the things she could have said, of all the things she should have said, what she did say was, "Sounds good. When's it gonna be done?"

"Hmm, you just can't rush a thing like that. It takes time, you know. Should be about done later this year."

"Well, that's a pretty solid deadline, Shakespeare. Since you're going to be writing all afternoon, I'd better run to the store and get some supplies, some paper and pens," she said, quickly fleeing the subject of her disdain.

"How about a soda?" yelled Billy.

"Oh yeah, a soda. We need to keep you alert."

"Yeah," he echoed as Rita sped off.

Driving away, she thought, *I express my deepest concerns with our relationship, and all he can say is that he's writing a book.*

It was then that the voice came. It was her voice, just a more understanding version. *People do write books*, it said.

Not stupid people, answered the first voice.

Yes, they do, confirmed the second.

Yeah, well the ones they write aren't any good.

What's good to you may not be good to others, and vice versa.

I'd just like to see him finish it, sustained the first voice.

The voices then came together to proclaim, *That'll be a mighty cold day in hell!*

As Rita drove, she laughed. The life she'd been living was strange, about as strange as the voices. As the mental banter receded, Rita made a decision to see it through. She couldn't vouch for his skills as a writer, but if life experience had anything to do with it, she thought that it might be good. Billy was lovely and peculiar, but he was also doomed to learn things the hard way. She knew that. Maybe he knew it too. Maybe that's why he just kept bumbling along.

Rita cursed the cheap screen door again as she entered the house with an armful of groceries. It seemed like she was always bringing Billy things. She'd decided on the way home that it was high time for him to offer something up. If he'd actually been working on something, she wanted to see it. She wanted proof.

"Hey, honey," she chimed, "give me a preview of this latest chapter so I can decide whether I'm going to stay with you or not."

Rita sounded serious. She hadn't yet spoken in those terms. Sure, he knew she was disgruntled, but so was every other girl that he had ever gone out with.

"It's not my usual way of doing things," he mumbled, "but what the heck?"

So, with that, Billy stepped back and in a hushed voice asked, "What did we name the book the last time?"

"'Ending in Redemption,'" she answered.

"Yes, that's correct, my cherished and patient audience. 'Ending in Redemption.' So without further ado, I give you Billy Winslow!"

Billy applauded and prompted Rita to do the same as he tore into the latest entry.

Chapter 8
Along for the Ride

It's what he'd always wanted, a place to call home. Flash was tired of the road. He was tired of the one-night stands, the bad deals, and the lies. Sure, she had made things complicated, but she'd also attended to his softer side. She cared about him, and that's more than he could say for the toothy predators at the gates.

Instead of letting her go, Flash wanted her to stay. She could tighten his armor. She could hand him his sword. She could look longingly over the meadow and see the peaceful village. She could sustain the vision and give him something worth fighting for. For a tired old soldier, this would be his last war. It would be his last trip. It was do or die, and he decided to bring this pretty lady along for the ride.

He finished and she clapped. His writing wasn't horrible, although her role seemed a tad domesticated. She wanted a sword too. It seemed like she might need one.

Silence dominated the moment as he awaited a response. There was none so he asked, "So, what do you think?"

"Aside from the one-night stands and the things that are going to get out of hand, it's not too bad. I mean, is he going to get himself and the girl killed?"

"No," he said with a grin. "She's going to save him."

She is, eh? thought Rita.

"So, do we have to name it again?"

"What do you think?"

"I think, for some unknown reason, you probably want me to."

120

This was her territory, or at least the one she'd been assigned. *Rita Polli, the Great Namer of Books. How odd*, she thought.

"What's the heroine's name?"

"She doesn't have one, at least not yet. She needs one, though."

"How about, 'Saved by Grace?'"

"Genius!" declared Billy. "Both beautiful and smart."

Billy kissed Rita's forehead, selected another sheet of paper, and in twelve-point bold text typed:

"Saved by Grace"

The Stakeout

In the beginning, darkness gave way to light. From light emerged understanding. From understanding arose ignorance. That same ignorance fueled the two as they lay in wait, peering through the shrubs, hoping that Van would hurry up with those chicken tenders he'd promised.

"Man, I'm hungry," said the young bum with a hand on his abdomen.

It felt like he hadn't eaten in days. Like the next thing he dropped into his mouth would sound a metallic *ping* as it careened through the empty cylinder that used to be his stomach.

"You think Van was telling the truth about those chicken tenders?"

"Why would he lie about that?" asked Edwin.

"Why does anyone lie about anything?"

Edwin twitched as he felt another episode coming on. It was getting old, constantly having to explain things to a kid.

"Look," started Edwin, "I've had people lie to me about money. Women have lied to me. People lie about where they've been or what they've done. They lie about what they're gonna do."

"Hell!" exclaimed Edwin, "I've had people lie to me about pretty much everything. Where they live, what they drive, where they work, what they weigh, who they know. I've had people lie to me about messing people up and about getting messed up. But come to think of it, you know what anyone has yet to lie to me about?"

To mitigate any further damage, the young bum meekly answered, "Food?"

"Yeah, food!"

"Hey, you guys need to keep it down. You're supposed to be under-cover," sounded Van as he appeared with a pan of chicken strips and barbecue sauce.

"I was undercover till the young bum asked if I thought you were lying about the food!"

"Why would I lie about that?"

"Never mind," muttered the young bum.

"You're not supposed to be arguing, you're supposed to be watching."

"Tell that to Edwin," countered the young bum.

"In the industry it's called surveillance," corrected Edwin while Van and the young bum cringed.

"Well, whatever you want to call it, do it quietly. We don't want anyone to call the cops."

"Sure thing, commander," agreed Edwin.

"Roger that," added the young bum.

Edwin and the young bum had been given the task of staking out the restaurant to see who clocked in and out first and when might be the best time to seize the poor lad. To Edwin, this is what they'd come on board to do. To the young bum, they were being used. He wasn't completely sold on the deep-cover mission or the damn greasepaint that Edwin smeared across his face and onto his favorite fishing shirt.

"Well, why'd you wear your best shirt out here?" asked Edwin.

"I figured we'd be watching, not dressing up for Halloween."

He had a point. The greasepaint may have been a tad unnecessary, but Edwin wouldn't admit it.

The day vanished quickly as an anxious hum echoed from the dark-ness. Edwin, now a little drowsy, rubbed the thick black paste off his face and onto his shirt too.

The young bum laughed. *Serves him right.*

Somebody put Edwin in charge. The young bum didn't know who, but peering angrily at the old man, he figured that Edwin put Edwin in charge. He didn't know why he ever listened to the guy, but he did. Maybe it was because whenever he tried to do something on his own, he failed. Maybe that's why they were both sitting in the bushes, because neither one of them could do anything right. It was a sobering thought, one he quickly dismissed. Edwin was an idiot, simple as that.

"You take the first shift, bum. I'm gonna catch some zzzzs."

The young bum didn't know there'd be two shifts. He figured they'd be out there for a few hours and then done, but when he looked left, Edwin was fast asleep. Thinking of the girl he'd seen earlier, the young bum settled in as well. He wondered where she was and if she'd be at the beach tomorrow. He glanced again at the restaurant and then back to Edwin. He liked this hiding out stuff—it was pretty kicked back. He then noticed a block of cars stream into the parking lot and knew they were in for a busy night.

With a line already out the door, the Chowder House was full to capacity. Billy was tense. Van was hiding something, and Steve was his normal arrogant self. It was seven thirty, and the place was packed. Servers sprinted between the bar and their tables as Van slammed the pots and pans. An early meltdown led to a quick break as Steve slid by and remarked, "What are you doing out there, Van man, taking a piss? Make sure to wash your hands. Oops, I forgot, you're the dishwasher!"

It was then that Van felt the weight of Steve's fate. The die had been cast. He couldn't stop it even if he wanted to. It was a scheme borne of perhaps the most ancient embedded emotion—anger.

As Van wallowed in more disgust, Billy rounded the corner and asked, "What the heck is Keller doing here?"

Van didn't know. No one told him. He was in the dark, out of the loop. Amazed at how quickly things were moving, he needed an answer.

"The man's gotta eat, doesn't he?"

Billy was irate. There were too many questions and not enough answers. Keller's presence in the dining room also reinforced what he'd suspected: there was another party involved.

"If you're double-crossing me, you're going to get beat."

Van wasn't afraid of Billy. He had other things on his mind, namely the two guys watching the place, and now the guy who'd just walked into the place.

"I don't think I like your tone."

"You don't need to like it. I got you into this thing, and I can just as easily get you out of it."

Now he's decided to bare his teeth a bit, thought Van as he saw a little anger in the eyes of a comrade. He stepped back. He didn't want to, but to preserve the status quo, Billy had to feel like he was in control.

"OK, boss," muttered Van.

In the kitchen there was a time for everything: a time to prep, a time to joke, a time to complain, and a time to flat-out work. That's what they were there to do, so their short conversation was put on hold. Steve, on the other hand, was just starting to talk.

From a secluded booth in the darkened restaurant, Keller knew exactly who and what he was looking for. As he eagerly fixed a flame on a waiting candle, Steve arrived and remarked, "Looks like we got a self-starter here."

Far too advanced for idle chatter, Keller flashed a puzzled glance.

"Get it, a self-starter?" he repeated, motioning toward the candle. "It's not my best material, but not my worst either."

"God forbid," muttered Keller. "I suppose for the twenty-fifth time tonight, you're going to announce your name along with an array of tantalizing fried-to-oblivion seafood specials guaranteed to keep us coming back for more."

"Wow, not only a self-starter but a deep thinker as well. The fish comes sautéed, broiled, baked, poached, cooked in parchment paper, grilled, seared, and, in some cases, not cooked at all. What I'd planned to do was to take a drink order, but if you'd prefer to hear the dinner specials, I'd be more than happy to rattle those off too."

"Yes, of course," sighed Keller. "We'll take a carafe of white wine and two of the broiled seafood specials with rice. The lady would prefer oil and vinegar for the house salad, and I the bleu cheese."

Perfect, the guy got the message. Keep it short and sweet and maybe they wouldn't be waiting the rest of the night for their food.

"By the way," added Keller, "what is your name?"

In no mood to be treated like a sap, he looked straight at Keller's girlfriend and answered, "It's Steve."

"Well, Steve, could you please bring us some water?"

"Right away, sir," replied Steve, his eyes still fixed on Emily.

The pair never failed to attract attention, and tonight was no exception. Keller had done some shameful things over the years, but not even Emily was ready for what he did next.

Nearing the halfway point in their meal, Keller summoned Steve. "Steve, would you be so kind as to send for a manager?"

Steve knew better than to ask why. He'd let the manager deal with it.

"Hi, my name's Phil," announced the overly attentive manager. "Has everything been to your satisfaction tonight?"

"The dining was exquisite until I found this in my dinner," said Keller, pointing to a soggy German cockroach resting listlessly on his plate.

"It probably came out of his hair," remarked Steve.

"I heard that, Phil," replied Keller. "I did not come to this establishment to be insulted and fed bugs."

He was getting louder, and Emily was getting more embarrassed.

"Obviously, sir," said Phil, "we'd like to comp the meal and invite you back for another dining experience, on the house, of course."

Pointing at Steve, Keller snarled, "That would be fine, as long as he will not be our waiter."

By this time news of the bug had filtered into the kitchen. Billy knew the culprit. Keller had been planting bugs in food for years, but the cooks checked the plates anyway.

"You ain't gonna find anything," yelled Van. "Those plates are clean. Put two and two together, and you guys are still going to get three. The guy put the dang bug in the food."

They accepted it, and Phil looked the other way. These things happened. Most of the time the house won, but tonight they got beat.

Emily was irate. It took everything she had just to sit there while Keller finished his wine. Turns out they should have waited a few more minutes because as they walked out, a big guy and a pretty lady walked in. *Wouldn't want to tangle with that guy*, thought Keller as he brushed past.

As they did every Friday night, the big guy and the pretty lady split the double doors to find their son, Steve. Surely, if Keller missed it, a detail of such epic proportions would be noted by the guys watching from the woods.

A last call echoed from the bar as the Chowder House powered down. The waiters tipped the bussers while a few of the staff stuck around for a shift drink. Van held court while Billy slipped out the side door. His feet had gone ice cold and he was done. The time was right. He could write the rest of it out on his own.

Jim, Donna, and Steve headed up the stragglers as the restaurant finally went dark. Steve told of the odd couple he'd waited on. Of the rude patron who looked like he had survived a shipwreck. Jim similarly recalled the two guys who showed up at the dealership with the same look. "It almost seemed like they were casing the place."

"All this guy wanted was a free meal. He stuffed a bloated cockroach into a pretty piece of grouper. Phil had to comp his meal," said Steve, as the significance of the two incidents went unnoticed.

Donna had sensed something was up. She put it on Mick the other night, but the feeling had yet to subside.

After a short ride home, Steve headed out, and Jim and Donna went to bed. As they retired, Donna voiced a concern. Where it originated she didn't know. Why it occurred she couldn't say. It had more to do with a mother's intuition than any kind of logic.

As if the words were guided, she hurriedly said, "Maybe Steve should take some time off."

"Why?" asked Jim. He wasn't against the idea but wondered about the reasoning.

She couldn't describe it. She didn't want to. All she wanted was for her son to return home safely every night.

"Because I feel like something's going to happen."

The night was dark. It was like a black glaze had been spread across the heavens. The chirps and rattles of dusk had gone silent as the forest finally got some rest.

"Oh no, man, no," mumbled the young bum as he woke from a vivid dream.

A quick visual revealed unfamiliar surroundings. A more in-depth assessment confirmed he'd fallen asleep.

Edwin lay beside him, still snoring. Instead of watching they'd been sleeping, which was problematic, one: because they were supposed to be collecting information. Problem number two was that he'd most likely get blamed. Forget that Edwin was supposed to be some sort of a military expert. *What kind of an expert falls asleep on a secret mission? A fake expert, that's who*, thought the young bum.

"Edwin, get up!" he said with a not-so-gentle shove.

"Errr," muttered Edwin as the rude awakening set in.

He took in some scenery as well before figuring out what happened. A face smeared in greasepaint first came into view, and then the restaurant. The cars were gone, and the lights were out. He'd slept through his shift. *Ahh, the young bum must have gotten it*, he thought.

After a yawn, Edwin again focused on the young bum and casually asked, "So what'd ya get, bum?"

"Nothing. I just woke up myself."

Edwin could blame him, but the guys on the other side were going to blame Edwin, so they could all go ahead and play the blame game.

"You were supposed to wake me up, man!"

"You weren't supposed to go to sleep. You stepped forward, you wanted the responsibility, then you get up here and conk out. I just don't see it."

This was different from their regular back and forth. It had implications. However Edwin arranged and rearranged it, the result was the same: he came out on the bottom. A look of concern framed his deeply lined face. The young bum was staying put. He held all the cards.

"Well, we're the only two who know about this," said Edwin, "and for now I do believe we need to keep it that way."

"Glad you came to your senses," replied the young bum, as they staggered out of the woods.

It was late or early, Billy couldn't tell. He felt dull. Instead of sleep there was a blur. The steady creak of a ceiling fan counted off the seconds. A half hour turned into an hour. The pillowcase grated across his face as he tossed and turned. Unable to sleep, he decided to write.

In the uncomfortable darkness, Billy felt sickly inspired. Awake and alive, he slipped away from Rita and made for the spare bedroom. Adrenaline coursed through his veins as he angrily typed.

Chapter 9
Down in Flames

Flash abandoned the mission. He jumped ship. He went from being one of them to being not one of them. He went from being on the inside to being on the outside. He went from being with them to being eternally against them. He'd come to terms with something they already knew: that he was getting set up.

Flash was in no mood to get burned by a bunch of amateurs. After all, he was the captain and they were the crew. He was the chef and they were the cooks. He was the owner and they were just renting.

The circle was closing and he needed an out, but he wouldn't go alone. As far as Flash was concerned, they could all go down in flames.

Billy finished at dawn, his tortured thoughts summarized in a couple of searing paragraphs. The ceiling fan continued to pulse as he collapsed in a cold sweat. Rita mopped his forehead with a cool towel and said she was worried.

"I don't feel so good."

"You don't look so good."

"I need some sleep."

She softly agreed and in a hushed voice said, "What you really need is a wake-up call."

That's it, thought Billy as he rushed back to the typewriter to finish the night's work. Snatching a fresh sheet of paper, with an unyielding spirit and a splitting headache, he feverishly typed:

"Wake-Up Call"

Hornswoggled

Billy woke to an angel at his bedside. That was it, he had died and gone to heaven. He didn't count on getting there. If anything, he felt like he'd end up somewhere in between, in the middle, mediocre.

So there she stood, a glimmering jewel reflecting good onto his not so good, injecting sense into his nonsense and, at the moment, adding comfort to his discomfort.

The sickness made him weak as he gingerly asked for the time.

"It's five thirty," answered the glowing apparition.

"Five thirty, I was supposed to be at work two and a half hours ago."

"I called Phil and told him you had a fever. He didn't sound too happy, but I couldn't get you up."

"Maybe I should go."

"Suit yourself. I don't think he's expecting you, though. I told him you looked really pale and that you wouldn't budge. He actually suggested I check your vital signs, and I told him they weren't all that telling even when you're awake."

"Glad to see you two were yocking it up while I was in a coma."

"I missed a shift to watch you lay there and mumble about being in between something and something else. I think you said a rock and a hard place, real original."

She was doing it again, getting angry.

"Please," begged Billy. "I'm going through a lot right now. I've got some not-so-nice guys planning to do some not-so-nice things. So, unless I can change the flow of this sinister tide, I could end up in the middle of something deep. I could already be in the middle of it."

Rita listened but couldn't be of too much assistance. She knew Billy tried. She realized he had a good heart. He was a lot of fun and she loved him, but the time had come to give him some advice.

"It's true, they say you gotta write about what you know, but you can't go instigating a story. What did you think would happen?"

"I didn't instigate it. They brought it to me."

"You went along with it. I mean, if someone brings you a beehive, are you going to smack it with a baseball bat?"

Billy hadn't heard of anyone other than a beekeeper possibly gifting a beehive, but he got the idea.

"No," he answered.

"No," she repeated. "You're putting yourself in danger and even worse, you're putting me in danger."

"This is dangerous stuff," he feverishly replied. "I'm not in the business of playing it safe, and neither are you."

She thought Billy was sick, but now he seemed to be firing on all cylinders.

"I don't want to be bored, but I'm not going to put myself in harm's way for something that may or may not pan out."

"It's not only my dream. It's yours too, to do something great, to be distinguished. It comes at a price. You can't just poke it with a stick. You gotta reach out and grab it; you gotta get close to it. If you want guarantees, you're with the wrong guy. But I can promise you this: what I do is going to be done with style, and what I make is going to be made well—it's going to last."

Billy's conviction was intoxicating. It was a shame he couldn't muster up as much enthusiasm for something normal. Write a book about a dog, or a mission to space, not about binding someone up and throwing them into the trunk of a car. Rita couldn't change his mind, though, and wasn't sure she would even if she could.

Billy was on his back as Rita stole a quick glance. In his handsome face rested memories, mostly of the good times. The romance was still there. She was still excited to see him, but what she said next came as no surprise.

"We may not make it through this," said Rita.

"I know," answered Billy.

Across town in a bland, orderly apartment, Van jumped out of the shower. Billy wasn't at work, which was nothing unusual. At this point he was just a pawn in the game, the most disposable piece. *He's gonna get disposed of*, thought Van. Tonight, the crew would travel to Keller's for their final meeting.

Edwin and the young bum knew that Van was on the way and wondered how things would go. There were two of them and one of him. They figured he'd whine a bit and then come to his senses. It was his choice. He could make it difficult, or he could make it not so difficult.

Van moved seamlessly through the dark, empty streets. Tonight he was tense. He was there to assess what they'd seen. He needed to be briefed on their surveillance. Van had lobbied for a Saturday stakeout in order to miss Jim's Friday night dinner date, but the suggestion fell on deaf ears. He could only protest so much without drawing suspicion.

In the pit of his stomach, Van felt like he might have to come clean. He didn't want to, not until the time was right, and the time might never be right. Van hoped that what they didn't know wouldn't hurt them, but he knew that in this case, it very well could.

Reaching Edwin's apartment, the door was ajar, so he let himself in. Van expected to see the two talking, or at least arguing over who could hide from the cops better, but they were just sitting there.

"What's up, guys?" asked Van.

"Nothing," answered Edwin.

"Nada," was the young bum's reply en Español.

"Nada, eh?" repeated Van, sizing things up. It didn't look good, but he wouldn't give anything up without a fight.

"So, what'd you get?" he sternly asked.

They both shifted a little as if things had gotten a bit more uncomfortable.

"It was dark," answered Edwin.

"The place is completely lit," said Van.

"Ahh, we were kind of far away," added the young bum.

"You had binoculars," answered Van, holding up an imaginary pair of binoculars.

"We had to be careful not to be seen," said Edwin, a little louder than before.

"Who's going to notice two guys squatting in the bushes from a hundred yards away?" was Van's final and most bewildered reply.

There was no answer; none was expected.

"Wait a second," snarled Van, "you guys fell asleep."

"The young bum did," offered Edwin.

"You did too, Edwin!"

"Just restin' my eyes, kid," was the word from the old salt.

They had crashed out on their assignment. It was too good to be true, a get-out-of-jail-free card. They expected him to be angry, so he'd get angry.

"You, a special forces soldier," sneered Van.

"I was in the air force."

"You were a dishwasher in the air force."

"I can't tell you everything I did."

"That's the problem. You can't tell me anything you did!"

Van then turned his ire on the young bum and said, "And what about you?"

"Huh?"

"I'm surprised you didn't try to grab the old man's package out there under the stars and all!"

"What are you tryin' to say?" asked the young bum, taking a step forward.

"I'm not trying to say anything," answered Van.

Edwin then separated the two and said, "Look, Van, I blamed the young bum and he blamed me. Now you're blaming us, but the guys in the trailer are going to blame you."

They all had something to lose. There was a lot that could be used against them—stolen surfboards for the guys, and a dead body for Van. If Keller and his gang sensed anything suspicious, there was no telling what they'd do.

"Well, we need to tell 'em something. They'll expect it. Saying that everything looked normal is gonna be too mechanical. We can't just lie to them, they'll sniff it out. They're liars."

Edwin and the young bum didn't understand. Maybe everything had been normal.

"Get a pen and a piece of paper, bum," ordered Van as the young bum snapped into action.

"Edwin, draw a diagram of the restaurant."

"Right away, sir," was Edwin's immediate response.

Van then began to craft his most ingenious hoax to date.

The two watched as he mumbled. He needed something scandalous. He needed to turn one thing into another. In short, he'd have to employ a certain measure of deceit. Keller wanted information, so he'd give it to him.

"It was seven o'clock when I took my first break, hmm, then I saw Steve pass by and ahh, that's when he met his boyfriend!"

"What?" exclaimed Edwin.

"Wow!" added the young bum.

"Yeah," murmured Van in a devious suspended growl.

He'd done it. They all knew what it was. Smoke and mirrors, sleight of hand, in a word, misdirection. Could it work and, more important, would it work? "Do you think it'll work?" was the first and most obvious question, and "Is he really gay?" was the second.

"Yes" and "no" were the answers. "He's got a smoking hot girl-friend," added Van. "Don't ask me how."

Nobody bothered to, and it didn't matter. All that mattered was they were back in business. So, it was decided that Van would be the one to pass on the bogus testimony. Neither Edwin nor the young bum could be trusted. It was too complex. It was too dangerous.

On a patch of grass along the rocky driveway, Rita started her car. She'd left without saying good-bye. Billy hoped she'd return. The way things were going, he wasn't sure she would.

Billy swore as the garbage truck deliberately sped away. A black cat had recently appeared in the neighborhood, and Rita started to feed it. The neighbor's dog was gone, done in by old age. Billy had known it from a puppy, fifteen years to be exact. *Fifteen years and what have I done?*

No woman could enter a room like Rita. Huffing and puffing, dumping her gear on the counter all the while complaining about a bank teller on downers. "I sat in the drive-through for twenty minutes to cash a check for twenty dollars!"

"I could have loaned you the money."

"That's not the point, but thanks anyway," she said, noting the generous nature of the offer.

Knowing he needed something better, Billy spun Rita around, kissed her on the cheek then went on to compose one of the final entries.

Chapter 10
Gone Wrong

With a beat-up car and worn-out pair of shoes, Flash stared at the lady he was about to lose. She'd fit in well with the ones he'd already lost. Almost everything he ever had was gone. He'd get it then it would be gone.

He'd tear his shirt open if it would help. He'd scream at the top of his lungs if it would do some good. He'd blame somebody if he could. But it all came back to the image in the mirror, the one that looked like his father.

It wasn't the end. It wasn't what was wrong with the world. It was just another thing gone wrong.

Billy took a break and let it sink in. He could handle the minor setbacks but had hoped to avoid the real life-in-ruins stuff. It could be on the way, though.

Similar to his father, Billy was also accident prone. Talented, edgy, and sometimes out of control, they both shared the same larger purpose. Billy Sr. went north to buy a fishing boat and never returned. Gone to the chaotic pulse of the sea, it was a tragic end for someone who had more to give. Billy was young when it happened, but it still changed everything.

He showed Rita some old pictures, and she remarked at the likeness they shared. "Although he was more handsome than you," she quipped.

Rita studied the photos, the ones where Billy's dad held a little tyke in coveralls. She looked again at the ones where he stood alone.

"You two are practically a mirror image."

"That's it. You've done it again!"

"I've done what again?"

"You've named this great manuscript."

"I did?"

"You did."

"What is it?"

Billy waved a single celebratory sheet of paper and said, "Here it is!"

Rita looked to the page uninspired and read:

"Mirror Image"

The Setup

Something was awry.

A critical detail was missing.

Crucial data was being withheld.

It could have made a difference.

It would have changed everything.

To say things looked normal would be too predictable; they wouldn't buy it. It was a matter of manufacturing the right story, striking the right chord. It was mathematical: in order to subtract, they'd have to add. To add, they'd have to subtract. For the truth to remain hidden, they'd have to lie. The truth being that two dummies fell asleep and they were about to kidnap a maniac's son.

Although Keller was overconfident, he still had the makings of a career criminal. With a highly piqued sixth sense and the absence of a conscience, he was still in control.

Keller shouldn't have had to do all of the legwork. He had the résumé. It wasn't as if he'd left everything to chance. He grilled Van and even blackmailed the hell out of him. He blackmailed the other guys too. He sent his top lieutenants to stake out Steve's dad's car dealership and even visited the restaurant where Steve worked. Heck, Steve even waited on him. It was all basic: borrow a brat for a few hours and then get his former best friend sent to jail for a very long time. If it was all so simple, then why had the twitch returned?

In the past something always turned up, a last-minute phone call, a warning from an old friend, or a gut feeling. The feeling was there, as was the time to expose any additional details. A thin alien smile slid across Keller's face as the thought of using force quickly became an option.

But barring any unforeseen developments, the mission would continue. Everything was falling into place. Things were going too smoothly. Everyone was seeing what they wanted to see; everyone besides Billy, that is.

Keller saw a wiseass kid without any backbone. Randall saw a chance to remove Keller, and Freddy saw an opportunity to get rid of Randall. Edwin and the young bum were in it for the money, and Van was trying to save his hide. To say that a lot was riding on this last meeting was an understatement.

The road to Keller's seemed darker and the potholes deeper as Van moved swiftly along. Edwin didn't have a problem with the pace, but the young bum was struggling.

"If we speed up, we could probably drop him."

"Shut up, Edwin," hissed the young bum.

"Both of you shut up," growled Van. "Behind that door a few tough guys are gonna be staring a hole in you. Stay calm, speak when you're spoken to, and don't give any extra details. I'll do the talking, is that understood?"

"Sure thing," agreed both Edwin and the young bum.

In the darkness Keller's glowing trailer seemed to have a pulse. From a distance it looked small and dangerous. Van hoped the meeting would go quickly, and he said as much to the other two.

"I'm gonna keep this short and sweet," hissed Van. "We're not going to spend any more time in there than needed. I don't really want to be there in the first place."

Standing in front of the mildewed edifice, they knocked, and the door opened to a comfortable living space. Van's mission was to make it uncomfortable.

"Well, hello, my friends," said Keller in a sinister tone reminiscent of Dr. Zachary Smith from the sci-fi series *Lost in Space*. He had the maniacal grin and vicious eyes to match. Van laughed as he pictured a robot flailing its cheap metal arms and warning, "Danger, Will Robinson!"

"Is something entertaining?" asked Keller with a quick scan of the room.

Randall and Freddy followed suit as if to say, "Yeah, funny guy, what's so funny?"

"No, just thinking about what I have to say is all."

"This should be good," muttered Keller.

"What's with the negativity? We're supposed to be in this together," said Van, who for some reason was feeling pretty loose.

"We are not in this together," replied Keller.

"OK, Burger King, have it your way."

"Burger King?"

"Yeah, Burger King," repeated Van. "You put it together, you stack it up, you know, make it look pretty."

"Burger King," said Keller again, as a disturbed look eased into a grin.

So amused with his new status, he turned to Randall and exclaimed, "I'm the new Burger King!"

"Greetings, Your Highness," announced Randall, not really sure what to make of the levity.

"Long live the king!" added Freddy, somewhat relieved that he didn't have to throw the guys out.

Keller then looked to Emily and asked, "Would you, lovely and beautiful Emily, consider being my Burger Queen?"

"Yes, of course, my generous king," answered Emily.

Edwin and the young bum just snickered while Van showed a wide toothy smile.

"Ahh, enough of this tomfoolery," said Keller. "We are here to put the finishing touches on a rather delicate undertaking."

Up until now, no one had even mentioned the word *kidnap*, perhaps to ease the gravity of the task, considering it to be more of a loan or an exchange. It was a sanitized version of the truth, one that Van would have to destroy if he were to be taken seriously.

"Let's get this straight," he announced, "what we're taking part in here is a kidnapping. It's a serious crime. It's not for the faint of heart."

He and Keller then locked eyes, and for the first time, Van felt like he held equal footing. It was up to Keller. The cards were on the table. They were no longer making vague references to a mysterious chore. This was the real thing. He could pull out now and they could all go home. Give up the incriminating photographs and bid the troops a fond farewell, but Keller couldn't do that, and Van couldn't tell Keller the truth about Steve's dad. He was too deep into the lie. Keller had pictures of him posing with a corpse. Who was the stiff, and more important, where was he?

"Well, what did you discover?" asked Keller in a neutral tone, too neutral for someone trying to flush something out.

What did he know? This was going to be the tricky part.

"I think you've met my associates, Edwin and the young bum."

Keller nodded as the other two mumbled in agreement.

"You see, these guys were watching the restaurant from the bushes."

"Brilliant," said Keller. "Go on."

"Everything seemed pretty regular for a restaurant."

"Everything?" asked Keller with a raised eyebrow.

"Uh, yeah," they muttered.

"Yeah, everything," said Van.

"What time were they there?"

"Five thirty to ten."

"Did they see me enter and leave?"

"Yeah."

"Was Emily with me?"

Van nodded.

"What was she wearing?"

"Sandals and a strapless blue sundress."

"Is that what she was wearing?" was the question quickly directed at the two.

They hadn't the faintest idea, but weren't about to disagree.

"Yeah, you got it," answered Edwin.

"Yup," agreed the young bum.

"How could you see what she had on her feet from the bushes?" was the question designed to expose the truth.

"They had binoculars," answered Van.

"When and where does Steve take his breaks?" asked Keller.

"He takes a break before the dinner rush at roughly six to six fifteen, then another at nine around the northeast corner of the building by the dumpster."

"Is he ever visited by friends, family, or other?"

That was it. Keller provided a perfect segue into the bogus testimony. Edwin and the young bum knew it, and so did Van. He wasted no time.

"If by other, do you mean his boyfriend?" Van rhetorically asked.

"Hmm, enjoys the comforts of another man, does he?" mused Keller to no one in particular. Why it was important, he couldn't tell. What it meant, he hadn't a clue. All he knew was that he had sensed the same thing.

"That's what I thought!" he finally exclaimed.

Van winced.

Edwin and the young bum gave each other a slight glance, and Emily shook her head.

"These guys picked it up," said Van. "I've worked with the guy for a year or so and was none the wiser."

"Some would rather keep such things hidden," instructed Keller on discretionary matters. "For instance, Van, I don't suppose you'd tell me if you happened to yearn for the touch of a man."

"Uh, don't suppose I would," answered Van. He hadn't given it much thought.

"Hmm, yes of course," muttered Keller. "We'll have to make sure that his special friend isn't in attendance when we carry out what Van so bluntly characterized as a kidnapping."

Everyone agreed, especially those who knew his special friend wouldn't be in attendance, as Van declared, "Well, it's getting late. We better be getting out of here, Keller. It's been fun, I mean, it's been real."

"Keep yourselves available. Further instruction will be issued as we work out the final details, is that understood?"

"Aye, aye, captain," said Van.

"Keep us posted," added Edwin.

"Yes, I will, as you said, keep you posted," replied Keller with a cackle as they shut the light aluminum door and took off.

"Man, he bought it!" exclaimed Van.

"Worked like a charm," agreed Edwin.

"You had those guys eating out of your hands!" added the young bum.

"I sure did," he chuckled, although he knew the victory would be short lived.

Van had a feeling that they, like Billy, were being set up for a fall, a fall he just wasn't willing to take.

Content for the time being and with an ever-important errand to run, Keller picked Freddy to ride shotgun. Keller would often leave one of the two alone with Emily. Most of the time it was Freddy. Truth be told, Randall couldn't remember a time when it wasn't Freddy. In the past, such a detail would have troubled the second in command, but tonight it didn't because things had changed.

Randall had questioned Keller's judgment a time or two. He spoke up when he probably shouldn't have. In short, the two had splintered. Not to mention the suspicious division of funds. Keller had two cars while Randall and Freddy were still riding bikes. The trailer was full of things he didn't deserve—the leather couches, the thick glass table, and above all, the girl. He'd left the two alone without a care in the world, a glaring reminder of his arrogance—as if the last thing he had to worry about was Randall.

She sat on the couch, and he knew he'd have to trust her. He thought about making some small talk but decided against it; there'd be time for that later.

"Look, Emily, I'm starting to get a bad feeling about this."

"You don't say," she said in an uncertain falsetto.

He was relieved. Had she answered differently, he would have had to adjust his plan. Randall decided to go all in.

"Look, I've seen the guy's dad. He's a monster."

"Steve's not gay either," replied Emily.

"What?"

"Yeah, that night at the restaurant he slid me his number. I think he did it to spite Keller, but he also wanted me to call."

"I'm sure he did," agreed Randall. "Did you?"

"I thought about it. I mean, he's cute, but he's not really my type."

"But you didn't tell Keller."

"Didn't think I needed to. I get hit on all of the time—he doesn't seem to care."

The new information was compelling, to say the least. At first blush, it seemed like one of three things had happened. One, Emily was lying, which he thought to be highly unlikely. Two, Steve was pretending to be gay, which he dismissed almost immediately, or three, Van was lying about Steve being gay.

Of the three dangerous scenarios, the last seemed to make the most sense. The way he said it, coming in all cavalier and confident. He had to give him credit, though—it was quite a show.

But why the deceit? thought Randall. If they lied, it meant they were covering something up. If they were covering something up, it meant they'd made a mistake. If they'd made a mistake, it meant that something was going to go terribly wrong. The next question was one of tremendous importance.

"Are you going to tell Keller?"

"Should I?"

The question loomed large. He needed to be creative. If he was too abrasive, she might get insulted. If he answered too quickly, she might be tentative. If he was too brazen, she could have a change of heart. She had to trust him. He had to be her friend. This had to work, because if it didn't, there would be trouble.

Not overly inventive, Randall asked, "Do you want to?"

"Do you want me to?"

"It's not really my place to say. Hmm. I don't know that I would."

"Then I guess I will."

"I don't think you should."

"All I was asking for was an honest answer," she said.

"It's not an easy question," he replied.

He wanted to kiss her, but it was too early. She admired his ruggedly handsome features and thought he'd clean up quite well. He trusted her. He didn't have a choice. Instead of a chance encounter or an enchanted evening, it seemed like the first thing they'd share would be a dangerous secret.

Van, Edwin, and the young bum finally got to a more comfortable spot when Edwin asked, "So what's the big deal?"

"What do you mean?"

"What's with the cover-up, the suspicion, the bad vibes? I mean, what's going on?"

"Yeah, what'd we miss? If Steve's not gay, then what is he?" asked the young bum.

Van didn't have time for this. He wanted to tell them to shut up, that everyone had a job to do and theirs wasn't to ask questions.

"Don't worry about it, just shut up and have a drink."

It wasn't quite the answer they'd expected. In the past such a reply would have caused a disturbance, but Van had bought them some more time, so Edwin decided to employ a little diplomacy. Instead of getting irate, he said, "What we're wondering is the same thing that Keller's wondering."

It was a sly remark. *Checkmate*, thought Van.

With some more theatrics and heated discussion, Van probably could have made the question go away, but he was spent, both physically and mentally.

"There is one detail I've kind of omitted. I mean, Billy didn't take the news too well."

"What news?" asked the young bum.

Yeah, what news? thought Edwin.

"I can tell you, but at this point, if you tell the other guys, you could get us into a lot of trouble."

There was silence as they pondered the phrase "a lot of trouble."

"I think we kind of need to know," said the young bum.

"Yeah, it would have been kind of nice to know something before," sputtered Edwin, now waiting for the other shoe to fall.

"Well," started Van, "Steve's dad was a college football player turned professional wrestler. He's kind of a local celebrity."

It all made sense now. Keller was on to something. He'd just been digging in the wrong spot.

"At least he's not in his prime," replied the young bum.

"Yeah," added Edwin, "he's probably all wrinkled up and bent over."

Van didn't respond.

"He is all wrinkled up and bent over, isn't he?"

"Not really, he's in pretty good shape."

"Pretty good shape?" queried the young bum.

"Really good shape."

At this point, Van didn't have the stamina to sugarcoat it. It was late. He was tired, and it was time to come clean.

"What I'm trying to say is that he's a big dude—big and scary."

That conniving little weasel, thought Edwin.

"What did you see that night?"

"What night?"

"The night we fell asleep."

"The night you blew your assignment?"

"Yeah, that night," replied Edwin, his head lowered in shame.

"He was there."

The gravity of his mistake now set in. Had he seen him, he could have blown the whistle.

"I could have shut the whole thing down!"

"Keller wouldn't listen to you, man. He'd throw you on the scrap heap with the rest of them. You don't get it. This thing is going to go off with or without you!"

"Well, why didn't you go ahead and target a Green Beret, or better yet, a Navy SEAL?"

"I think the police chief has a daughter," added the young bum.

"Yeah, we ought to shanghai her on the same night. I mean, what were you thinking?"

"I had a bad night."

"When have you had a good night?"

"Enough with the sarcasm," growled Van. "Steve pissed the wrong guy off on the wrong night, and I vowed to teach him a lesson."

"Couldn't you have just greased the plates up or something?" offered the young bum, thinking more in terms of sabotage.

"Do you guys want to listen or what?"

"Do we have a choice?" countered Edwin.

"Yeah," answered Van.

Edwin made a broad motion with a bony arm and said, "Go ahead."

"As I was saying, Steve pissed off the wrong guy on the wrong night, and the next day I told Billy that I wanted to bag the kid. Instead of laughing it off, he basically tried to take the whole thing over. Well, fast-forward a day or so, and I'm hanging out with Keller. We're having a drink, and I decide to tell him about the plan that me and Billy made."

"Billy and I," corrected Edwin.

"That's what I meant, professor," growled Van. "Anyway, Keller hears the plan and wants in, except with a twist. We'll kidnap the kid. He'll get the money, and Billy will get arrested. It sounds all well and good. The only problem being that I get stuck as the double agent, stringing Billy along. I think you guys know the rest."

"Well, why didn't you tell him about the kid's dad?" asked Edwin.

"I waited too long to pull the plug, and he caught me unawares. I mean, I slipped up, and as you both know, he's a crafty old fox. Remember how he got you guys loading up the stolen surfboards?"

"Yeah," they chimed in disgusted unison.

"Well, he's got a picture of me too."

"What did he get you doing?" asked Edwin.

"Yeah, how'd he fix you up?" added the young bum.

"He got me loading something into the trunk of a car."

"Must have been a bag of money," said Edwin.

"Nope."

"A bale of weed?" guessed the young bum.

"Worse," answered Van.

"A pound of cocaine!" exclaimed Edwin.

"Even worse."

"What could be worse than that?"

With a slight resignation to the facts, Van calmly admitted, "He's got a picture of me loading up a dead body."

"Wow" and "whoa" is how the guys voiced their shock.

"Yeah," added Van.

"I didn't know the guy was that heavy," said Edwin.

"I didn't know either, but it was a hell of a way to find out. Anyway, I've got to follow this thing through, but you guys don't. I'll handle Keller and the pictures—you can take off."

Van was serious. He had no problem confronting Keller and his goons. The old Van would have been scared to face the dragon, but the old Van was long gone.

They trusted Van to do as he said. They heard the sincerity in his voice. They felt the resolve. They knew they could walk away.

"OK, thanks a lot," said Edwin as he moved for the door.

The young bum quickly blocked him. "No one left behind—isn't that the code you live by?"

"It's the code I live by. I don't die by it."

"Let him go, bum. You ought to go too," said Van.

Although mildly flattered by the show of loyalty, Van didn't want to mess the kid's life up any more than it already was.

"I'm not going anywhere. I'm staying."

"Suit yourself," replied Edwin as he moved for the exit.

He'd planned to make a beeline for the store, but was struck by a couple of scenes: memories of the young bum as a child running through the surf while he shared a cocktail with the kid's mom. He wondered where she was. Van was the first guy he'd met at that dive bar on the beach. He sure appreciated that cold beer after his first shift. He'd been down to his last dime. Edwin walked slowly back to the door and paused. With a new sense of purpose, he knocked, and after a few seconds, Van answered.

"Forget something?"

"Guys, I've got something to say. There were three musketeers, and there are three of us."

Edwin then walked toward the two, put out his hand, and said, "All for one," as Van and the young bum joined to exclaim, "and one for all!"

"Man, Edwin, we thought you had taken off for good," said Van.

"Didn't figure on seeing you again, at least not that quickly," added the young bum.

"Ah, I was just messing with you guys."

It was a lie. They all knew it, but decided to have a drink all the same.

Through the revelry that ensued, they resolved to keep the kid safe and to keep themselves out of jail: two things that were going to be extremely difficult to do.

On Cedar Avenue, Billy and Rita settled in for the night. Billy noticed the softness of her skin as they touched. Sick of the same old thing, Rita wanted to talk about the future. Billy didn't. He thought that hers would be good while his probably wouldn't.

Any fool could see she was something special. Billy could see it. She didn't think he was a fool, but he did, especially after haggling over her clutter again. He couldn't walk through a room without tripping over a pair of shoes or stepping on a shirt. He yelled this time, a vicious reminder of the stress he was under.

She never left in such haste. He was usually the one waiting, pacing the living room while she changed jeans for a third time.

"Hey," was all he could say before Rita stormed out.

"I was...kidding."

I was just kidding, he thought, but there was something else, something deeper. He wasn't completely joking, and she hadn't cared to ask why.

"Ho-hum," he unconsciously chimed, "might as well use the time wisely."

That's what Flash would do, thought Billy.

Putting Rita firmly out of his mind, Billy decided to write. Thinking of the past with a heavy heart, he injected his woes into Flash.

Chapter 11

Past Bye

The walls were closing in.

    All he could see was the past.

    All he knew was yesterday.

    He couldn't go anywhere.

    He couldn't do anything.

He was a prisoner of a time that had been unkind.

A time that had made him weak.

A time that put him here.

Not in the future, but in the past.

One day he'd say good-bye to the days that kept him enslaved, to the clouded images that held him at bay. One day he'd say good-bye to the past.

The writing was cathartic. Whether he'd be able to make sense of it was another thing. He felt that all too soon, he might have to.

As Billy finished up, Rita had yet to return. She was his good luck charm. How soon her absence made his heart grow fond. He had to call her. She needed to name the book. The phone rang for the fifth time, and he hoped it wasn't too late. He was about to hang up when her mother's sugary sweet voice answered, "Hello."

"Hi, Jillian, how are you doing tonight?"

"Fine, Billy, how are you?"

"I'm OK," he lied. "It's not too late to call, is it?"

"No, honey, I get plenty of calls at one a.m."

"I was hoping to get in touch with Rita."

"Of course."

"Did she talk about me?"

"Not this time."

"Could you possibly put her on the line?"

"Let me see if she's awake, Billy."

He heard some rustling in the background, hushed voices with one saying, "Just talk to him."

Her mother seemed to be on his side, although maybe she was spurring Rita on, encouraging her to put the final nail in the coffin.

"What?" barked Rita.

"Ah, how's everything going? I mean, were you gonna call?"

"What is there to say?"

"Is that it? Are we breaking up?"

"Why don't you tell me?"

It seemed like a yes or no question, so he said, "No."

"It sure seemed like we were."

"Look, I'm sorry. I don't want to fight. I just want you to come home."

Even though he was wrong, and she was still mad, she'd most likely relent.

"I'm staying here tonight. We can talk tomorrow."

"We need to talk tonight."

"About what?"

"About the book."

"Oh, about that."

"Don't sound so enthusiastic."

"I wasn't trying to sound enthusiastic."

"Well, you didn't."

"Well, I'm not," she said, getting irritated all over again.

"Hey, honeybee," offered Billy. "I need some help."

"Let me guess, you want me to name the book."

Why he kept asking for help, or why he thought she even cared, was a mystery. It felt like a charade. Where he was taking her, she didn't want to go.

"So, what's going on?"

"What I wrote, or what it means to me, is that he's wallowing in the past," he said. "The past is getting in the way of the future. The book is getting to be less about a kidnapping and more about this guy. Don't ask me why—it just seems to be working out that way."

After a brief silence she said, "'Past Due.'"

Excellent, he thought.

"I love you, butterfly. See you tomorrow," he said through a long, lonely dial tone.

Thinking painfully about what he owed, Billy took out a blank sheet of paper and typed:

"Past Due"

Bad Blood and Betrayals

Soft moans drifted from the bedroom as Billy and Rita crashed into one another. They made love furiously, as if they were hurting each other. The act had an intense effect, but it didn't make her feel good.

"What's wrong?" asked Billy.

"Nothing."

It was the kind of nothing that meant everything.

"Don't you want to know what the nothing is?" said Rita.

"I figured that when you said nothing, it really meant nothing."

"If you had to ask, you must have thought something was actually wrong."

"Is that what we did, something?"

"That's just it—I'm not sure what it was."

I know what it was, thought Billy, but he didn't say it.

"I was giving you some space. I didn't think you needed me to ask a bunch of questions."

"You don't need to ask a bunch of questions. You need to ask the right ones."

Billy was stumped. It seemed like whatever he said was going to be wrong, so he chose his words carefully. "How are you?"

"Not good," answered Rita.

"Did I do something wrong?"

She thought of where to begin but knew that it wasn't all him. It was true that lemonade came from lemons, but so did other bitter things.

"No, Billy. It just doesn't feel the same. The me, the you, the whole thing just feels out of whack."

"OK, so what's the problem?"

"You're just so indifferent. You're OK with whatever happens. You don't seem to want to admit that we're not doing well."

With a heavy heart Billy finally said, "OK, Rita, we're not doing well."

Butterflies flutter. Flowers bloom. Seasons change, and people fall in love. Randall was hopeful in the new day. From the moment he awoke, a whistle echoed throughout the neighborhood. Freddy thought it suspicious for a guy who'd been demoted to act so jovial, but it didn't raise a red flag.

So, Randall walked on, skipping and laughing, moving fearlessly through enemy territory. He felt no guilt or remorse, only feelings of passion for Emily.

Could it be love? Could there be true love in the midst of deceit, or was it a general distaste for another that brought them together? If it were love, would it be clear as a mountain stream, or murky and thick like runoff barreling headlong into a storm drain? Was love different for those on the other side, for the ones who had fallen, or was it the one universal truth, the moment where all were equal? Randall didn't know, but he sure hoped to find out.

Through a trusted friend, Emily arranged a meeting, and that's where Randall was headed. Gone was the scraggly beard save for a thick mustache placed perfectly on his rugged, tan face. In a Hawaiian shirt, jean shorts, and flip-flops, the man looked sharp.

Keller had eyes all over town, so Randall had to be careful. He went to a phone, called a number, and was given an address. Quickly finding his way to a short square building, Randall sounded a chime and was promptly buzzed in. He briefly entertained the thought of being set up but quickly dismissed the notion. He wasn't the only one out on a limb. She also had a lot to lose.

Emily's unit was at the end of a long hallway, all the way down—the same place he'd be going if things didn't work out. Randall knocked, and after an extended three count, the door swung open. It wasn't Emily who answered, but an older version with a fat stomach and scraggly hair.

"Hey, handsome," she said with a wink.

"Ah, hello, ma'am," replied Randall in his best respectful greeting.

"You can call me Laney," countered the lady in full flirtation mode.

A greeting like that might have worked last week, while stranded in the desert, but now at the oasis, he'd drink from only the finest cup.

"I guess you probably know that I'm here to see Emily."

"Sure do, sweetie, just let me know if she's too boring for you."

"Mom!" sounded Emily.

"OK, OK," growled Laney. "God forbid I should have any fun."

"You've had your fun, probably too much of it!"

"Not by a long shot!"

On her way out, Laney turned back to Randall and said, "Good luck with that one."

"Go to your room and stay there!" chimed Emily. "Close the door, or I'll call your probation officer."

"You wouldn't."

"Yes, I would," sneered Emily. "It's like this every day with her, it's exhausting."

Randall recalled what it was like to have a woman in his life. It made him feel like a man. Instead of a handshake or a distant hug, he moved quickly in and gave her a strong kiss. Emily resisted slightly and then settled. She knew it was coming, just not so fast.

As Randall eased up, Emily put some distance between the two. She fixed her hair, straightened her top, and then thought about Keller. If he'd seen what just happened, there's no telling what he would have done. There was no turning back now.

"I expected a hug, maybe a kiss on the cheek," she said.

"I'm sorry, Emily, I couldn't wait any longer."

"Don't apologize," she replied as she grabbed him back for an even deeper kiss.

"Why don't you two just do it, for God's sake," sounded a jovial voice from behind a closed door.

"I told you to shut your trap, so shut it!" yelled Emily.

"Stay out, crazy!"

"You haven't seen crazy!"

"She didn't have a bad idea," suggested Randall.

"Is that what you want?"

It was a loaded question. Yes. No. There wasn't a good answer.

"I just want what you want."

There was much to do before they went any further.

After a moment of collective silence, she said, "I—I'm worried, Randall. I've never had to do anything like this."

"It's uncharted territory for me as well. I didn't think it would go this far. I figured Keller was just blowing off steam about Billy again, but I guess he's finally gone off the deep end. I just wish he wasn't taking anyone with him."

In a way, Randall felt responsible. At the moment, he couldn't tell the difference between right and wrong. Had he fooled them? Was he fooling her? Was it his fault? If he'd done something different, could he have kept it from turning tragic? As much as he rolled it over and rearranged it, the result was the same. Randall was resigned to do his part, but he didn't want to hurt anyone else.

"Look, Emily, you don't have to do this," said Randall in a final effort to make sure she was doing it of her own free will. He didn't want to influence anything ever again. If he could have, he would have just disappeared.

Emily was also experiencing a wide range of emotions.

"He's lucky I haven't called police. I probably should."

They both probably should have, but they couldn't. It's not how they lived.

After a drink and some more small talk, Emily rattled off the vague details of the mission.

"Sometime in the evening, on a Saturday, after they take Steve, they're going to call his parents. Keller wants the exchange to happen in the wee hours of the morning."

"How much are they going to ask?"

She shifted slightly, giving the impression that the question was a bit uncomfortable. It seemed like every time she moved, a different curve surfaced. He never saw a woman complement a couch like Emily. That she was willing to do what she was about to do made her even more interesting.

"They're going to ask for a million, 'a nice round number' is what he said."

"So, he thinks they'll have that much cash just hanging around?" wondered Randall.

"He figures they can get it from a bank," she said, rolling her eyes at the notion.

"If they had to round up that type of dough, they probably could. The guy's a local big shot, probably has his own set of keys to the bank."

"Hmm," she cooed, caring not whether they could or couldn't. That she'd soon be free from the petty crimes of an amateur was all that mattered.

Randall shed his visor, settled his unruly hair, and proceeded to ask the most important question of all. He didn't expect her to know, but if she did, she'd be worth her weight in gold.

"So, how are they going to do it?"

"The other guys that came over, they're going to take Steve and Keller's going to collect the ransom."

"I'm expected to be with Keller's group, I suppose."

"Correct. The guys holding Steve will be waiting for a sign that you all got the money. Keller's gonna shoot off a flare or something. When they see the flare, they're supposed to stick Steve in Billy's house."

To Randall it meant that whoever paid the money would get Billy's address. They could then save Steve and arrest Billy. He'd go to jail, and they'd go to the islands.

"So, Keller thinks we'll be able to waltz up, put in a request for the cash, and then head on out?"

"If you want your child alive, don't call the police. I think that's the way he put it."

The words hit home and Randall took a deep breath.

"He's just stupid enough to try it."

"He's going to have the kids on the lookout," she added.

The neighborhood kids that Keller employed from time to time knew the place blindfolded. If they were hidden, they wouldn't be seen.

"So, where's the drop supposed to be?"

"Circle Drive," she answered.

"Just like I thought," replied Randall, "the boat's going to be in the water."

"There's another part of the plan. Keller had me leave the room, but I could still hear."

Now this information particularly caught Randall's attention.

"What were they talking about?"

"How to get out of town," she said with a sad finality.

"The night before, we're supposed to check into a motel in Fort Lauderdale. I'll stay there while they double back to get Steve. He's booked a plane to the Bahamas that same morning. From there we're to disappear into the Caribbean. The passports arrived last week. He plans to be a suspect, but figures Billy's arrest will be enough."

The way she spoke of it was odd, almost as if he wasn't included.

"They're going to double-cross me?"

"They're going to double-cross all of you."

Randall was incensed. That he planned to double-cross Keller didn't matter. He tried to be a good friend, but Keller's recklessness had forced him into the role of a pariah.

That's just like him, thought Randall. *Nothing but bad blood and betrayals.* It was time to connect the dots.

"Can your mother be trusted?"

"She hates Keller with a passion. He stole all of her jewelry one night when she was passed out drunk. She wants him in jail more than anyone."

Randall felt sorry for the other guys but couldn't risk telling them. If he tried to torpedo the mission and failed, he'd pay the price. Emily couldn't leave; she had to stick with Keller. As much as he was opposed to it, Randall would have to show, at least until Steve's dad arrived. He figured that's when things would get interesting.

Similarly stuck, and charged with the danger that lay ahead, Emily and Randall slept together. The next day they'd have to face Keller and pretend they hadn't. Things were starting to get dicey.

Just as he said he would, Keller contacted Van to deliver the final orders. With intense dark eyes and deep commanding speech, he looked more like a cult leader than a small-time cook. All that seemed to be missing was a few hundred devotees and a healthy supply of tainted Kool-Aid.

"So, they're going to be on Circle Drive," said Van.

"What if we don't see the flare?" asked Edwin.

"He said to feed the kid to the fish, to get rid of him," answered the young bum, repeating Keller word for word.

"We ain't gonna feed the kid to the fish, I can tell you that right now."

Edwin and the young bum added a "Hell no" and a "No way" to the conversation.

"I'll take him right back to the restaurant no worse for wear. He doesn't know you guys, never seen you before, and he's not going to know I had anything to do with it. He's going to walk outside. You guys are gonna scoop him up, and then I'm gonna clock out. We're going to wait for the flare, then lock the kid up in Billy's house. Once they get the kid and arrest Billy, we're home free. I'll be at work the next night, and you'll be hunkered down waiting on a payday."

Not altogether naive, the young bum asked, "What if Keller steals our cut?"

"Then I'll kill him."

Van's answer stunned no one. True or not, it's what the guys wanted to hear.

Billy hadn't heard anything else and hoped it had all blown over. *Flash got out of town*, he wrote.

The Snatch

Rita spent the morning looking at pictures of her father. There was nothing distinct about the day, nothing she could put her finger on. She'd been thinking about the past and then opened a box. It was there where she saw the photo album, an old album full of old pictures.

There was an honesty in the soft quality of the snapshots. Instead of clothes, it seemed like they were wearing costumes—her father in bell bottoms and Rita wearing her favorite yellow shorts, with bangs, spindly legs, and all. *What were we thinking?* she affectionately thought. Then there was her mother, looking as glamorous as ever. Rita and her father were the only ones who shared that same goofy smile, the one she used to hate. She loved it now.

Her thoughts drifted back to Billy and how he reminded her of her dad, strong and smart with a great laugh. Aside from all of the nonsense about art imitating life, he really hadn't done anything that bad. He really hadn't done anything at all. That was more of an issue than his odd behavior and strange friends.

She finally let her guard down and wanted to be in love. Maybe she was in love. Maybe it was with Billy. Today, instead of wanting to leave, Rita wanted to stay. In essence, she was giving it another chance. The pictures gave her a lift, and she resolved to be a little more patient. After all, it was most definitely her call.

Billy came home smelling like battered shrimp and tartar sauce. Rita detected some salt and pepper as well. *Delicious*, she thought. As always after a busy Friday night, Billy walked through the door a beaten man.

"Had a beer already, I see," she cheerfully said. "Are you going to open one for me?"

"You seem rather spry for someone who was writing my last will and testament ten short hours ago."

"A lot can change in ten hours."

"A lot can change in one hour. It doesn't mean it did."

"It doesn't mean it will either," she replied.

"I hope it does."

She then grabbed the beer, walked to the front porch, and ever so slightly whispered, "It might and it might not."

As distant stars illuminated the crowded sky, Billy and Rita went outside to talk. It reminded her of a night they'd spent beneath a similar astral display. He probably didn't remember, but she did: when he'd said that he knew something made the stars, and that the oceans were no cosmic mistake, and neither was he, or she for that matter. That was when he was attentive rather than preoccupied.

Lately Billy had been acting more like a snake oil salesman than a romantic, but now that all of the nonsense was behind him, she was beginning to see his softer side again. He hadn't talked about any projects or had her name any books in a while, so Rita decided to ask a few questions.

"So, what about those guys you were meeting up with, or should I say conspiring with?"

Rita was gorgeous beneath the shimmering sky. Billy didn't want to spoil it by talking about those freaks, but he figured he owed her as much. After all, he was one of them.

"When it got busy, Steve started in on Van again."

"That doesn't sound too good."

"It wasn't. I had to break them up as usual."

"Poor Van," she muttered.

"I don't feel sorry for him. The guy's made my life miserable for years. Let's change the subject."

"Good idea—let's talk about the stars."

"Do you remember that night?" asked Billy.

Rita hushed him and affectionately answered, "Yes."

Back at the restaurant, Van cleaned the kitchen mats as Steve stacked the last of the glasses. Throughout the night, Steve felt like he was being watched. He'd turn a corner, and there would be Van. He'd look over his shoulder only to see Van quickly look away. He'd walk out back and who was sure to follow, none other than Van.

"You're creeping me out, Van," said Steve to the newly stealthy dish dog.

Van just gave a sly look, content that all too soon Steve was sure to feel a measure of discomfort. *He deserves it*, thought Van.

Edwin and the young bum started out the night by drinking. Edwin suggested it would be a good way to prepare, so they swilled spirits and composed a list.

"We're gonna need a tarp," said Edwin.

"And some string," added the young bum.

"We're gonna use tape. Gotta shut the kid up somehow."

"How about some rubber gloves?"

"Now you're talking," replied Edwin as he scrawled *rubber gloves* onto a thin yellow pad.

The where, the when, and the why had been established. All that remained was the how. That had been left up to Van and in turn assigned to Edwin.

Edwin should have kept walking that night, but in a world that had stripped him of nearly everything, all he had left was the one thing that could finally leave him with nothing: loyalty.

"OK, bum, here's how it's gonna go down."

The young bum was all ears as he leaned in to better hear the details.

"What time does the restaurant close?"

"Nine."

"Twenty-one hundred hours?" queried Edwin.

"Yeah, nine o'clock," repeated the young bum.

"That means we're going to have to set up at nine thirty."

"How are we going to get the kid?"

"Thought you'd never ask," answered Edwin. "Gonna use a snare, a lethal design from the jungles of Southeast Asia, over 100 percent capture rate."

Of course, thought the young bum, *the more things change, the more they stay the same.*

"It's gonna take two guys, a spring, some fishing line, and a can of beer."

"A can of beer?"

"You can use a can of beer," affirmed Edwin, "in place of the lethal cans of orange soda that the kids in Saigon used to sell."

"Oh yeah," replied the young bum, "well, what was the name of the soda?"

"You don't need to quiz me on every freakin' detail! Can't remember, anyway—smoked a little too much of the stuff over there, if you know what I mean."

"I think you smoked a little too much of the stuff over here."

Edwin's blood began to boil as he cursed the fact that he'd somehow lost his army service revolver. *Might have had to use it on the kid,* thought Edwin through a hateful glare.

Returning the glare, the young bum extended it through a long, uncomfortable silence, but it didn't matter. In a few short hours, in the darkness before dawn, all would be forgiven.

All Steve remembered was seeing two guys that looked like Van and then slipping on a piece of pineapple from the Cape Caribe, his least favorite sauté dish. He also recalled the slight touch of an aluminum can as it careened dangerously close to his face and then nothing: black.

The can landed, but rather than hitting Steve, it smashed brutally into the young bum's head. So, with the young bum down and Steve presumably out, Edwin snapped into action.

"No time for a break, bum, grab the tarp!"

Wanting to kill Edwin, the young bum instead spread out the tarp, and they rolled Steve up and shuffled him into the woods. Adrenaline-laced air shot through their lungs as they fought desperately through the thicket. Finally at a safe distance from the restaurant, Edwin turned to the young bum and exclaimed, "We did it!"

"We didn't do anything," replied the young bum. "He slipped."

It's all he could say. He didn't yet know where to place the blame for the brutal head strike. The can exploded on impact and left his hair a wet, sugary mess.

"I ought to kill you for hitting me with that can," growled the young bum.

"I didn't hit you with it," replied Edwin, which was basically a technicality.

"It was your stupid idea."

"It would have worked."

"It might have," sneered the young bum as he checked for blood.

"You guys need to keep it down," hissed Van as he pushed through the woods. "The restaurant's closed and everyone's gone. I called Keller, so now it's time to boogie."

All three bikes were ready and waiting, two without any alteration while the third had a trailer for the cargo. They gingerly slid Steve into a board bag and then covered him with brush.

"Doing a bit of yard work," said Edwin.

"Yeah, taking out the trash," added Van.

No comment was made by the young bum. None was needed.

A length of chain and a lock had been provided for when they got to Billy's. Their orders were to lock him up and then to run. Of course, Keller planned for the police to go in that direction as he and his crew crept quietly out of town. Then the authorities could make Billy's acquaintance, and he theirs. Quite lovely, it seemed.

Steve woke to the smell of moss and wondered where the hell he was. He was alive and moving. It was a bumpy ride as he again fell out of consciousness.

They arrived at a secluded spot and looked to the sky. It was there that the flare would show. If it didn't, Steve would stay right where he was and they'd be gone. They had a four-hour window, so it had to happen fast.

Upon closer inspection of the young bum, Van asked, "What the hell happened to you?"

"I got hit with a can of Coke."

"Tangled with Edwin's snare, eh?"

"If you call getting beaned in the head by a stupid trap set by a dummy tangling with something, then I guess I tangled with it."

"He came under friendly fire," growled Edwin.

"Still reading those Vietnam books, I see," muttered Van.

"Yeah," agreed the young bum, "he said they used cans of orange soda over there, but guess what?"

"What?"

"He couldn't remember the name of the soda he drank every day."

"I didn't drink it every day!"

"Well, how often did you drink it?" asked Van.

"I was under stress over there. I was in the theater of war!" stammered Edwin.

"You might have been in a theater somewhere," snapped the young bum.

Arguing late into the night, Steve had nearly been forgotten when a stern "errrr" along with a weak thrash came from the woodpile. The night's earlier events were all but forgotten in the muted sounds of distress. Surrounding their cargo, they gazed tenderly at the protrusion, opting to stall instead of engage.

"What should we do?" hissed Edwin.

"I can't speak—he knows my voice. You're going to have to do the talking," whispered Van.

He didn't know what to say, so he said the only thing that could make any sense to a guy taped up and thrown into a bag.

"Do you need something to drink?"

"Arrrg!" was the answer.

"What'd he say?" whispered Van.

"It sounded like he said 'yeah!'" offered the young bum.

Edwin had selected a cheap bottle of whiskey for the task. He knew there was water in it as well as a natural sedative. It wouldn't be bad for the guys to take a swig either.

Throughout the course of the night, two things had become painfully obvious to Steve. One was that he had most certainly been abducted, and the second was that his abductors were some of the biggest idiots on the planet. He was in a board bag, on a bike trailer, beneath a stack of wood being force-fed whiskey. *I need to get out of this alive*, he thought.

The phone rang at the Linon residence sometime after twelve. Jim often got late-night calls from the dealership, although tonight it was an unfamiliar voice. The voice he didn't recognize was one he'd soon hate.

"Is this Jim Linon?" asked the stranger.

"Yes, it is. Who may I ask is calling?"

"It's your new partner."

Jim's senses were now piqued. Something didn't seem right. Steve hadn't come home, and now this suspicious call.

"That's impossible, chum. I don't have an old partner."

Keller winced. "Let's just say that we have a common interest."

"Listen, pal, I'm not one for heady conversations in the middle of the night, so maybe you could get to the point."

Keller was somewhat surprised. For a car salesman, the guy sounded pretty gruff.

"You'd like to get Steve home tonight, and I'd like to help you get him home."

"What exactly are you saying?" asked Jim.

"I'm saying that your son has been kidnapped."

Jim heard the words, and they made him feel dull. Left with only muscles, tendons, and rage, he was now a man without a heart. Embarrassed to be completely helpless, he'd have to play it cool.

"I'd like very much to get my son home tonight, so how might we be able to do that?"

"Now that sounds better. I was hoping for your assistance."

That was it. Only silence so Jim would again have to speak, but what to say?

"How can I help?"

"Thought you'd never ask," answered the caller. "I trust that you have access to large amounts of cash on short notice."

It sounded like the caller had done their homework. Jim had a safe at the dealership, although he doubted he'd have to open it.

"OK," countered Jim. "What are the terms?"

Keller liked the no-nonsense approach. Things seemed to be going quite smoothly. He foolishly thought that if it worked once, it could work again.

"Two bags containing five hundred thousand dollars apiece. Arrive at 700 Circle Drive no later than three a.m. Rest assured, the location will be heavily fortified, so for the safety of everyone involved, please come alone."

Through a delayed response Keller was forced to ask, "Any questions?"

Empowered with a sudden feeling of invincibility, it was now Jim who'd stall. He was glad to hear that everyone's safety was of such concern to the doomed gentleman on the other end of the line.

A simple "No" was the grave reply as Keller now thought he could be in for a confrontation. But the eventuality had always been there—hence the thugs and the tricky location. Keller still held an advantage, but for some reason, the fellow didn't seem shaken. *Who is this guy?* wondered Keller.

Jim sat on the edge of the bed as Donna shifted.

"Was it Steven, honey?"

He heard the question but didn't answer. He didn't know what to say. The whole thing was his fault. Donna even warned of the incident. *How did she know?* he thought.

With a long-held belief that good things rarely happen in the middle of the night, she asked, "Is our son OK, Jim?"

There were no words to say. There was no way to say it. As if their lives had been too charmed, here was the boulder barreling down the hillside, or the plane making a crash landing. In other words, it was now their turn.

"Steve's been abducted, honey."

"No!" she begged as if to will it away with one strong word.

Wound in a full embrace, Donna sobbed uncontrollably. She was angry and threatened. The tears came from a helpless place.

"It's my fault," said Jim.

"Don't say that, Jim. You've been the best father and an even better husband. I know you can fix it. I know that you can fix this, Jim!"

He had to fix this, but how? The thought of paying a ransom never crossed his mind; the thought of crushing someone's skull had. They were in one place, and Steve was probably in another. He'd have to call the sheriff.

It was another late-night call, something the sheriff had unfortunately gotten used to. He caught it on the second ring and heard a deep, concerned voice say, "Jake, it's Jim, there's been an incident."

"What's going on, Jim? Another broken window?"

"Wish I could say it was, Jake. This time it's more serious."

"Well, go on, good buddy."

It was hard for Jim to think it, not to mention say it, but he had to. It was the second time.

"Steve's been taken, Jake."

After a short silence, the sheriff said, "We need to set up a command center and establish contact. We're going to have to get a fix on them."

"Got it already. 700 Circle Drive at three a.m., two bags with five hundred thousand each."

"Can you handle that kind of weight, Jim?"

"I can, but I'm not gonna."

The sheriff knew that Jim had the money, but he also knew Jim wasn't one to be told what to do.

"We've got to stall them. Let the law handle this. We don't want anyone to get hurt, least of all Steve. He's got his whole life ahead of him. He's a good kid!"

"He's a good kid, but he's my kid and this is between me and them. I called you and I didn't have to, but Donna and I could sure use your help."

Sheriff Jake Williams didn't believe in vigilante justice, but it seemed like this thing was going to happen with or without him.

"OK, we'll need to set up a perimeter. Unmarked cars and undercover officers. I've got a couple of guys who are really good at being invisible."

"One car—the one you're in. I'll have Mick drop me off at the 7-Eleven on Banana River Drive. I need you to be there too."

"That's not enough, Jim!"

"It's got to be. It's a closed circle, real hard to sneak up on. I'll get Steve's location and then give it to you. Grab your two-way radio, switch it to channel one, and show up after three as the guy getting gas."

It went against everything the sheriff had ever known, but all he could say was, "OK, Jim, I'm the guy getting gas."

Back at the Linon residence, Jim walked quietly to a door. Behind it lay the various punishing things of his past. Among the clutter, Jim knew exactly what he was looking for—something shiny from a dark time.

From the packed closet came a large black cloak, a red demon mask, and a huge golden belt. It was a championship belt, and it was his because he had been the champion. It had avenged before, and so it would avenge again.

Naked and clearly reflected in a cold silver mirror, Jim shattered his sunken image. Splintered glass wedged into familiar cuts as he tasted blood from the jagged wounds. He touched some random items and made a low, guttural growl. If he were a wolf, he would have attacked something; a bull, he would have smashed something; a bird of prey, he would have snatched something from the air. As a man, he felt equally dangerous and would again rely on violence for survival.

Keller was equally tense as he summoned the scouts, along with Freddy and Randall, to the trailer. They'd arrive at the staging area by boat and then disperse, the scouts digging in and Keller to greet the poor sap with the suitcases.

As they quietly boarded the boat, Randall kept his distance. They neither noticed nor cared. It was taken for granted that he had nowhere else to go. *Man, are they going to be surprised*, thought Randall.

They glided up to the dock in silence as Freddy dutifully tied off. Large oaks wound through the undergrowth like giant studded serpents while glowing eyes dotted the still, muggy night. It was remote and quiet with ample spots to hide, so it was there they'd wait. It was 2:00 a.m.

The scouts scurried throughout the neighborhood as Freddy fiddled with the flare gun.

"Man, this thing looks like a real gun, especially in the dark."

"It is a real gun," sneered Keller.

"I meant a gun that shoots bullets, real bullets."

"As opposed to fake bullets," remarked Randall. He couldn't resist.

It was nearly three as the sentries took cover and the crew donned their disguises. If anything other than a man with a couple of bags of money showed, they'd signal and then disappear. Keller hoped it wouldn't come to that, but at this point no one knew who they were, and he wanted to keep it that way.

Randall cautiously eyed his watch as a glowing 2:57 radiated from the timepiece. *Time to split*, he thought.

"Uh, Keller, I've got to take a leak. I'll be right back," said Randall, shuffling past Freddy with a nod.

"What?" snarled Keller. "Hurry up, this thing is about to happen!"

Randall turned back with a smile and said, "No problem, boss, wouldn't miss it for the world."

The sudden feeling of bravado passed as the clock struck three and only he and Freddy remained. Keller motioned Freddy into the palmettos as they waited on their much-celebrated guest.

"Guess punctuality isn't this chap's strong suit," muttered Keller.

Early on Sunday morning, Jim and Mick drifted to a stop in the parking lot of a beachside 7-Eleven. Wearing wrestling boots laced to the knees, a large billowing cape, and a full-face mask, Jim had officially flipped. Mick knew what was at stake, so he stayed quiet.

Jim switched on the two-way and gave a quick, "Radio check."

"All ears, good buddy," replied the sheriff.

Jim's black cape then rustled to life as a quick walk turned into a run. Getting closer and now at a full sprint, he reached the lone street in a dark blur. The lookouts moved to tell Keller, but it was too late. Whatever it was had already arrived.

Alone and alert in the early morning hours, Jim looked more like a superhero than a man. His muscled torso glistened with sweat while the cape snapped his back like a whip. Although Keller and Freddy were hidden, he seemed to be staring straight through them. Keller was in shock and wondered if this character was lost. Halloween wasn't for another few months at best.

There were any number of questions he could have asked such as, "Where's the pudgy white car salesman?" or "What's with the black underwear and boots?" but in Keller's infinite stupidity, he chose to further anger the large, cloaked gentleman by saying, "I was expecting Wonder Woman, but you'll do."

Fear had a purpose. Realizing they didn't have any, Jim guessed it might go easier than he thought.

"She took the night off but sends her regards."

With that Jim released the larger of the two duffels and inched invisibly forward. He saw the gun and identified it as a flare; strange but still dangerous. When he struck, it would have to be hard, and it would have to be fast.

While keeping an eye on the bizarre stranger, Keller knelt to unzip the bag. Neither he nor Freddy had detected the slight advances, and for that they'd pay. And where was Randall? There wasn't any time to sort him out. That would have to happen later.

The sack, now completely open, revealed not cash but gold! *That'll do quite nicely*, thought Keller as he read, "Southern States Wrestling Champion. Whhha," was all he could say before being clubbed in the head with a vicious open-hand slap. Another quickly followed as Keller's large frame suddenly went limp.

Watching from the woods, Randall flinched as the lookouts scattered.

With Keller down, now Freddy was in the line of fire. After witnessing the brutality of the first two strikes, he thought, *To hell with that, I'm gonna shoot him with this fake gun.* As Freddy raised his arm to take aim, the masked man struck. Propelled by an ancient, animalistic fury, Jim crashed into Freddy with the force of a small automobile, knocking him clear into the air and ultimately out of breath. The gun discharged, but instead of firing into Jim, it shot straight into the sky, a perfect Mayday signal. A detail not lost on Randall, who recognized it as the sign to mobilize the other party. Now he knew what he'd do.

Out of Town

The signal wasn't lost on the others either—the ones across the river with Steve. Unaware that anything had gone wrong, they snapped into action.

"Look, there's the flare!" exclaimed Edwin. "Time to go!"

"Damn straight," whispered Van. "Let's get rid of this kid!"

"You're going home, Steve," added the young bum.

Half-drunk and exhausted, all Steve could muster up was a weak, "Ugh."

Jim still had his hands full as the two he'd beaten were beginning to show signs of life. Struggling to his feet with a guttural growl, Keller feverishly rushed the costumed character. In his opinion, they needed to shut this guy down and get out of town quick.

Measuring Keller's fanatical advance, Jim had the perfect move. Catching him in midflight, Jim hoisted Keller high overhead and drove him straight into the ground.

Then, in a moment of sheer instinct, he snatched up his championship belt. Its thick custom leather was soft and familiar. The shine hadn't tarnished, and as Jim turned to smash an oncoming Freddy in the face with it, he duly noted that the belt was still solid.

Unbeknown to Jim, the flare had been a sign to move Steve, so Van, Edwin, and the young bum coasted their bikes to the back of Billy's duplex.

"Can't we lock him outside?" asked the young bum with perhaps the best idea.

"They want him inside, so he's going inside," answered Edwin.

In no mood to change the plan, he started testing the windows for any that might be unlatched. The young bum followed suit as Van walked to the front of the house. *They're giving Billy too much credit*, he thought.

"All right, Bum, here's what we're gonna do."

The young bum cringed as Van said, "You ever think of trying the front door?"

At the wooded lot where Jim had again beaten his opponents into submission, the two were incapacitated and hopefully ready to cooperate.

"You guys are done," he said. "I could kill you, but I'm not going to."

"Uh, thanks," muttered Freddy, immediately being met by a kick from Keller.

By now he had the two pegged as amateurs, but amateurs could be dangerous, and he needed to get Steve.

"Where's my son?" asked Jim, giving them the benefit of the doubt. A direct question met by a direct answer, then he could go home, and they could go to jail.

"We were merely out for an evening stroll before being accosted by a violent masked brute," wheezed Keller. "We need medical attention immediately."

"I am your medical attention," growled Jim, grabbing Keller by the throat. "Now where is my son?"

The lookouts had scattered as Randall silently made his way to the dock. He didn't care what happened to Keller, but he didn't want Freddy to take any more punishment. They'd go to jail, or maybe get off on a technicality. He didn't know. What he did know was that he was going to end it right now.

Over at Billy's house, the crew was poised to land Steve in his final destination.

"I was about to check that," said Edwin in response to Van discovering the unlocked door.

"Come on, slide him over here," he ordered, motioning them to slide Steve into the house.

"Who put him in charge?" whispered the young bum.

"Let it go," replied Van. "We've got bigger fish to fry."

At this point, Steve was pretty sure he'd survive. All he could do now was hope for a speedy resolution. *Maybe my dad will kill these guys*, he thought. If that happened to be the case, he wouldn't be upset.

Rita woke to the struggle as a gravelly voice whispered, "Here, here, move him over here!"

"Wake up, Billy, there's someone in the house," warned Rita.

"Uh, it's the dog."

"It's not the dog, stupid. You don't have a dog."

"What happened to the dog?"

"Nothing happened to the dog. You never had one. Now, wake up!"

As Billy's dream of a noisy canine evaporated, he said, "It sounds like someone's in the house."

"That's what I've been trying to tell you!"

"Oh man, they're here!"

"It's not only them," she guessed. "They've got something with them."

Of course, Rita was first up as she grabbed a powerful flashlight and ran into the living room. Menacing shadows moved quickly throughout the room as one of the shadows issued a stern warning.

"Better excuse yourself, little lady, this happens to be a man's detail."

"That would be fine," she boldly replied, "if there were any men here!"

She was prepared. She had something they didn't. *Guess men don't carry flashlights*, she thought as the strong beam cut into the eyes of the closest assailant. Keeping the blaze fixed on his scorched retinas, Rita reached for that stupid old boomerang from the thrift shop. And as she buried its sharp edge deep into the crease of Van's mouth, he sounded a garbled scream and instantly fell back.

Rita then grabbed a smooth, heavy object and flung it violently toward the head of an unlucky long-haired intruder. The paperweight landed with a dull, fleshy thud as the young bum again hit the deck. While Van cradled his gashed mouth and the young bum struggled to rise, Rita yelled, "You guys had enough?"

With that, Edwin quickly snapped into military mode. *Retreat, retreat*, he thought.

He then grabbed Van and a dazed young bum and headed for the door.

"Beat it!" said Rita.

"Yeah, get out of here!" added Billy, stumbling out of the bedroom.

"Till we meet again," yelled Edwin in admiration. She'd put up one hell of a fight.

They were gone, but something was left behind. Zipped up in a board bag and making sounds of distress was Steve.

"You happy now?" snapped Rita.

"No," answered Billy.

Still trying to discover the whereabouts of Steve, Jim was about to pound it out of his captives as Randall set the boat adrift.

"Hey, masked man!" he yelled back to land.

In one quick movement, Jim was at the dock. He hadn't seen anyone else. It was a shock. He had taken two of them but probably couldn't have taken all three. The boat was out of reach. He wanted to beat whoever was on it but instead asked, "Who are you?"

"Right now, I'm your best friend."

"I don't have any friends out here."

"You do now," said Randall.

"Steve's going to be at 162 Cedar Avenue. He'll be unharmed."

Jim heard the number and then the crank of an outboard. He turned to radio the sheriff and then back to get a fix on the boat, but it was gone. Randall wasn't going home, though. He was off to Fort Lauderdale by van. He'd heard it was a good time of year to go, even better with a pretty lady and a full tank of gas. He needed to get out of town and fast.

"That was Randall Daniels, and this was all his doing," said Keller as Jim spoke to the sheriff. The sheriff dispatched the marine patrol, most likely too late, and then headed for Cedar Avenue to retrieve Steve.

"Is that so?" replied Jim. "Who are you, then?"

"I was going to ask you the same thing."

"I'm Jim Linon, former Southern States wrestling champion from 1987 to 1990, the owner of Gentleman Jim Motors, and more importantly, Steve's father."

Keller then turned to Freddy and asked, "Was this not a detail that you considered to be of at least minor importance?"

"I didn't know," replied Freddy.

"Hmm, I'll bet I can guess who did."

Back on Cedar Avenue, things were getting even more complicated. Billy went for the lights, and Rita pushed him back. He wasn't thinking, but she was.

"Leave the lights off," she said as she focused a beam of light on the bloodstained floor.

Billy's head was spinning. He didn't expect this, especially not now, without warning in the wee hours of the morning.

"I must have been set up. What the hell am I gonna do?"

"Get him out of the house, stupid," was her first order.

The board bag that held Steve suspiciously resembled the one that had been stolen from his car as he pulled it quickly toward the door.

"You gonna help?" he groaned.

"I'm not touching that thing."

"Suit yourself," said Billy as he threw Steve into the neighbor's hibiscus hedge. "There you go, hang out with Jeb."

"Why did you say that?" asked Rita, incensed that Billy would add insult to injury at a time like this.

"I'll probably be going to jail soon, so I might as well go there a wiseass."

Rita mulled it over. He probably deserved to, but she wasn't going to let her man go down.

"Wrong," she ordered. "If you got set up, that means the cops are on the way. You've got about five minutes to wipe up the blood, pack a few things, grab your passport, and get into that car over there—it'll be running."

As Billy raced to fill his pack, he couldn't believe something could be so stunningly strong and beautifully brutal. As if she hadn't already, tonight Rita earned her stripes. He'd miss her.

Billy bounced feverishly into the Camry as Rita stuck it in reverse and motored south. The other car approached from the north: an unmarked police car. More police cars then followed: the marked kind.

Rita continued south on A1A and was soon headed west. She took the scenic route, just in case the cops were looking for a tall blond bean pole and a gullible brunette. They were headed to the airport. Billy was going to Mexico.

Van, Edwin, and the young bum spent the morning ducking from hedge to hedge, Van cradling his gashed mouth and the young bum stumbling along in a pained stupor. On their egress, they both entertained the same thought of how to kill Edwin and get away with it. Because Edwin let them get beaten back by a girl, Keller would probably hold out on the ransom. Billy had most likely hauled the kid off and gone back to bed.

"Now we're not going to get our cut 'cause of Billy and that damn lunatic chick," growled Van.

"She was no ordinary girl," replied Edwin. "She must have been special forces of some sort, highly trained at any rate."

"It's more like you being non-special forces," snapped the young bum, now dreary from the pain and lack of sleep.

"Back in Nam the women fought like tigers, more brutal than the men."

"Well, we're a hell of a long way from Nam, and you didn't do anything besides run like a dog," said Van.

"I could have saved your life. She was coming back for more!" exclaimed Edwin.

"Well, maybe we should go find her so she can kill you," muttered the young bum.

"She probably could," agreed Edwin. "She probably could."

In the early morning hours, the three decided to split up. They'd have to lay low for a while.

Jim was happy. He had gotten his son back and had been able to break out a few of his old moves in the process. *Old guy's still got it*, he thought. Aside from fingering Billy and Randall, Keller and Freddy went mute, deciding, of course, to exercise their right to an attorney.

While Rita gunned the Camry west, she guessed the only smart thing that Billy had done through the years was to keep his passport current. Probably for one of those surf trips he wanted to take but never had.

In that moment, and for one last time through the night dimly lit by the highway lights, Billy caught Rita's eye. Scrawling into a beat-up old notebook, he was more attractive than ever. In the relative darkness, he was perfect. He was a dreamer and she a believer, but dreams die, belief fades, and people move on. Like gamblers, they had stayed at the table too long, winning the small hands only to lose the larger ones, destined to be together but also to fail. It saddened Rita to think of it that way, and she knew that fighting off the tears would be hard.

There went her damn sentimental streak again. The guy had basically gotten a kid brutalized, and here she was, admiring his solemn glow. It was the romantic version, not the others she'd conjure up from time to time. But it was now, and Billy was leaving, so of course she'd think fondly of him, perhaps even love him, although in the end, she'd leave him.

In the early morning hours, they wound deliberately through an empty parking garage and into a spot. Billy grabbed his backpack while Rita made note of the parking section, and then they headed off to a ticket counter. It was a somber passage through the airport with Rita looking as gorgeous as ever and Billy exuding charisma even in his darkest hour.

They scoured the board for the earliest international departure and spied one to Cancún, so the question to Billy was, "Where do you want to go?"

"Do I have to go to Mexico?" he asked. "I don't speak any Spanish."

"They all speak English there," she said with a wink.

He didn't really have to go Mexico, but it's where she wanted him to go, and more importantly, she was paying for it.

"OK, Cancún it is."

They booked the flight then waited. She was still mad, then she was sad, then complacent, and then she'd go back to being mad. Maybe it was the only way for them to split, in an instant and against their will. It still felt like she was experiencing another loss, taking another blow, losing another man.

For Billy it was happening too fast. He needed to get out of town, but Mexico? He'd trust her, though; she'd been right about everything else, and plus, she was paying for it.

Billy looked at Rita, and she looked down. *Congratulations, dumbass*, he thought.

He moved her head up and said, "Look, Rita, I really tried."

She shook it off as if to say, "I don't want to cry over you."

Now Billy's head dropped. Light sniffles broke the quiet, prompting Rita's breath to stagger as well.

"You made me think that I was special, that I had talent. I wanted to show you I did, but instead, I showed you I didn't. I was stupid and selfish and I'm sorry. It was a grave mistake, one that I'll regret forever."

She wanted him to stop, but he didn't.

"Don't view this as a failure, I mean, 'us' as a failure."

She did.

"Don't think of it as the end."

It was.

"We'll be together again."

They wouldn't.

Weaving gently toward the gate, a sobering call went out for Billy's flight as Rita's tears stained the side of his face for one last time. As his section was called, they were ripped apart, and she was finally free. Left with only wasted time and tears, it was still difficult to let go.

Rita then watched him bounce away, his long blond hair moving in all different directions. It was like him, unruly and original, and as he turned to issue a final farewell, she was also ready to say good-bye.

"Hey, Rita," called Billy. "I'll see ya soon. You're gonna make me cry again if you keep that up."

She wiped a tear away and asked, "Can't you move any quicker?"

"I thought you'd come to your senses," he answered with a parting smile of absolution.

Rita then watched from the window as his plane idled along the tarmac. Moving slowly at first, it eased into a sprint and then arched powerfully into the air. And in an instant, along with all of the different parts of her, Billy was gone. It was quiet as she stood in the aftermath of all that had happened. It was a different place to be, out of love, on the run, and alone. An odd sense of accomplishment followed the other pained thoughts. She'd beaten them back and come out on top. She wondered what it meant.

Moving drearily through the airport amid the grays, the browns, and the dingy plastic seats, Rita barely recalled leaving. In her current state, finding the car was a major accomplishment as she pulled her hair back and shoved her bag into the passenger seat. Of course it did a somersault, spilling into every crevice imaginable, so now she'd have to deal with that when all she wanted to do was go home and go to sleep.

Following a quick cleanup with the last of her bits and pieces back, Rita noticed one last item. It was a notebook. It was Billy's notebook. Not meaning to pry, she couldn't help but notice the quirky name she'd once furnished.

The passage read:

Of the ways in which Flash had damaged his life, this was definitely the worst. Deceived and double-crossed by a pack of wild dogs, the woman he loved was gone and he was on the run.

He'd have to go where the air was clean and the water clear to heal and to forgive. He hoped to be forgiven, but that wasn't his call.

All he knew was that starting over was getting harder, the finish line farther, the light in people's eyes darker, and the cross he'd have to bear larger. He was enraged and wanted to strike. But who was there to strike besides himself, the lonely man, the one underwater and out of breath?

That was it. Tears welled up again as she thought of her handsome ex-lover writing about his shattered life. She wanted to help.

PART II:
RITA'S REBELLION

Coming Down

With the sun barely up and most of the city still asleep, Rita returned early. How they found Billy such a convenient flight was a mystery, more proof of life's painful symmetry. Through a deep breath, she searched for calm, but all that came was a sad smile.

Pulling safely into a single-car garage, she collected her bag, entered the apartment, and then collapsed onto her childhood bed.

For what seemed like days Rita slumbered, waking and then again lapsing into a sound sleep. As she uncoiled the twisted sheets and dislodged her face from a flattened pillow, it seemed early. The door was open, so Rita knew that her mother had visited. Thin rays of light cut through the bedroom blinds and reflected onto a white wall. It was the morning, and she was alive.

Rita yawned, collected a towel, and then settled into the best shower in recent memory, maybe the best ever. Draped in a white robe with her long, damp hair twisted into a bun, she made her way into the kitchen. As if recovering from an intense sickness, Rita moved with a keen sense of awareness. Everything glistened and was new to the touch. Her movements were slow and deliberate, and worries, for the moment, few. The note on the counter read:

"Good morning, baby, didn't want to wake you. There's fresh-cut fruit in the refrigerator—help yourself and stay as long as you like. Will be back after a golf lesson and cocktails. Love, Mom."

Golf, thought Rita, *what's the point?* She promptly shredded the note and delivered it into a waiting trash can. The story would have to be that she'd been living with her mother for a while. They'd iron that out later. After a cup of coffee and a generous helping of fruit, Rita was off to the beach.

Under a floppy hat and wearing a large pair of sunglasses, it seemed like she was in a strange place and maybe in danger. The feeling was intense, the ground fertile and new. Something was happening, she just didn't know what.

After a short, careful walk, Rita reached the beach access. It was deserted, so she scurried into the dunes unseen. Beneath her toes, the early morning sand was cool. She looked to the sea, and it was flat. Gone were the thick waves piling up along the coast. It was the calm after the storm. The destruction had been minimal, the casualties few. She'd lost something she didn't really need, but it still stung. And what about the men she had beaten? Were they out for revenge or behind bars? Hopefully the latter.

Rita settled behind a sheltered ridge to arrange her towel and other needed effects: flip-flops, sun block, and what was left of Billy's so-called book. When she first arrived and was alone, before going anywhere else, she went to the beach. And so it was that she was there again. The rustling sea oats and sea gulls that had kept her company before also did the same. Rita laid back and through the tint of her sunglasses examined the sky. Beneath it, she had no regrets. Billy hadn't harmed anyone. It wasn't even his idea. He may have provoked it, but he never would have done it. They did.

The thoughts now came. The levee had broken. Like dangerous water descending on a helpless town, her mind was awash in conjecture. Maybe she did him a disservice by carting him off. Maybe he should have relied on the courts to declare his innocence. Maybe he wasn't innocent. Maybe she wasn't. Maybe it was all her fault. Maybe she had driven him to do something foolish. A new light illuminated her ugliness. A different lens magnified her mistakes. Now she was the one who felt like a jerk. It was bound to be that way for a while, the back and forth, a typical breakup, although it seemed to be anything but that.

She was sad because she loved him, but an old boomerang, a heavy paperweight, and a quick trip to the airport drastically changed her tack. The questions would come, and she was ready. The call was sure to arrive, and she'd answer. It seemed, as Rita began to leaf through Billy's old notebook, that something was left undone. Would it be the two of them? What could possibly be next: bank tellers, hurriedly scrawled handwritten notes, and dark sunglasses? She could do the driving, she guessed, as thoughts of them together again made her weary. She dropped Billy's notes and began to doze, this time a restless nap as the beach began to fill.

As the day wore on, one thing became evident: she was going to have to tell her mother. Rita hoped Jillian would be somewhat receptive and not too hard to find. The lady had a calendar to rival any big-city socialite. She was always taking a class, having a lesson, or attending a meeting. She knew a lot of people and, more importantly, she talked to a lot of people. That's why Rita needed to talk to her.

Still in hiding, Rita's slow walk turned into a jog as she peered around the hedges, hoping to see a certain car in a certain spot. It was there, and she was amazed. Now she'd have to duck the neighbor and get into the apartment as quickly as possible.

Jillian caught Rita from the corner of her eye and immediately gave her a deep hug.

"How's everything, honey? You slept like the dead. I was worried, but I know you've got a lot going on, what with that handsome man and all."

She'd go into a fake Southern drawl at times, forgetting that in most parts, Florida was barely considered the South.

"Oh, cut it out, Mom. You've got twice the social life that I have, and you know it."

"Maybe," she playfully submitted, "but it hasn't always been that way."

"I know," agreed Rita.

Together they were impressive. Like purple mountains or deep golden canyons, they were always in the right light, always a perfect picture. There were different sides but none bad. They were smart enough to laugh at just about anything, but thoughtful enough to know what wasn't funny. As Rita began to explain the unexpected visit, she hoped her mother's sense of humor was intact.

"Look, Mom, Billy and I are no longer together."

"What?" heaved Jillian in surprise. They seemed like the quintessential star-crossed couple, meant to be at odds but also together. She liked Billy. He was likable.

"He did something stupid. I mean, we did something stupid, and now he's gone."

"He's dead!"

"No, Mom. He's in Mexico."

"Oh, thank goodness," was her first response.

The next was, "What's he doing in Mexico?"

"He's in hiding."

"Ah," murmured Jillian.

"That's why I'm here. He's gone, and I need a place to stay."

That was the easy part. Rita knew the door was always open. She was more reluctant to deliver the next request.

"I also need your help. It could involve the cops."

"Oh," offered Jillian. She was all ears.

"It started with a phone call and a bad idea," began Rita, as she ran through the story with her mother, saying things like "how devious" and "he was such a wild card."

When Rita told of how she had beaten the intruders back, Jillian said, "Good, they deserved it!"

There were plenty of "oohs" and "ahs" and "you knows" to go around. With some laughter and even a few tears, it was a good release.

For the first time in a while, Rita felt close to her mother. In a way, it seemed like a new beginning. She hoped it was.

After all was said about what had been done, it was understood that when the authorities came, Jillian would say as little as possible and be flirtatious if it could help. She was to say nothing about the breakup and if asked, would say only that Rita had been living with her for a while. Furthermore, Rita asked Jillian to take her calls and forward only the ones from friends, work, or the police. To avoid any extra tells, Rita didn't want to speak to Billy. She didn't even want to know if he called. She thought that it might be one of the questions and wanted to answer as truthfully as possible. Jillian pledged her support, and together they were sure to be a potent team.

As a credit to Jim's mild celebrity status, little was made of the kidnapping. The intent was to lure any of the accomplices out of hiding. In terms of an ongoing investigation, the trail was still hot.

Aside from Keller and Freddy, who had since been booked and denied bail, Billy Winslow and Randall Daniels were the prime suspects. The other gruff voices, foreign to Steve, had also gone unmentioned by the two in custody, who had since come down with amnesia.

Without the luxury of a deep, restorative sleep, Van had to get ready for work. It was four thirty, and he was scheduled in at six. It was an eventuality anyway; whether the kidnapping had been a success or not, he'd have to show. The only difference now was that he didn't know if his name had been mentioned. He didn't know what happened to Billy. He didn't have a clue what became of Keller and the others. Completely straight, shocked into sobriety, he'd been forced to draw a few iffy conclusions.

The plan was for Billy to be singled out as the ringleader. If the authorities had arrested him, they'd most likely be looking for everyone else. The idea was for Van to deny any involvement. Where was the proof? Plus, the owners loved him. He was like a pet, a challenging one at that, but for the most part predictable. Or so they thought.

Desperate for sustenance and badly in need of a change of clothes, Van moved in a zigzag pattern toward his triplex. As he eased the door open and silently vaulted in, he was once again, and only for a moment, safe.

With a wild stare and insanely dry mouth, Van snatched a beer from his aged avocado-colored refrigerator, cracked it open, and gulped it down. It was sure to be another tough night.

He quickly downed two more before sadly reflecting on his situation. It never should have happened. If it hadn't been for Keller and a dead guy, it never would have. Now, with a bad night's sleep and a jaggedly cut mouth, he was off to work. Not exactly ideal, but not altogether damning, it was something he could explain.

Edwin and the young bum went south to disappear. It was unknown if Steve could make a positive identification even if faced with the two. And why would Keller incriminate them? They could incriminate him. Maybe it was all for naught and the kidnapping had been a success. In that case, they'd be owed some money.

Van made his way to the restaurant and noticed an unmarked car in the parking lot. It wasn't altogether unexpected as his favorite drink had, once again, made him ornery and confident. If asked he'd say that he got into a bar fight at Dino's. Case closed. If there was evidence, he'd be arrested. If not, they could send him home. If they wanted him to work, he'd work. It was that simple.

Rita also went in to work. Although the media was quiet, the town was buzzing. Steve was recovered early Sunday morning with a large goose egg and a blood alcohol level twice the legal limit. He was checked into the hospital, rehydrated, cleared of any concussion symptoms, and then released into the care of his parents.

Randall and Billy had disappeared. Keller's friends blamed them, but no one really knew anything more. Most of the speculation, of course, involved Billy.

"Was bound to happen one of these days," was one common sentiment.

"Not surprised," was another.

Rita just took it all in—she wasn't talking. After the news broke, her boss, Carmine, rushed her.

"Yo, what happened to Billy?" he asked.

"Billy who?"

"Billy your boyfriend, that's who."

"What happened to your girlfriend?" answered Rita. "The one that wasn't your wife?"

Carmine then backed off with a nod of understanding. It was the first question about Billy, but it wouldn't be the last.

They dragged Steve, taped up and stuffed into a surfboard bag, out of a hibiscus hedge. It was Billy's bag, but he'd reported it stolen. His car was broken into, and the complaint surfaced as the sheriff began a background check. Speeding tickets, suspended license, drunk and disorderly, community college, construction work, restaurant work, there wasn't a whole lot there. No one was talking.

"Haven't seen him," they said.

"Gone walkabout," said another.

Billy didn't show up for his shift and had basically fallen off the face of the earth, but that wasn't illegal. All the sheriff had was a pair of mutes, a board bag, a locked-up old duplex, and a name given by criminals. The name was Rita. Rita Polli, the girlfriend, as she had been described. Current or former, it was a place to start.

He called in the morning and left a message. Rita wasn't under any obligation to respond, although from Sheriff Jake's experience, most did. After a day or so, she also replied and a date was set. Since Rita worked nights, they'd meet in the afternoon, on a Wednesday, a rather unassuming day. There were some questions surrounding the disappearance of her boyfriend, Billy Winslow. Something that, unbeknown to the sheriff, Rita expected.

Sheriff Jake figured it would be a routine meeting, one where he'd set the tone and control the tempo. He'd ask the questions, and she'd crack. They'd be done before lunch. She'd sing like a canary. With a badge on his belt, he'd leave the gun in the car. *Who knows?* thought the sheriff, *depending on what she'll admit to, she might be taking a ride.* It was wishful thinking for a man who'd been spending a lot of time alone.

Wearing slacks, leather boots, and a short-sleeved shirt, the sheriff slogged through another humid afternoon. Of course, there were no spaces in front of Rita's building, so he had to park at the clubhouse. A mere quarter mile away, it was no problem in shorts and a pair of flip-flops, but in full work gear it was nothing short of torture.

Fit and trim into his fifties, Jake's thinning blond hair was a matted mess by the time he reached Apt. 201 of the Ocean Sands condominiums. Sweating and now slightly winded, he pressed a plastic doorbell only to be greeted by one of the most beautiful women he'd ever seen. She seemed to be his age as well, which made it even worse. He should have been picking her up for lunch, not interrogating her daughter.

"Decided to take a swim before the visit, eh, sheriff? How informal," noted Jillian with a hearty laugh.

"Ahh no, no, I only swim in triathlons or when I'm training for one," he awkwardly claimed, a lie, although he did run nearly every day.

He extended a thick, sweaty hand, and she took it lightly. "Sheriff Jake Williams," he said.

"Well, let me get you a towel, sheriff. I'm Jillian, but I guess you didn't come over to meet me, shame," she added as she pressed a fresh-smelling towel into the sheriff's chest.

As he mopped his forehead in the strange beauty's kitchen, his confidence was slowly being sapped. A glass of water quickly appeared, which he was, of course, prompted to take.

"Thanks for the hospitality, Jillian." He almost wanted to say, "Have a nice day and call if you need anything," but he had a job to do.

"Is Rita available?"

"Of course, Sheriff Jake."

"Call me Jake."

It just came out. He didn't want to be too formal. Their plan was working. Jake didn't stand a chance.

Jillian then led him into the living room, into Rita's lair. And there she sat, still and sullen with dark hair and bright-blue eyes against a white wall. A loose shirt fell into all the right curves as a pair of tan, muscular legs draped comfortably across the couch. She shot him a quick glance fraught with pain and a hint of sadness and then turned away. Jillian was there to make him comfortable. Rita wanted to make him uncomfortable.

"I'm Sheriff . . ."

"Sheriff Jake Williams. I heard you from the other room," offered Rita as she set a devastating gaze on the stranger.

"Rita, be nice to Jake. He has a couple of questions for you."

"So, what's on your mind, sheriff?"

Great, now she was asking the questions. He had to get on with this thing.

"I'm here to talk to you about your boyfriend."

She glanced quizzically.

"Your ex-boyfriend?"

She nodded.

"OK, so your ex-boyfriend, Billy Winslow," he acknowledged.

It was part of his game but she was hip, so he decided to get it over with.

"Look, Ms. Polli, can I call you Rita?"

She shrugged.

"OK, Rita, Billy's a suspect in the abduction and torture of a local teen. I was wondering if you had any information on his whereabouts."

He studied her face for any clues, and there were none. She was ready. She knew more about it than he did, although in the context they seemed like some pretty serious charges.

"No, I don't."

That was it, no hesitation whatsoever, no follow-up, and not even a hint of assistance. This was going to be more difficult than he thought.

"Did you live with him, Rita?"

"Yes. My name wasn't on the lease, but I stayed with him from time to time over the course of a few years."

He knew the answer to the next question, but just had to ask, "Were you with him on Saturday night, on the twenty-fifth of June, I believe?"

"I don't think so."

"You don't think so?"

"I don't believe so. We've been broken up for a while. I can't recall the dates and times, but there have been a lot of dates, and a lot of times. Our last real breakup was a few months ago."

She wasn't exactly intimidated.

"If you weren't with Billy, where would you have been?"

"I would have been here."

"When was the last time you saw him?"

"It's been a couple of months."

"In what way, what were you doing?"

"We slept together."

"But you were broken up."

"Yes."

The sheriff let it linger. She studied the crease of his pants, the starchy dress shirt, and tacky boots. He was smart and intuitive, but he didn't know anything; nobody did. They couldn't.

"Some folks have put you and Billy together a couple of weeks ago."

"Not a real shocker," she said. "We still talked, but I haven't seen him in a while. He's kind of all over the board."

He felt her stare, and it was uncomfortable—her haunting eyes and perfectly blank face. Her right index finger danced lightly on a bare thigh. She wanted a cigarette but had quit, of that he was quite certain.

"Have you heard from Billy lately? Has he called?"

"No," she answered. It was the truth.

"Steve heard a lady that night. He's willing to testify that a lady was present."

"It wouldn't surprise me," she replied, which was also the truth, because it was her.

That was it. It's all he had.

"Well, thank you, Rita, I appreciate your time."

Spying a key ring from the corner of his eye, the sheriff had one last request.

"You wouldn't happen to have a set of keys to the duplex, would you?"

Knowing physical cues could often be as damning as verbal ones, staring straight ahead, Rita answered, "No, I don't."

Damn, he thought, *should have grabbed them when she looked away.*

Softened by the day, the heat, and the beauty, he was off his game.

Rita gazed through the sliding glass doors as the sheriff flipped out a card and placed it on the table.

"Call me if you hear anything."

"Sure will," she said, breaking her stare for a moment, then back to the terrace.

As Jillian entered the room, he was done. He knew less now than before. Yes, she was his girlfriend. Sure, they had broken up, but she couldn't remember when. There was no paper trail, no prints, no pictures, and most important, no Billy. It would have to be a waiting game. Sure, he could get into the apartment, but what of any evidence collected? The landlord hadn't let him in, and he knew how the courts felt about an illegal search, fruit from a poisonous tree. Although he did wonder if there was any fruit there.

"I hope my daughter was able to help," said Jillian in a sexy rasp.

That snake, he thought. "Oh, of course, Jillian."

He said nothing else. There was nothing else to say.

"Here, let me walk you to the door, hon," offered Jillian, with the sheriff delicately in hand.

And then like a dazed fighter being pulled off the canvas and pushed out of the ring, Jake made his exit. It wasn't a good feeling, and as he left, Jillian's soft touch remained. He was smitten.

But as one door closed, another opened.

"Hello, young man," said old Mrs. Haines to a not-so-surprised sheriff. She was probably in her eighties, so to her he could have seemed young.

"Hello, ma'am," replied the sheriff.

"It's so nice to see you again," she added, which caught him a little off guard.

"Have we met, Mrs....?"

"Of course, we've met. I'm Mrs. Haines. Are you coming in for a soda today?"

No, he thought, but then changed his tune. She might have some information on the sexy girl next door and the disappearance of her ex.

"Sure, Mrs. Haines, I could use a cold drink."

Jake then followed her into the apartment and was instantly met by the stale odor of old things.

"Here's a nice soda for you, young man," offered Mrs. Haines, brandishing a lukewarm diet Dr Pepper.

The apartment had to be about eighty degrees, and she was wearing a sweater! Between the smell, the soda, and the heat, he felt sick. The two next door had beaten him and then tricked him. He was stuck.

"Did you know Michael?" asked Mrs. Haines.

"Uh, no."

"He was my son. He worked at the cruise ship terminal until they discovered he had a brain tumor."

"Oh."

"He was walking on the beach one morning and suddenly passed out. My husband, Richard, painted this," she said, pointing to a decent rendition of a farmhouse in Ohio. "He did all of these," she continued in a grand sweeping motion.

"Ah, Mrs. Haines, before we go any further, would you mind if I ask you a few questions about the neighbors?"

"Oh, them," she sneered.

"Yes, the ladies, if you don't mind."

"Should have known."

"Have you seen any young men over there lately?"

"Oh, there's men in and out of that place all the time."

"Have you noticed a younger guy hanging around, one with messy blond hair, kind of tall?"

"They're all tall, and quite rude, I might add."

"OK, but there's one I'm interested in, muscular, with broad shoulders."

"He might have been there yesterday."

"And the daughter, you know the younger one," inquired the sheriff.

"Yes."

"How long has she been living there?"

He was expecting to hear "a couple of weeks" or that she'd just moved in. He'd tap the phone. He'd stake out the place. No one could outrun the long arm of the law.

"Oh, her," answered Mrs. Haines with a confused look. "She's lived there for about twenty years."

"Are you sure?" asked the sheriff, thinking Rita couldn't be any older than twenty-five.

"Are you calling me a liar?" barked Mrs. Haines.

"No, no," offered Jake, beginning to get the picture, "it just seemed like she was younger than that."

"They're always being loud, not like my son, Michael. He was well behaved."

"Oh," sounded the sheriff, pondering another dead end, the second of the day. He was off to a pretty poor start.

After another two hours of Haines family history, Jake was finally allowed to leave. As he walked slowly back to the car, breathing in some fresh air, he felt like he needed to take a run. It seemed to be what Billy had done. He just wondered where.

Jillian shuffled through the apartment, thinking about the sheriff and whether she'd see him again. If she wanted to, she probably could. Rita was thinking about Billy, wondering where he was and how he was doing. *Flash on the run*, she thought.

Contact

On a busy street in the city he now called home, the confusion was normal. Things moved in a different way, quicker and sometimes more deadly. There weren't many people to trust; a smattering of humanity is all that would come. In other words, the cavalry wasn't on the way.

A large blond American with a backpack and very little money, Billy was left beaten and now more broke than before. As the alcohol wore off and the dings on his face began to throb, the phrase "Welcome to Mexico" came to mind. It was supposed to be a tourist destination. *They need to work on their hospitality over here*, he thought as another key phrase popped into his head: "trial by fire."

They saw Billy that morning. A few guys from the States noticed an out-of-sorts gringo and offered him a place to stay.

"Stay off the back streets, amigo," one said.

Going forward, the advice would serve him well.

The girls were starting to look his way, but the guys were still wary. Billy was settling in but still felt lost. Would he be left like this, unknowing but alive, down and out but at least free? Had he lost Rita? The loose ends kept him unwound.

Like an inmate, he spoke of his beautiful girlfriend who he'd surely see when he got out. She was smart and sophisticated, and they'd surely start a new life together once he did his time.

They listened. Some asked a few questions, but didn't ask the same one he didn't ask, which was, "How did you end up here?" Don't ask, don't tell seemed to be the rule down there. At least until one of them broke the ice. He was still too new.

Billy called once a week, on Rita's day off, but was beginning to feel like she didn't want to talk to him. Which was a shame because he wanted to hear her voice, at least one last time—for her to tell him it was over, or to just say something, anything. Maybe they could joke around. He also needed to know what was going on back home. He hadn't spoken with anyone else—it was too risky.

The next call came in at dusk, a lonely ring on her day off.

"This is a collect call from Billy," sounded his voice over an automated recording.

"Would you accept the charges?" was the burning question.

"Yes," she answered.

It was a miracle, or a lifeline at least. Billy was elated, but at the same time suspicious. Where in the heck had she been? Rita clutched the receiver and felt a rush of anticipation. Why did she even take the call? Why didn't she hate him? The things that made her wonder also made her wary. It felt like going home, or maybe wondering if there still was one. She guessed that it was probably the same for him.

As his voice came through the line, Rita suddenly felt irritated, late, and in love. She guessed that whatever happened, she'd always love him.

"So, you ship me off to Mexico and then give me the cold shoulder?"

"Hello, Billy," said Rita.

"Hey, I know I messed up, but I'm paying the price down here. Believe me, it hasn't been easy."

"It doesn't seem to have humbled you much."

Whatever he did or said was going to be wrong; he was used to it. Now she'd act indifferent. It meant she still cared.

"Is that what you want? A broken man?"

"I'd like a man with a brain. Is that too much to ask?"

In a way, it was. A real man should act, and do, and explore. If that, to some, made him look stupid, then so be it.

"Because I love you, I'm not going to take offense."

He just threw it out there; perhaps she'd concur. She wanted to but didn't; maybe at another time, in another place, but not over the phone to a fugitive in Mexico.

Rita heard the clatter, the steady pulse of traffic and voices, mostly loud, all speaking Spanish. It sounded like he was in a marketplace or something, a far cry from Cedar Avenue.

"It sounds like you're in the middle of a carnival over there. Decided to pick the busiest time of day to make a call?"

"It's never quiet here. All the phones are in public places, although I haven't had to speak into one yet."

"There's a reason for that."

Hmm, that comment confirmed the worst. He thought maybe he had slipped through the cracks, that Keller and his crew were arrested and the case was closed. It was wishful thinking at best. He was quite certain that if he hadn't been a suspect before, Keller would have been sure to make him one.

"I miss you, Billy. How are you doing?"

"The first couple of weeks were rough, but I'm OK now. Got a job at a local resort setting up beach chairs and umbrellas, and of course the usual cleaning," he said with a sigh.

"What, did you expect them to make you the general manager?"

Billy laughed. He wondered what he'd do without her counterbalance. It was an odd type of punishment that the voice he had so often ignored was now the only one that mattered. It seemed only fitting to provide her one last lament.

"It just seems like my talents are still being wasted."

She could have said something else, but it wasn't the time or the place, and they had all suffered.

The call couldn't go on forever and they probably wouldn't end up together, so Rita decided to tell him how she felt. Her voice was confident and intelligent, and when she gave a compliment, it stuck. Like her eyes, it was deep and decisive, and he'd never get sick of hearing it.

"Look, Billy, I've never met anyone like you. I'm glad you're alive. I don't mean that in the physical sense, but in the sense that you have dreams and ideas. You're unconventional and unpredictable and smart and funny, and not bad to look at either."

She chewed a pinkie nail in remembrance as he puffed out his chest.

"You really spoiled me. We had a lot of fun. You cooked me a lot of good food and put up with my moods." It rhymed, but she hadn't meant to. "What I'm trying to say is that you were sweet and kind, and I'm sorry that I was so hard to deal with."

Her words gave comfort. Billy often felt like Rita would have been better off without him, like he was holding her back. It made him feel better to know that it wasn't true, vindicated in a sense that he hadn't ruined her life.

"It's OK," he replied. "Good people are often difficult."

"Thanks, Billy, I didn't want to be thought of as a tyrant."

"Never, I'd take it all back if I could."

"I know."

"Are they looking for me?"

"Yes. I had a visit from the sheriff."

"The sheriff!"

"Yeah, the only one in Brevard. You've been listed as a person of interest in the kidnapping and torture of a local teen."

"I did none of that! I was just clowning around. They went behind my back, and it got serious. I don't know how it happened and don't care to know because if I ever find out!"

"Easy, Billy. What's done is done. You got too close to the flame. You got burned. That's why I helped. I've had thoughts that maybe I shouldn't have. I mean, I hurt those guys."

"Believe me, they deserved to get hurt."

Billy was seething. At the moment, they were the last thing he cared about. His life had been shattered. He had done it. He wanted to know if there was anything left.

"I need to know if you still love me, and if I should come home."

"Yes, I love you, and no, you probably shouldn't come home."

It was a bittersweet statement. Of course, she loved him, in a universal sense, but he knew she meant more. It was just hard to let go.

"Are you going to wait for me?"

"I don't know, Billy. I'm not in a very good spot either. I've got the law breathing down my neck and my mother trying to get me into every cocktail party east of the Mississippi. I need to take a break. I hope that's a good enough answer for you."

Wow, thought Billy. It was almost worth it, just to hear Rita say that. She had left Chicago a spoiled suburbanite only to become a true Southern outlaw. Somewhere in his heart of hearts, he knew he had succeeded, and he also knew their run was most likely over.

After a lengthy exhale and a silent good-bye, he needed a few of the details.

"So, what do you know about their investigation. I mean, what do you think they know?"

"My guess is they don't know much. You haven't been charged with anything."

"That's a plus."

"I didn't want to seem too curious. But they've probably got someone in custody, someone a lot closer to the whole thing than you."

"Probably Keller."

"That weird guy who always had it out for you?"

"Yeah," said Billy, now resigned to his fate, and the fate of his love life.

"What do you know about the sheriff?" he asked.

"He's smart. Don't push it, stay gone."

"Sounds like you want me to."

"I want you to stay safe. I'll handle the apartment. Mrs. Johnson loves you, of course."

"Don't all women?"

"I guess," agreed Rita, "bad judgment isn't solely reserved for men."

"Ouch," replied Billy. "Touché."

More than her smoldering looks, he'd miss her sharp wit. Billy leaned on a wall as Rita sat on the couch in a pair of shorts and a tank top. They should have been together instead of discussing the details of a botched kidnapping. She didn't know what to do and neither did he. At this point it was basically all guesswork.

"But seriously, in my opinion, you should wait until they get a conviction and then ease back into town. Or you could declare your innocence. I'm sure they'd like to talk to you—just don't mention me."

"Only if it'll get me some time off. You'd visit me in the slammer, wouldn't you?"

"That's not my style, but you could probably find someone who would. It takes all kinds."

"That it does," said Billy, scanning his new surroundings. "That it does."

After another brief pause, he asked, "How long do you think this whole thing will take?"

"It's hard to say, but I'll keep you posted. They're being really hush-hush, and I'm not going to ask any questions. Eventually it'll come out. When I know, you'll know."

Man, that was final, it was cold.

"Oh, and ah, one last thing," stammered Rita.

"Anything," said Billy.

"You left your notebook in the car."

"That stupid thing," he growled. "Ditch it, throw it away. I never want to see it again."

"I was actually thinking I might be able to do something with it. I mean, with your permission, of course."

"Sure, be my guest."

"That doesn't sound much like a vote of confidence."

"It isn't—the thing's blighted. Get rid of it," he snarled.

She understood. It hadn't brought much joy, but he had put a lot of work into it. It seemed a shame just to toss it out.

"OK, OK, calm down," said Rita.

Although they may have wanted to, they couldn't talk anymore. He was tired of standing, and she was also bushed.

"Well, call me in a month or so."

"You'll accept the charges?"

"I guess I could," she playfully agreed.

"Hey, Rita?"

"Yes."

"They really pushed our hand, didn't they?"

"They sure did."

"Bye, Rita."

"Bye, Billy."

Ending

Billy was gone. Rita wouldn't see him anytime soon. They were no longer together. She'd been left with pretty much nothing. Or was it really nothing? She glanced at the notebook. It's true that it was in bad taste, but a mischievous smile widened as Rita thought, *What if I finish this thing myself?*

It's not what she wanted to do. It's what she had to do. With a broken heart and a lot of the good she'd known gone, Rita needed redemption. A sign that he was good and that she was good and that their time together would count for something.

Rita wanted to be writer. She must have stuck it out for the material. It was also for love, she acknowledged, but how could she rid herself of the criminal element? *Embrace it,* she thought.

Electricity filled the air. The time for reflection had passed. Out of an old shoelace and a piece of cardboard, Rita fashioned a Do Not Disturb sign. She called out sick for the next two weeks, fired up an old computer, brewed strong pots of coffee, and went to work. The days merged. The clock was a blur. It was a timeless era with trips to the kitchen and bathroom only. Rita's hair was a mess as she sprinted by her mother at all hours of the day and night. She didn't speak or sleep and then as the dust settled, there was something to print. Completely strange and instinctive, she finished in a little over a week. Now it was time for another monumental slumber.

Sun shone through the bedroom blinds as Rita finally woke drowsy and dehydrated. Not so lonely in the morning anymore, she was getting used to waking up alone. Stumbling into the bathroom with greasy hair and stained pearly whites, she thought, *Perfect*. Being attractive was often tiresome. Instead of a mad genius, or a grubby artist, all she could be was a pretty girl, so the change was good. The looks that defined her were gone, and it was cool to be someone else.

Today Rita felt different—hopeful without any hope and desperate with no real desperation. It was a strange feeling. Where to go? What to do? She wrote a book, so now what? She'd see it through. She'd go to a city and throw her hat into the air. *Better brush my teeth before I do all of that*, she thought.

Rita didn't want anyone to see it, didn't want anyone to read it. In a way, it was contraband. In a sense, it resembled something that may or may not have happened.

She wasn't even looking. It came as a surprise, a chance encounter of sorts, a mystic transaction perhaps. On the table was a newspaper. Although Rita rarely read it, she did that day. The arts and entertainment section, needing to be entertained, she guessed.

Among the pictures and reviews, she spied a workshop for prospective writers at a bookstore in Orlando. Far enough from the beach to be completely anonymous, it was there where she'd unveil her masterpiece.

Gone were Rita's fashion concerns of the past. Condensed into a pair of cutoffs, some old Birkenstocks, and a V-neck T-shirt, her style reflected the way she wanted her life to be: functional. Of course, the dolphin earrings and jangling bracelets remained, along with a soft tint on the lips and a light floral scent. Deciding on a looser pair of jean shorts and a ponytail, the cleavage would have to stay, if only slight. Starting her car for the first time since its last fateful journey, Rita was ready to go.

Heading west, Rita wondered if she were the only one driving tentatively about, full of questions and uncertainties. Everyone else seemed to know where they were going, and they were going there fast. A sharp beep reminded her of that as she drifted through an off-ramp and then onto a cluttered side street.

Among the strip malls and cracked blacktop, Rita was looking for something clean, something free from the rainbow stain of petroleum and the scatter of cigarette butts. She was looking for something new, something without the smear of greasy hands and the restrained look of minimum wage. And there it was: square, beige, and inviting stood the new bookstore. Pulling into a hot parking lot filled with hot cars, Rita felt remarkably average. A sharp contrast to how she felt at the beach—better, like staring across the ocean, limitless.

Following a light stroll, she pulled open the double doors and was instantly hit by a wave of cool air. At a glance the paradox was immediate—a large store that was packed to the gills with small things. Rita stood beneath the bright lights with her book and wondered what to do. Everyone besides Rita seemed to have some kind of direction, so she decided to ask.

The girl behind the counter seemed aloof but not altogether unhelpful. With the cultivated look of a librarian, she appeared less like a cashier and more like a person in transit.

"Excuse me," said Rita in a soft voice so as not to alert the others to her foolish pursuit, "could you tell me where the writers' workshop might be?"

The question loomed large as the cashier gave Rita the once-over. She stalled on the copy as if to say, "You don't stand a chance. You don't even look like a librarian, or work in a bookstore."

"It's in the back of the store under the banner."

So, Rita did an about-face and trudged back to a large banner that said An Afternoon with Writers. *Sounds encouraging*, she thought.

The books for the seminar were neatly stacked as Rita pondered buying a book that she didn't really want. With that in mind she picked one up, walked back to the girl in the fluffy blouse, and dropped her money on the counter.

"*How to Get Published*," said the starchy counterperson. "Should be a good read."

"You can bet on it," returned Rita with a wink.

If she was going to waste her time, she'd do it in style.

Rita's second approach was more successful as she took a seat among her peers. From notebooks to folders to a few sheets of paper, every-one had something to offer. Some of the manuscripts were worn while others, like hers, looked brand new. Although she figured that in a few months it would probably be covered in a healthy swath of dust.

So, the workshop began with the authors of the how-to book bringing laughter and chuckles to the room with their tales of working in the industry, and the idea that a select few in the room could end up there as well. Rita was also amused until it came time to submit a writing sample.

She ran—or fled was more like it—away from something, possibly the truth. It just wasn't what she had imagined, under the lights in a plastic chair, the book's demise before it ever had the chance to flour-ish, its death before it even had a chance to live. She'd bring it back to life. She'd nurse it back to health, but more importantly, she'd get it out of there!

Rita moved past the others without a single glance and then exited into the heat. The sidewalk was wide and white, and she was pensive. Maybe she should have stayed and sought some advice. Oh, well, at least she'd taken the first step. The book was sure to need some work, and luckily, she had a trusty how-to manual. *It shouldn't be long now,* she thought in jest.

Against the city's skyline, the midday sun released a hazy, metallic glow. Thirsty and depleted, Rita wandered over to a health-food store for a vegetable juice. The store was nice and the line at the juice bar long. She was destined to get some satisfaction now, or maybe not. The large gentleman in front of her was doing his best to obscure an already small menu. She'd move left and he'd move left. She'd move right and he'd move right.

"Ahem," she signaled loudly.

The disruptive gentleman then turned and said, "I'm sorry. I noticed you walk in and wondered if you'd smile if I did something stupid."

"Did you get your answer?"

Through her irritation, she noticed something that made her a little less guarded. He was rather good looking.

"Most definitely," he answered, "next time I'll have to be more creative."

She wanted to say there wasn't going to be a next time but instead said, "Sounds good."

Rita figured that would be the end of it, but the guy continued. With an outstretched hand and a sparkle in his eye, he brazenly announced, "Corbin Flake at your service."

She blurted out a sloppy laugh, and he was a bit taken aback by the stunning beauty and her unlikely candor.

"It's better that Corbin Flakes, isn't it?"

"I suppose," she agreed.

As she spoke, he noticed something in her voice—a low-level ping that rang out below everything else. It caught his attention. Moving closer to the counter, it was now his turn.

"Why don't you let me get your order? It's the least I can do for disrupting your afternoon. I'll move on after that."

"You promise?"

He nodded sideways in a "What do I have to do to strike up a conversation?" gesture, and Rita of course returned the nod.

She was striking, fearless, and strong. He wondered where she'd been made, struck from the finest metal, a Greek goddess, a Roman empress, and why she had walked through the door today. There had to be a reason. He was intrigued and, if nothing else, persistent. He'd give it one last try.

As he handed her the drink, there was time for one last attempt. He had to make it count. Another quip wouldn't work. Any type of invitation was sure to fail. A stupid question would be better than no question at all as he said, "Can I at least get your name?"

Rita took a swig of her carrot juice and with a frothy orange mustache replied, "It's Rita."

Now he was the one to snicker at the sight of Rita wearing her drink.

"What?" she snarled, using her forefinger to remove the unwanted tint, all the while under the close scrutiny of her new friend.

"I could have gotten you a napkin, that's all."

"Look, I don't want to be rude, but I've got a long drive home."

Corbin couldn't let her leave.

"Well, what brought you to Orlando today, and to walk through that door over there," he stammered, "and straight into my life? I need some kind of an explanation."

Rita exhaled. He had worn her down.

"I came over for a workshop at a bookstore. What about you?" she indifferently asked.

"Oddly enough, I was working in that building today, doing a reset for the owner, or for my father. What I mean is my father's the owner, and I help him out from time to time."

"So, your father owns a glorified strip mall, eh? What do you do, mooch off him?"

It was his fault. He asked for it. All she wanted was a drink. He intervened, so now he'd pay the price.

"I wouldn't say that," replied Corbin. "My father's an entrepreneur, and I've kind of followed in his footsteps. We enjoy the hands-on stuff as well."

She was impressed. He took the jab without so much as a stutter. She'd allow him to proceed.

"Well, what's your story?"

"I make investments. I'm what you might call a venture capitalist."

"So, you're rich."

"That's kind of relative."

"That's something a rich person would say."

"Let's just say money isn't something I've had to worry about, but enough about me," he countered. "How did the book come out?"

Corbin dabbled in entertainment, mostly as a middleman, getting the right people to the right places. Always on the lookout for new talent, he'd drop a business card almost anywhere, including in line for a smoothie at a co-op.

"What book?"

"The one you're holding."

"That's not a book—it's a manual."

"I don't mean the how-to book. I'm talking about the other one."

"How do you know it's even a book?"

"Because you bought a book on how to get published, so it's an assumption on my part that the rather crude-looking manuscript below the polished one is a real live work of fiction. Am I wrong to have assumed that?" asked Corbin, sensing he had her at least a little bit interested.

Rita made a slight movement, added an "ahh" into the mix, then replied, "Yeah, it's a book."

"What's it about?"

"It's about a kidnapping."

"Hmm," murmured Corbin.

"That's what I thought," snapped Rita as she started to leave.

Corbin also moved to slow her exit. He needed something good.

"Look, you're the artist and I'm the guy who's always sizing things up, so just give me a chance!"

He said the right thing to buy a few more minutes, but she was about to set him straight.

"You talked to me. I didn't talk to you. I'm holding these stupid books so you can see exactly what I'm doing. I don't have a clue who you are or what your agenda is, but I can promise you this, I'm no target, so if you're looking for a quick score, you need to look somewhere else."

"You're right," he conceded, "I could be making this up, but I'm not."

I could take you for a ride in my father's jet; see if I could make that up, he thought, but he didn't dare say it. Rather, he pulled out a business card that read

Flake Industries and Entertainment:

Don't Fake It—Flake It!

Rita snickered, and Corbin smiled. If nothing else, at least the card held some entertainment value, but at the moment, she didn't seem to want to fake it or flake it.

Taller than her with light eyes and brown hair, everything about Corbin seemed honest. He had impeccable bone structure and smiled at the thought of them having their first fight. She was going to be a challenge, he knew that. This afternoon he wanted two things—he wanted the girl, and he wanted the book. Now how to get them? Ask two questions, she'd answer no to one and yes to the other.

"Look, Rita, I know we may have gotten off to a rocky start, but I was wondering if you'd let me take you out to dinner, one of these days, when I come back into town?"

Without a moment's hesitation Rita answered no, and explained, "I live over on the beach anyway. It's pretty far."

She was still too complicated. There was a lot to sort out, what with Billy, her mother, and the sheriff waiting in the wings.

"OK, well what about the book?"

"What about it?"

"Can I read it?"

Rita considered the request without the slightest notion that she was about to hand it to someone who could probably get it published. Corbin actually wanted to start a publishing house and was in the process of reviewing material. He was intrigued, to say the least.

"I guess," she answered.

Relieved that Rita agreed to the one request, he instantly became more businesslike.

"Thank you so much for your trust, Rita. I know it's a big step, to hand it off to a stranger, but I'll take care of it, I promise."

"I've got a few more copies. Someone's going to have to read it, so it might as well be you." She looked at the card and read, "Corbin Flake, if that's who you really are."

"That's who I really am, if you'd like to see my driver's license."

She raised a finger in a "quiet" gesture. "I've really got to run, Corbin."

The moment was fleeting, and she was leaving. Maybe it was a dud. How could he at least get a hold of her?

"Oh, by all means, I'll be in touch. Is your information in the copy somewhere?"

"In the front flap," said Rita as she walked off. If he was a psycho, she could just change her number.

He immediately scanned her contact info then glanced up to watch the leggy beauty disappear. As Corbin thumbed through the book, he wondered why she'd been so standoffish. Girls usually came up to him, but she was different, refreshing. A little angry, even. In the fast-paced and often shallow world of finance, he'd been searching for a companion, and for a simple, down-to-earth venture they could call their own. It was a long shot, but staring across the parking lot, he felt like he found the girl. She'd be tough to bring in and easy to lose. He'd have to proceed with care.

On a marshy stretch of highway headed for the coast, Rita was relieved to be going home. As the day edged further into dusk, the thin, winding river and solemn pastures would soon be bathed in a purple glow. No matter what changed, the water stayed the same, hiding whatever wanted to hide and showing only what was meant to be seen. Although she didn't want to, Rita couldn't help thinking about the handsome stranger. Was he that way, seemingly calm on the surface without a hint of what might be lurking?

Still relishing her independence, Rita wanted to be alone. She wanted to suffer and to be sad and then to be happy and never have to suffer again. She yearned to know how the tragically tortured soul could see the world so beautifully. It gave her hope, and as the sun rapidly set, that was about all she had.

Beginning

The sun rose and then set. Then it rose and set again. The same sun that bathed the ugly dinosaur and shone on the cross at the crucifixion still worked. It reminded Rita of how much there was still to do: to get a career, to get married, to have children, to have fun, to struggle, and then eventually to die. She couldn't do it all in a day, so instead she decided to have some toast and tea.

As Rita crept into the kitchen, she'd yet to receive her mother's standard overzealous reception, so the coast seemed clear. It was a nice place to be in the morning, quiet and relaxed with just the right amount of natural light. She could open the windows for a cross draft and lift the blinds to see strangers walking dogs and strange cars driving by. Rita toyed with the idea of calling the sheriff for a chat about harassment, but decided against it. He was only doing his job. She also wondered if the case was closed. It had been a couple of months and still no word of any arrests. Time was moving quickly, especially with so much undecided.

To the chagrin of Jim Linon and Sheriff Williams, Billy's apartment had been emptied and scrubbed clean. They approached the landlady with a second request for access, which was this time granted.

"Any idea when he might be back?" asked the sheriff as a formality.

"Your guess is as good as mine," she answered as more of a formality.

Rita still worked at the restaurant, but only in a limited capacity. She'd been tinkering with her book and beginning another. A drastic departure from the first, it was more of a travel journal based on early family trips to the Upper Peninsula of Michigan.

For her latest installment Rita decided on St. Simons Island, Georgia. It was a quick car trip for a "girl on the run," which was set to be her new brand. Her mother would tag along for the first chapter, appropriately titled "Mother Knows Best."

As they were packing, a call came in which Jillian, of course, rushed to answer. She always enjoyed exchanging pleasantries with Billy.

"Hi, sweetie," slid provocatively from her lips as Corbin stalled.

Mistaking it for a phone sex line, he nearly hung up before the voice again said, "Hello?"

"Ah, hello, um, I hope this is the right number. This is Corbin, Corbin Flake. I was wondering if Rita might be available."

"She might be," answered Jillian. "What might this be about?"

"It's about a book," answered Corbin.

Jillian covered the receiver and excitedly mouthed, "It's for you. It's about a book."

"What?" sounded Rita as she moved for the phone. "This is Rita."

"Hi, Rita, it's Corbin."

Corbin, Corbin, she thought.

"It's Corbin Flake, from the health-food store. Ahh, I bought you a drink and took your book."

"Oh yeah, that annoying guy who tried to pick me up."

"I was trying to get to know you. It was the only way I knew how. If I offended you, I'm sorry."

He listened. She was still on the line. He still had a chance.

"Ah, I guess it's OK," she said with her arms tightly crossed.

He was quite good looking and charming to boot. She wouldn't let him know it, though, at least not yet.

"So, to what do I owe this great pleasure, Mr. Flake."

This lady is something else, he thought.

"Are you sitting down, Rita?"

"No," she said, even though she was.

"Well, you might want to."

"I might not want to."

"OK, don't worry about sitting down," he said. "We read your book, and we want to publish it."

Instead of saying "Wow!" or "No way!" or anything else exclamatory, she cautiously asked, "Are you sure?"

"Yeah, we're sure."

He expected her to be happy but understood the reluctance. She was unfamiliar with the process. How would it be handled? What about the compensation? There were probably a million questions, one of which was, "Do you think anyone will read it?"

It was a valid question.

"We're willing to take a chance. I've drawn up a contract and plan to be in Orlando in a couple of days. Would you be free on, say, Wednesday at three?"

"Who is 'we,' anyway?" asked Rita. She wanted to know more about the publishers.

Usually there would be a company with a name. He hadn't mentioned anyone at all. She wasn't going to give it away. She'd burn the darn thing first.

"Oh, so sorry, Rita. When I say 'we' I'm referring to myself and a few partners. We don't have a name, but we do have a New York address and with any luck, we'll be able to publish your book if you're not too stubborn about it."

The nerve of this guy, she thought, although she was somewhat attracted to the notion that he wasn't completely intimidated. Whoever ended up in her camp needed to have a little fight.

"Well, excuse me for asking a few questions. You're nothing more than an acquaintance, a rather problematic one at that, making some pretty suspect claims."

Now she had done it. She struck him in the heart. No one was going to accuse Corbin Flake of being a fake.

"I'm a businessman and a good one at that. I'm prepared to offer you a sizable advance and a share of all copies sold, if that's something a cynical, headstrong, too-big-for-her-britches little girl could agree to."

"You don't know where I've been," she snarled.

"It doesn't matter. It's not important. What's important is where you want to go. We can go there together, but you've got to give me a chance."

He realized she was hurt and that he wasn't going to get anywhere with a slick sales pitch. Fighting fire with fire was the only way he'd be able to cut into her defenses.

"Whatever book we publish is going to be our first, and I want it to be yours."

She thought it over, all the work that had gone into it: the ruined relationships and the people on the run. It was hers and it was Billy's. It could remain theirs, or she could ship it off for all to see. She could open their closet to the world or to whoever wanted to buy a cheap paperback from a rotating rack of supposed best sellers.

Against her better judgment, Rita trusted the new guy. She was going to have to trust someone, especially with what she wanted to do. She couldn't do it alone. Corbin passed the first test, and the sound of a generous advance had a good ring to it.

"You said Wednesday at three?"

Corbin clenched a fist in celebration. His first writer, the beautiful Rita Polli. Something told him she'd be worth the trouble.

"Ah, yeah, Wednesday at three. I'm flying in early to take care of some business. I can be at the beach in the afternoon."

"OK, but don't be late. We've got business to attend to as well," she replied so as to sound equally engaged.

"I won't be, and I'll call Tuesday to confirm. If anything changes, I'll give you plenty of notice. I don't ever want to waste your time."

That sounds nice, she thought.

He was also interested in her. She knew it. She may have been interested in him. She wasn't sure. She'd let him publish the book, but would she let him steal her heart? What about Billy? It's what he had wanted all along, but with its doom and destruction, would he give it his blessing? He'd have to know. She'd have to tell him.

Between work, worry, and all of the things that make a day, Tuesday swiftly rolled around. Among other calls, news of investments, and more calls, Corbin needed to call Rita. The phone of course rang off the hook.

"Hello," trilled sweetly through the line and this time Corbin recognized it as Jillian. Rita still wasn't answering the phone, and Jillian was getting tired of being an answering machine.

"Hey, Jillian, it's Corbin. I was wondering if Rita might be available. It's about our meeting on Wednesday. I was just calling to confirm."

Jillian prompted Rita to take the call as she firmly resisted. Why leave a perfectly good man on the line? Her mother didn't get it.

"Ah, Corbin," started Jillian, "Rita's busy at the moment. Is it OK if she calls you back?"

With Rita shaking her head and flailing wildly, Jillian stood firm. She had a feeling. Rita could stay as long as she liked, but sooner or later she was going to have to move on.

"I'd be delighted," replied Corbin. "Anytime after six."

"I'll see to it that she calls."

"Thanks."

It seemed like he had the mother's approval. Now all he needed was the daughter's.

Jillian smiled. Happy in her thoughts for a moment, the happiness was short lived as Rita stomped into view.

"Why in the heck did you tell him I'd call?"

"Because you will, and if you don't, I will. He's flying in from New York to see you. The least you can do is talk to him."

"That sounds like a threat."

"It is."

Rita grimaced. Things had been going well, but it seemed like the armistice had been lifted. She trudged into the bedroom and dove into her puffy bed. Maybe her mother was right. Maybe it was time for her to make the call, but what to say?

Aware that she had something to do, the rest wasn't exactly restorative. The clock showed a bit after six, so she grabbed the phone and dialed. It rang, and she squirmed. It rang some more, and she nodded in a told-you-so gesture.

Just as she was about to hang up, a jovial "Corbin Flake, at your service" sounded through the receiver.

She laughed slightly.

"Sounds like Rita," he said. "Glad my name is at least entertaining."

"How did you know it was me?"

"I figured you'd be antsy, that you'd want to get it out of the way. You wouldn't call at six, but not long after."

"How'd you know I'd call at all?"

"Because if you didn't, your mother would have."

"How do you know that?"

"Because she knows what's best for you."

Rita was infuriated, and Corbin was amused. The conspiracy was afoot. He was weaseling his way into her life.

"Well, I'm calling."

"I'm enchanted."

"You're on thin ice."

"Does that mean you'll be home tomorrow?"

She wanted to say no, but reluctantly said, "Yes."

If he wasn't mistaken, they seemed to have a fair amount of chemistry. Rita felt it too. She'd fight it, though.

"I'll be there at three with some papers for you to sign."

"Maybe."

"Oh, of course," agreed Corbin. "We'll go over all of the business type stuff. It's easy to understand, especially for a smart girl like you."

She sat upright. Was he taking a shot at her?

"OK, but don't be late."

"I won't be," he affirmed into a dead receiver.

Just when we were getting somewhere, he thought. He'd be doing it anyway, regardless of a personal interest in the client. He just happened to be interested in this one.

The following day a corporate jet with Corbin aboard landed at Orlando Executive Airport. Wearing a swank Brooks Brothers ensemble with a Swiss watch and Italian shoes, he was dressed to impress. Sporting a mild tan and a pair of Ray-Bans, Corbin turned heads, but he didn't notice. He was on the hunt.

He'd arrive by limousine with a bottle of champagne. She'd fall helplessly into his arms and then they'd elope.

Think again, said a voice.

She was a different kind of girl. Not one to be impressed. He looked in the mirror and a voice said, *Dress down.*

No limousine—a rental, the voice went on to say.

So that was it, he was off to the nearest Hertz to rent a car.

Headed toward the beach in a compact Dodge, Corbin felt somewhat ordinary. It was new territory for the self-assured young millionaire. In a common vehicle moving slightly over the speed limit, he felt remarkably human. For a boxy American model, the car handled well. The thought of driving it to meet a girl who hated him was laughable, almost stupid.

The terrain was flat and unfamiliar. To Corbin, it all looked the same. Past the pastures and the distant palms, through the pine thickets and over the St. Johns River was the Intracoastal Waterway. Corbin immediately felt at ease as he cranked the windows down to breathe in some thick, salty air. With the water came images of all things aquatic: slippery rocks and fishing rods amid the sooty diesel plumes of the outgoing ships.

He was close enough to be there soon, but far enough away to make a decision. How did he want to arrive? It seemed to be the theme of the day, so he knew better than to leave it to chance. He needed to do something different. It was now or never as the voice returned and said, *Walk.*

Walk?

Yeah, dummy, walk, it repeated.

Guess some exercise couldn't hurt. He had planned to take a swim and then catch a nap, but things had changed. Corbin and the little car took a wide right, and lo and behold, just around the bend was another Hertz. He was a bit suspicious but at this point decided to just go with it.

Pulling neatly into a parking spot, Corbin grabbed his gear and went in to return the keys. Eyeing the little blue car, the attendant smirked as Corbin raked his Rolex across the counter and asked, "Where's the beach?"

The guy then pointed east through a plate-glass window and Corbin sped off.

Across the highway and down a side street came a beachside road and then a boardwalk. Feeling woozy from the sun, the travel, and thoughts of the supernatural, Corbin forged ahead. Deciding to downsize, he threw both his shirt and his fancy watch into his trusty leather bag. Corbin then kicked off his shoes, licked his salty lips, and following Rita's directions, headed for Seventh Street South.

At the moment everything felt right. Although he looked out of place, carrying a leather bag and not much more, his engaging smile prompted return smiles from the young and old alike. As he moved along without a care in the world, a rising tide had gradually edged Corbin into the deep, soft sand. Now trudging instead of walking, the sun shone with a greater intensity as his dry mouth clapped painfully shut.

With his skin aglow in a light pink hue, the faster Corbin walked, the slower he went. His sparkling smile had vanished as he thought, *Where's the darn tiki bar?*

Corbin hadn't kept track of the time, but now that he was within striking distance, he'd take a peek. The watch read 2:45, and he still had seven blocks to go. That same stupid voice that told him to walk now told him to walk faster.

"I'm going as fast as I can," he said to no one in particular.

Slightly hobbled with blistered feet, Corbin winced with every uneven step. His skin felt cold and clammy and his shoulder was rubbed raw from the bag. As Corbin pushed on, he needed to get out of the sun.

Over a boardwalk and back on the road, he utilized a thin strip of grass to its fullest, searching for the Ocean Sands condominiums. A bronzed couple carrying beach chairs were his first clue.

"Excuse me, sir, is this the right way to the Ocean Sands?" wheezed Corbin.

"Sure is, son, straight ahead," answered the guy with a look of concern.

Surging forward with an animalistic kind of determination, he rounded the corner about five minutes late. *Hope she's still here,* he thought. Not only because he wanted to see her, but also because he could be in need of medical attention.

Getting closer to her building, he saw something on the second floor. It was hair, billowing locks, one woman standing next to another. Rita was on the left, so it had to be her mother on the right, both stunning, so it seemed.

Burned, dehydrated, and shoeless in an undershirt, Corbin weakly held up a tender arm and said, "Hi, Rita."

Rita whispered something to her mother and then moved down the stairs to get him.

"Sorry I'm late," hissed Corbin.

Great, I caused another guy to lose it, she thought, as she took his bag and slung his arm over her shoulder.

"Just glad you could make it," replied Rita. She meant it.

In the apartment, Jillian readied a glass of water along with a moist towel. He felt dizzy and fatigued, but the water stayed down, and he immediately felt better. Corbin had done it. He'd softened her stance. She had planned an icy reception but was now genuinely worried.

"This is my mother, Jillian," said Rita, not really sure how to play it.

They were relative strangers, yet there he was on the couch receiving care.

"Hello, Corbin," chimed Jillian.

"Hi, Jillian, pleased to meet you," he replied, attempting to stand but forced down with a touch from Rita.

"Not so fast, let's get something for that shoulder."

Now that he was inside and somewhat rehydrated, the redness of his skin started to show.

"You'll also need some aloe for the burn," she said, prancing through the apartment like a thoroughbred. He watched her walk and felt even better. If he was going to die, he wanted to do it here.

She returned to the living room and applied the ointment in slow, deep circles. It felt good, and Rita was fairly certain he'd be OK. As her concern lessened, she had a couple of questions, the first being, "What happened to your car?"

"Ah, I turned it in at the port," he replied through a pleasured groan.

"And what about your shoes?"

"I kicked them off."

"You didn't like them?"

"It was something spiritual, I think."

"Well, we're going to have to get you some shoes."

Nothing came back, and after a light shake there was still only silence. As Rita made her way across the room, something told her to turn, so she did. Corbin turned as well, or so she thought, so she returned to give him the once-over. He seemed to be asleep, so she cautiously let him be.

With a splitting headache, Corbin woke to darkness and strange surroundings. Where was he? Sore and sunburned, he'd been covered with a blanket, but he still shivered. He was in an apartment. It was Rita's. Small but comfortable, the couch had become his bed for the night. Did they ask him to stay? Unfortunately, no. A hint of embarrassment came as he realized he'd passed out. He checked for his clothes, and they were on. Relief. As Corbin woke, the odd events of the afternoon came into focus. Happiness and a plane ride, a pleasant drive to the beach and then that stupid voice, the walk from hell, and then collapsing shoeless at his first client's house. Not exactly off to a good start. A glass of water and a couple of aspirin sat on the coffee table, so Corbin took the pills, chugged the water, and then fell back asleep.

When he woke again, the sun was up. Noise came from the kitchen along with the smell of fresh fruit and coffee. *This must be the continental breakfast*, thought Corbin in jest.

Jillian was first on the scene. "Good morning, handsome," she said in a welcoming tone.

"Oh, you're too kind," replied Corbin. "Since when did unwelcome guests and pink skin become attractive?"

"She didn't say you were attractive," sounded a distant, irritated voice. Getting closer and now in view, Rita added, "She calls everyone handsome."

So, there was the rude awakening he'd anticipated. Jillian made a face as Rita passed and Corbin asked, "Is she always this pleasant?"

"Unfortunately, yes," answered Jillian.

As if the two were fools or common jesters, Rita shook her head and tediously asked, "How are you feeling?"

It was an interesting question. He didn't have a good answer. Corbin studied the place for a clue, for anything they might have in common. But as his gaze moved throughout the room, it always came back to her.

"I'm embarrassed, but other than that I'm all right."

"I'd be lying if I said I've never stayed in the sun too long," said Rita in their first real exchange.

Still in a nightshirt and a baggy pair of shorts, her subtle movements seemed choreographed. He had yet to see a flaw.

"I almost suffocated on my drive down from Chicago," she remembered. "I fell asleep on the beach the next day slathered in baby oil and nearly had to go to the hospital."

"Ouch," replied Corbin. "Surprised I didn't have the bright idea to cook myself as well."

They laughed, and for the first time, she noticed his eyes light up.

"I didn't exactly have my thinking cap on yesterday."

"You didn't have any hat on from the looks of it, or maybe you threw that away too?"

"No, I probably would have kept that. I mean, I don't know what happened. I just think with the travel and the lack of local knowledge, I mean, I thought there'd be a boardwalk or a place where I could get a pair of flip-flops or a drink of water. I didn't plan on showing up looking like the High Plains Drifter."

Rita laughed. She'd seen the old, painfully dry Clint Eastwood movie.

"I was thinking more like the Road Warrior, or Mad Max."

"Even better," agreed Corbin.

He was beginning to feel comfortable. It was nice to see Rita let her guard down. He couldn't tell if she was looking at him in a certain way, but he was looking at her that way.

"So, what brought you to Florida?" asked Corbin.

"My father was sick."

There went that, he thought as he quickly added, "Ah, you did say something about getting me some shoes, didn't you?"

"I thought you were asleep."

"Feverish more like it."

"Oh please!" she exclaimed before getting up to change.

"I see you've got a stylish undershirt. You wouldn't possibly have anything else so perhaps we could go out in public?" she sarcastically asked, in no mood for any more of his trickery.

"I believe there's something in this trusty old sack."

Tall with a moderate burn and an expensive pair of sunglasses, he'd fit in nicely as "the new guy."

Rita wasn't exactly embarrassed to be seen with him, shoes or not.

So, Billy was gone and Rita had graduated to a guy that she'd have to drive around. He was definitely going to buy his own shoes, that is, if he hadn't ditched his wallet too. This Corbin character was quickly turning into quite a question mark.

With his feet still tender, Corbin waited in the shadows.

"First stop, a surf shop. We've got to get you geared up for the sun," was her early morning rallying cry.

They went with the windows down. Rita was still, while her thick, unruly hair took flight. Wearing dark shades and shiny red lipstick, she looked like a sexy robot. With the mysterious tour guide, the car ride, and a light warm breeze, Corbin felt like he was hallucinating. He let out a minor laugh, which wasn't lost on Rita.

"There's no way to be fashionable in Florida—you might as well go for comfort," she said while battling her hair into a ponytail.

"You do a pretty good job of it."

"You're just saying that because I saved your butt and let you stay at my place."

"Perhaps," he agreed.

"Hmm," she muttered. They were almost there.

"We're heading to the place where I bought my first bikini. I was what the locals call Canada white. After a long Chicago winter, I was glowing like a bug light."

"Incandescent," added Corbin. "I know the feeling."

"I was pretty sure you could relate."

Little by little, she was letting him in.

Walking aimlessly through the crowded aisles, they visited a consumerist swath of destruction on the stuffed clothing racks. Deciding to keep his sunglasses, everything else would have to go. With shorts instead of pants, flip-flops for the feet, surf trunks for the beach, and a light dress shirt, Corbin was ready. A couple of bikinis, a sundress and a pair of Rainbow sandals completed Rita's summer wardrobe. As they passed the surfboards, Corbin handled some of the shapes, running his hands down the rails and testing the weight just like a surfer would.

"You know you're going to have to learn how to surf," remarked Rita.

"Is it anything like lacrosse?"

"Similar," she answered with a slight bump.

That was it, contact—the first real sign that she might be interested. Just as someone had shown her around, Rita now accompanied Corbin. They were like a couple, not in any hurry, playing off one another quite nicely. Taking a break from Billy, from the sheriff, and from herself for an afternoon was nice.

There were things to be discussed. There was something she'd have to say, but for now she asked, "So, when do you have to leave?"

"I don't know."

"What I mean is, when does your flight depart?"

"Not sure."

"Ah, a real man of mystery," she joked. "Shows up with no shoes, a sunburn, and now an open travel agenda. How marvelous."

"It's not like that. I was just thinking of taking a vacation, an open-ended trip."

"Well, where are you going to stay?"

"Here," he answered. "If you'll have me."

It was a bit presumptuous, but she was beginning to like his style.

"We'll see."

Following an afternoon at the beach and a short nap, Corbin suggested they go out to dinner, his treat, of course. The trio looked marvelous with Rita and Corbin more casual, and Jillian in a tight dress just to irk Rita. After dinner and drinks, Jillian retired as the two took a stroll on the dock. They discussed the day, the surf shop, and how thankful he was for her expert care. She said it was nothing, and that he would have done the same for her. Inching closer throughout the conversation, they were now together as Corbin moved in for a kiss.

"Look, I'm still kind of involved," said Rita.

"Ah, with who?" asked Corbin. He didn't see anyone around.

"The book you want to publish—it's his book."

That was a sobering thought. The mystery guy had the girl and the book. His only other question was whether to jump into the river now or later.

"Is that going to be a problem?" asked Corbin.

"Well, it's not his book," she explained. "He threw it away. He gave it to me."

"I can't publish the book unless I know who wrote it."

"I wrote it. He did the research, I guess you could say."

"So, you can't sign off on it?"

"It's just a technicality."

"Where's this guy now?" he asked, to hopefully have him sign a release.

The last thing he needed was intellectual property litigation. This little venture would be over before it started.

She stammered a bit before finally admitting, "Well, for lack of a better term, he was run out of town."

Before she didn't care, Corbin was just another guy with another story. Fine, look at the book, publish away. But now that he was here, she'd have to face the truth with regard to not only whose book it was, but was she still in love?

Corbin made it easy. He turned to her and said, "I don't care whose book it is—I just want a kiss."

This time she didn't resist. She moved into him as the first of many passionate moments followed. Sadly, it answered the question of love, and she was relieved.

Like he said, it was an open-ended trip, so Corbin stayed on for a few days. He fixed the faucet, replaced a doorknob, and painted the back deck—aqua, of course. When it was time to leave, Rita asked how he planned to get to the airport.

In true Corbin fashion, he answered, "Not sure."

So, she gave him a ride.

While Rita drove, Corbin studied her subtle, yet effective movements. Nothing about her was slack. Her arms were rigid, and her feet were at the ready as the car skillfully accelerated through traffic. As they continued on, Corbin was curious. He wanted to know about the voice and its accuracy.

"Had I arrived in another way," he paused, "meaning if I'd been flown in by a helicopter, or delivered in a limousine, would you have given me the time of day?"

"Maybe if you came in on a camel," she said, casually skirting the question.

"But where to find a camel?" he rhetorically asked as they moved along. "Take a right here."

"We're not going to Orlando International?"

"No, Orlando Executive."

"Never heard of it."

"It's not as big."

As they neared the facility, Rita saw a group of smaller jets, the kind that *people* own.

"Are you sure we're supposed to be here?"

"Unfortunately, yeah," he said with a forlorn look. "I don't want to leave, but it's about all the time I have for now."

That wasn't what she meant, but she didn't bother to elaborate. Rita was a touch gloomy as well—she'd gotten used to him. They'd gotten along quite well, among other things.

"Look, Rita, I had a great time, and I want to see you again soon. I'm going to leave some forms for you to look over. Once the ownership is figured out, we can take the next step."

He paused. That didn't sound right. "But that just pertains to the book, not to anything that happened between us."

Even worse, thought Corbin. He was new to the concept of mixing business with pleasure, but he'd have to hope for the best. At the moment, in relation to he and she, or to him and her, or to whatever they were, it was about all he could do.

"I know," agreed Rita. "Hopefully it'll work out."

He slid out the consent forms and handed them over. It seemed strange. Like an ending where there should have been a beginning.

"I hope so too," added Corbin in a rather bleak fashion.

Neither Corbin nor Rita seemed overly ecstatic as they shared a final kiss and a somber good-bye. In a final display of affection, he turned to the sad beauty, kicked off his flip-flops, and continued into the terminal shoeless. Rita laughed and waited to see a sleek white jet push into the twilight. Although a bit more refined than Billy, Corbin seemed every bit as crazy. Just odd enough to keep a girl like Rita interested.

The company was nice, but she was glad to be headed home alone. With the visit from Corbin a few things were cleared up, or one big thing. Most notably that she wasn't getting back together with Billy. Even if he resurfaced new and improved, she couldn't see it happening. It wasn't because of Corbin. She did want to see him again but wouldn't be crushed if she didn't. Her heart wasn't cold, just resolved not to be held back by any romantic inclination. She thought about the indiscretion and wondered if it even had been one. If it had to happen, it might as well have been with Corbin; at least he put in a little, or a lot, of effort.

Rita's thoughts swirled as she pulled her Camry into the driveway. Constantly reshuffling the deck was exhausting. The same cards kept coming up, the same unresolved issues: her life in flux. Maybe it would always be that way. She hoped not, because it was torture. She wanted a place to go.

As Rita walked quietly into the apartment, Jillian was in the living room pretending to read.

"You look tired," she said with a grin, knowing that the couch had remained unoccupied the previous night.

"I look tired because I am tired, Jill," replied Rita in a stay-out-of-my-business manner.

"Where's Corbin? I was kind of getting used to him."

"Gone."

Jillian put her book down. She had something to say.

"While you were away, Billy called. I told him you'd be back soon. He's going to call again. I'm just letting you know, dear."

And sure enough, just as Rita set down her keys, the phone rang. Hearing the shrill, unnerving sound, Rita's heart started to thump. She didn't want to answer but finally, on the fifth ring, she did.

"Hey baby, it's me," announced Billy, still trying to sound upbeat on a pay phone in a strange city.

"I know who it is, silly," Rita affectionately answered. "How have things been going?"

She didn't hate him—just the opposite: he'd been her first true love.

"How have things been going? Well, let's see," he said, "been eating a lot of Mexican food."

"I guess it's all Mexican food down there," she chuckled.

"Yeah, glad you didn't send me to Mongolia."

"Got something against Mongolian barbecue?" she playfully asked. "It wouldn't have been a bad idea, though."

"Aww, come on, Rita, I wasn't that bad, was I?"

"Compared to what, I suppose?"

The last comment made him feel alone. He'd hoped to hear something different, something soft. He had enough coins, but today he just didn't have the time.

"Compared to someone you didn't love."

Billy was used to the busy sounds of downtown, but the sound he wanted to hear had gone silent. She was pensive. Knowing he was on the run didn't make it any easier. He was in a bad way, and she was about to make it worse.

"Look, Billy, I've met someone."

The words hit like a brick. Billy slumped against the wall, trying to move it, but the wall, like everything else in his life, wouldn't budge. Now he'd lost everything, or the only thing that meant anything, but it didn't matter. On the streets in Mexico, there was always someone sadder and more distressed. There was always someone worse off. All he had to do was look around.

Billy fought the urge to say something hurtful and instead asked, "Well, how are you doing?"

Billy knew Rita, and he knew that it probably wasn't an easy thing to do.

"I'm OK, just taking it day by day. How about you?"

"I'm all right. I'm alive. I'm living," he said, picking up steam, "although I just found out I'm newly single. What's the guy's name?"

"It's Corbin."

"Of course."

"Why 'of course'?"

"Because it's lame."

"What's a good name?" asked Rita.

"Jeff, Kent, Bill, John, Joseph," growled Billy in rapid succession.

"Kent?"

"Yeah, Kent!" he exclaimed, red-faced and fanatical as the locals noticed the "loco gringo."

"Don't you think you're being a little extreme?"

"Yeah, I'm stuck down here eating beans and rice while you're living the high life."

"Look, I saved your ass not once, but twice, and if you would have displayed even the slightest concern for how I felt, things might have worked out!"

"I'm sorry," he muttered.

"I wasn't looking for it—it just kind of happened. I wanted it to be us."

"So did I," said Billy, "but I guess I just couldn't keep it together."

"You weren't supposed to."

The sky seemed empty. Colors froze in time, as a thin, liquid stain coated his face. She cried as well. Sobbed was more like it. It wasn't the first time, but she hoped it would be the last.

"Well, when am I going to be able to come home?" asked Billy.

"I don't know. I haven't heard anything. I'd wait for another month or so. I mean, you've made it this long."

He agreed. He wanted to make sure that the coast was clear, that someone had been arrested and it wasn't him.

"Are you still the most beautiful girl on the beach? I don't have any pictures, had to leave in a hurry."

"Yeah, we were kind of rushed. I've let myself go lately—late nights and not a lot of sleep."

"Doubtful," he said.

He could smell a fib. He'd done it a time or two.

"Oh, and there's something else, Billy," remembered Rita.

"What?"

What else could there possibly be? She'd already torn out his heart, made him cry, and left him stranded in Mexico with a yin-yang tattoo on the top of his foot, wasn't that enough?

"I finished the book. I've got someone who wants to publish it!"

"You what?"

"I finished it."

"You stole it!"

"You gave it to me."

"You butchered it."

"I corrected it!"

"It's supposed to be a true story!"

"Based on a true story!"

"You didn't get my permission," he said in a last-gasp attempt to retain artistic control.

"Do I have it?" she asked in all sincerity.

He'd told her to throw it away. Obviously, she hadn't. It got him run out of town, bruised, beaten, and distanced from all that he loved. Others had been hurt too.

Rita was gone, but a thin smile showed for what remained, sea-swept images and rain-soaked memories of soft pastel days. Her picture pasted over a collage of shiny, high-priced ads. Rita beautifully attached to a collection of expensive things.

She'd gone commercial.

Billy was glad.

It's what she'd always wanted.

"It's yours, Rita. I'm glad you finished it—you're an amazing lady."

There was no jealousy or envy, just the truth. She was flattered. He had always been the leader, the one who'd make a breakthrough, and in a way he had.

Not one to linger, Billy was going to have to get on with it. There wasn't much more to say, not at the moment, but for one last question. He just had to know.

"So, what did you name the book, Rita?"

She gave the wooden end table a light tap and said, "I named it 'Kidnapping Steve.'"

Epilogue

Early Sunday morning as the sun shone cautiously on a strange crime scene, Keller Finney and Freddy Blatt were taken into custody. Facing an immediate interrogation, Keller wheezed painfully through a couple of cracked ribs that he just happened to know the perpetrators of such a heinous crime.

"Billy Winslow and Randall Daniels took the poor child!"

He then developed amnesia and went quiet. It would now be up to the lawyers. Instructed to invoke their right to remain silent, Keller and Freddy did just that. They looked sadly on as the jury studied pictures of Steve being pulled from a flower bed. They were heartbroken as well.

There were other pictures too, pictures of Keller and Freddy bruised and bloody. Jim sat in the front row like a hulking vigilante who "took the law into his own hands!" The sheriff expected the worst, and now it seemed like that's what they'd get. The defense attorney fought like a rabid dog. He charged excessive force. He declared cruel and unusual punishment. He claimed false imprisonment. He cited diminished mental capacity. "I mean, look at them," he said.

"Their injuries were caused by blunt force, Your Honor, visited by him!" he exclaimed, pointing a long bony finger at Jim Linon.

"He may have even done it himself," continued the counselor, "a ploy to sell more cars, a deranged publicity stunt, a pathetic attempt get back into the limelight!"

The courtroom erupted as Jim rose to throttle the small man.

"Silence!" bellowed an aggravated judge as the gavel fell.

A verdict of not guilty was returned, which lead to the release of both Keller and Freddy. Empowered by the decision and relieved that justice had been served, Keller planned to hire a couple of the other inmates to handle his more risky endeavors.

"Captain Nemo and Suggs should fit quite nicely into an organization like ours. Pretty stand-up guys, I must say."

"Yeah," agreed Freddy, "when they weren't trying to steal my lunch."

"Healthy appetites, no doubt," added Keller.

With Billy on the run and a fresh crop of associates at the ready, things were looking up.

On that same fateful Sunday, with Steve in the hospital, Van had to go to work. With a face full of butterfly stitches, he wasn't sure what to expect. He didn't know who'd been caught. Something would have to be said, and it was up to him to make it as little as possible.

Van arrived at a quiet restaurant and instantly recognized an unmarked car in the parking lot. He walked swiftly into the kitchen, grabbed an apron, and headed for the dish room. As he filled the sinks and grabbed a rack of glasses, Phil and a guy who looked like a police officer made their way back.

"Hey, Van," said Phil, "I've got a guy here who'd like to have a word with you."

Van looked up and nodded. They weren't taking him in, so that was a good sign. Phil was nervous as usual, and the sheriff was fit and smart. With thinning blond hair and square shoulders, Van thought that he could have seen him out surfing.

"Hi, Van, I'm Sheriff Jake Williams. Do you have any idea why I came to talk to you today?"

"No," answered Van, staring him straight in the eye.

Through a quick visual, the sheriff determined that this Van character wasn't the type to crack. He also had quite a gash in the corner of his mouth. It was a good place to start.

"You got a healthy gash on the mouth there, partner."

"Got tagged in a bar fight."

"Which bar?"

"Dino's."

"So, when I ask the bartender if he saw you last night, he'll say that he did, right?"

"He didn't, never made it up to the bar. Put my quarters on the wrong pool table, I guess."

There was a fight at Dino's nearly every night. If the sheriff asked, he'd surely find that there had been at least one, maybe more.

"Where'd you go after that?" asked the sheriff.

"Went home to fix my mouth—I was losing a lot of blood."

As the sheriff nodded, a large individual with bloodshot eyes and a beer appeared in the background.

"Hey, Jim," said Van, just as cool as the other side of the pillow.

"Hey, Van," replied Jim. "I'll handle it from here, Jake."

"All right, Jim, I'll be in the other room if you need me." Meaning if they had to cuff Van, the sheriff was there to do just that.

"What's going on, Jim?" asked Van through a concerned growl.

"Steve was kidnapped last night, Van. He walked out back, and that was the last anyone saw of him."

No one knew this better than Van, but he acted surprised all the same.

"No freakin' way. Is he all right? I mean, what happened?"

"We found him this morning in a board bag. He was dinged up and dehydrated, but other than that, he's OK."

"Oh good," said Van.

"Yeah, it is good," agreed Jim, beginning to look like he might bloody the other side of Van's mouth. "I've got a question for you, Van."

"Shoot, Jim," replied Van.

"Did you have anything to do with it?"

Van recognized it as the man-to-man approach. Jim could be honorable. In his world, the truth had value and deals were done with a handshake. In Van's world, the truth was dangerous and a handshake meant nothing. To answer the question, Van would rely on an element of natural selection. He'd survive and flourish. He'd lie.

"No."

"Steve said the last thing he saw before blacking out was a couple of guys that looked like you."

"I didn't see anyone out there," affirmed Van. "Didn't hear anything either."

"Didn't it seem strange that Steve never came back in?"

"It was a busy night, Jim. I wasn't really paying attention to the waitstaff."

While Jim decided whether to kill or to believe him, he finally handed Van the beer and said, "I knew you didn't have anything to do with it, Van, just had to ask, you understand, right?"

"Of course, Jim. I'd be pissed too," answered Van, relieved to have escaped any further harm. The girl had messed him up bad enough.

He wondered where she was, and about Billy, that good-for-nothing fool.

Edwin and the young bum traveled a full city block before they heard the sirens. The menacing howl seemed to get closer by the second, and Edwin started to panic.

"We're hemmed in, bum. We gotta surrender!"

"We need to keep going," warned the young bum.

"We gotta lie down. They'll shoot us in the head if we resist!" insisted Edwin.

"They might shoot you in the head, pal, but I'm gone!"

At this point, Edwin could follow or stay behind. It made no difference.

As the young bum made a final push for the lights, Edwin, of course, followed.

"Hmph," sounded the young bum, "just like I thought."

"What?" said Edwin.

"Keep moving, sarge, we're almost there."

Finally at a convenience store, the young bum doused his bloody shirt and cleaned his face as Edwin ambled across the parking lot.

"Sit tight, bum, I'm gonna get you another shirt."

"Hurry up, old man. We gotta go!"

So, they needed to leave and there was Edwin gabbing to the cashier. Luckily the money changed hands and he made a quick exit. The young bum was about to grab him by the collar when a clean Buick LeSabre pulled up to the curb.

"Mr. Clark Gable, is that you?" asked the pastorally attractive lady at the wheel.

Is that me? thought Edwin.

It was that lady from before, the one who had given him a twenty after the young bum's failed flop. Edwin leaned into the car and noticed it had a full tank of gas.

"Why yes, of course it's me."

The troops were moving in, and he needed a way out.

"Ah, perhaps you could give me and junior here a ride," he said, motioning toward the young bum. "We're on our way to a church fund raiser and could sure use a lift."

"Oh, of course, Mr. Gable, why don't you and the young man make yourselves comfortable while I grab a box of donuts."

"We're kind of in a hurry, ma'am. These church folk aren't very tolerant of tardiness. If you don't mind maybe we could, ah, hit the road."

"Yeah," said the young bum, "we need to get out of here."

"Oh, I know what it's like within some congregations," she replied as the car motored off.

Peering into the rearview mirror, she couldn't help but notice the knot on the young bum's head.

"My word, Mr. Gable, your young friend sure seems to get hurt a lot."

"Yes ma'am, he's quite accident prone," agreed Edwin. "You can call me Clark if you'd like."

She looked him over as they drove away and said, "I think I'd like that."

The young bum rolled his eyes as Edwin showed a content smile. *Mission accomplished*, he thought.

Keller's old friend Randall, who'd incidentally surpassed Billy as public enemy number one, stayed in Fort Lauderdale. He hadn't contacted anyone and had no idea what happened to the rest of the crew. He didn't care what happened to them. All he wanted was his work and his new love, Emily. At peace with the way things went down, hopefully he saved Steve some grief. He wasn't able to save anyone else.

Jim was furious that Keller, Freddy, and whoever else was involved would never be brought to justice. The case was closed. They walked from the courtroom free men and rather quickly filed a restraining order against Jim.

Accidents happen all the time, though, he thought, but had the better sense to leave it alone, which lent only a small measure of comfort to his distraught wife, Donna. The whole thing had hit her pretty hard, and she suffered a lot of sleepless nights. She was angry with Jim and overly protective of Steve.

Donna barely let Steve leave the house and had grudgingly let Jim stay. Everything she had gracefully achieved was about to frantically unravel until she saw the bird. Too big for the nest and too innocent to know better, it dashed itself against a window over and over again. She clumsily reached for the bird as it tumbled down. She then cupped the fuzzy chick and it instantly flew away—away from the fall that could have damaged its wings and away from the hands that could have crushed it. Donna imagined it wasn't so different for her. That maybe life came down to a series of narrow escapes, flights from things that are dangerous. That maybe they were the lucky ones. She forgave

Jim. She told Steve to have fun and bought a pair of binoculars. Donna never imagined bird-watching could be so relaxing.

Jim changed too. In the shadowy events of that early morning scuffle, something stirred. In his soul, something was incomplete. In his mind, he knew what he needed to do. It started with a phone call and then moved on to an arena.

Jim walked back into the ranks of professional wrestling as a trash-talking, backstabbing, big-time promoter. King James was the new moniker, and he ruled over a stable of the most brutish kind. He was once again in the spotlight, and he liked it. With Mick Rider managing the dealership, the money continued to roll in quite nicely.

Aside from a few bumps and bruises, Steve emerged relatively unscathed. He went into the board bag a snot-nosed brat and came out a conscientious young man. He vowed to make a difference. He promised to make a change. He wrote a book on survival. *Alone in a Bag* was the title.

Alone in a Bag II quickly followed, making Steve a regular on the talk show circuit—not bad for a couple of hours of captivity.

Then there was Rita, the cunning femme fatale at the center of it all, the catalyst, or the reason it happened. She wasn't the real reason, but it could have been pinned on her. Billy ran. She wrote about it, and Corbin came along to pick up the pieces.

As the days passed, Corbin and Rita became an item. They reunited on a follow-up business trip and picked up where they had left off. Only this time, he was free to stay and explore some other ideas. His plans were for them. Hers were for something else, but that's how she was.

So, Rita, Corbin, and Jillian loaded up and headed north to begin *Nuts Roll Up*, Rita's latest novel. On the way, they penned a name for his publishing house and fell in love. For all creative endeavors, the company would be called Seashell Canyon, Inc. along with Penny Publishing, a subsidiary named after a dog.

Their wedding was quaint and elegant, with Rita wearing de la Renta and Corbin sensibly chic in Armani. Everyone was gorgeous, including Jillian and Sheriff Jake Williams, whom she ran into at a fund raiser for the local sheriff's department. Completely powerless against the will of the elder Polli, the sheriff had no other choice but to surrender. Although he still suspected that Rita knew something about the abduction, the case was closed, as was his interest in it. He told Rita she looked beautiful and, with a wink, whispered that Billy was in the clear. It was a bit of information she was sure to convey.

Published under a pen name and dedicated to bad ideas and to Billy, she felt justified in letting the facts speak. "It's a work of fiction," she'd been known to say, but between beachcombing in the Caymans and skiing in the Rockies, Rita was a little hard to find.

What began with a father and a sickness had come full circle. Rita became a writer. She also became comfortable in a private jet. They offered Billy a substantial sum of money for his contribution, or for his book, but he declined. What he wanted he could never have.

So, now Billy was south of the border playing spoiler. Rita hadn't forgotten how he had picked her up when she'd been down. Billy was probably the only one who could have—not some high-flying member of the jet set. She owed him a debt, maybe one that couldn't be repaid. Rita discussed it with Corbin, and they agreed. The papers were drawn up and inked.

Billy ambled up to the post office for his weekly mail call and received only a thin white envelope. From somewhere in New York, the name on the return address curiously read *R. Flake*.

"R. Flake," he announced, as he opened the letter.

Rita Flake? he thought as he unfolded a copy of something. It was a duplicate deed to the house on Cedar Avenue, fee simple absolute, free and clear, tax free for the duration.

"Drat," yelled Billy to no one in particular. "They got me!"

He couldn't give it back and he couldn't burn it.

On the back was a note. "This is just a copy," read the first line. "The real thing is in the CB PO Box #321-572. The coast is clear and the key will be there whenever you care to claim it."

It went on to say "Please accept this as a token of my appreciation. Love always, Rita."

For all intents and purposes, the book was finished. It was a wrap. There was but a minor detail left to uncover, a small bit of unfinished business. In an old shed across from Keller's, with some unknown fingerprints, the stolen surfboards were recovered and returned to their rightful owners.

Old Mr. Crawford, who'd passed as a result of natural causes, was delivered to the mortuary in the trunk of his own car while a roll of film fell harmlessly out of a box of evidence and into a waiting horde of pill bugs.

Made in United States
Orlando, FL
26 September 2022